DIVORCE HOTEL

B. R. SNOW

Copyright © 2012 B.R. Snow

ISBN-13: 978-0984967551
ISBN-10: 0984967559

Website:	www.brsnow.net/
Twitter:	@BernSnow
Facebook:	facebook.com/bernsnow

OTHER BOOKS BY B.R. SNOW

The Damaged Po$$e Series   Links

- American Midnight   http://amzn.to/1H6sgZV

- Larrikin Gene   http://amzn.to/10tqmMa

- Sneaker World   http://amzn.to/VUnhnP

- Summerman   http://amzn.to/SqukAk

- The Duplicates   *Coming Summer of 2016*

Other books

To Michael P. and Michael B.

So proud to call you Po$$e members.
Even prouder to call you friends.

If love is hell,
what does that make divorce?

1

John Germaine swayed in the early light doing his favorite thing; if doing nothing counted as doing something. Buried in his hammock, he closed his eyes hoping the morning silence would coax him back to sleep. But the silence nagged and John turned suspicious. He raised a hand to shield the rising sun and opened one eye. He looked left, then right. Not a sound. He opened the other eye and glanced at his watch. One minute to seven. John closed his eyes and hoped for ten more minutes. Thirty seconds later, all hell broke loose.

A leaf blower roared, and dozens of birds screeched. Cat meows triggered barking and demands for quiet. A pulsating bass line punctuated by three horn blasts initiated a mother-daughter will-not, will-too goodbye that was soon followed by a teenage screech about the inhumanity of man and clueless mothers. A door slammed as the car burned rubber and thunk-a-thunked away. Grinding gears battled with banging trash cans, and John cursed himself for again forgetting pickup day. The trash orchestra crescendo gave way to the next door neighbors.

"Because I didn't," a man screamed. "That's why."

His wife, also in fine voice, returned the volley. "And why not?"

"Because I was…busy!"

"Yeah, you were busy…at the bar."

"Jesus Christ. I stopped for one drink after work."

"You've never had one drink in your life. You were probably with some skank."

"You're unbelievable…And she's not a skank."

"What? Who's not a skank?"

"Uh, nothing. What was the question?"

"You sonofabitch."

"Lower your voice. You'll wake up the whole goddamn neighborhood."

"Too late," John said. He stretched and made a mental note to let his neighbor know he had a vacancy should it come to that. Another noise joined the party. John folded his arms behind his head and listened as the phone rang for a second time. Then a third.

"Answer the frigging thing."

The ringing continued. John sat up in the hammock and flipped face-down onto the overgrown grass. Making a mental note to call the gardener, he huffed and puffed as he speed-walked across the lawn. He made another mental note about getting to the gym at least once this decade. He slid the glass door open, entered the kitchen and saw Randolph Tut, GQ resplendent, sitting four feet from the phone reading the newspaper and sipping coffee.

Randolph glanced up from the paper. "Thanks. That was starting to get on my nerves."

John glared at Randolph, who had already slipped back behind his paper. He took a breath and picked up the phone. "Divorce Hotel." John shook his head in recognition. "Yes, Margaret…yes, Margaret…yes, Margaret." He held a hand over the mouthpiece and turned to Randolph. "How I wish I had a dollar for every time I've said-" He removed his hand from the mouthpiece. "Yes, Margaret. I do want to thank you for remembering my birthday the other day. I'm sure it had nothing to do with the fact that the alimony check is due." John poured himself a cup of coffee. "Of course, I liked it. It's every man's dream to have an autographed picture of his ex-wife. What am I going to do with it? I'm having it made into a dartboard." John jerked the phone away from his ear.

Randolph put the newspaper down and smiled.

"Margaret, do you remember when I said I do…? Well, I didn't. Oh, yeah…well, to death do us part to you too."

John slammed the phone and sat at the table. Randolph continued to smile.

"What are you grinning at?"

"Remembering the Alamo?"

"I should have known better than to marry a woman with 666 tattooed on her butt. At least you had the sense to only date her."

Randolph frowned. "Funny," he said. "I remember the tattoo, but wasn't it 999?" Randolph thought for a moment and shook his head. "Sorry," he said. "My mistake."

"Maybe she should have had it underlined so you wouldn't get confused." John grabbed the sports section and scanned the first page.

"Hey, I'm sorry. Besides I didn't even know you, she didn't even know you when we dated."

"Well, you were smart. I ended up married to her for seven years."

"You shouldn't have gotten married in California. No alimony here in the great state of Texas." Randolph shook his head. "I still don't know how you managed to hang in there that long."

"Well, my therapist told me there's a thin line between love and hate. Unfortunately, Margaret was always daring me to step across it.

The phone rang. John shook his head. "I wonder who that could be." He tossed the sports section on the table and grabbed the phone. "Divorce Hotel….Yes, I sent the check. I've already told you that four times. Jesus Christ, Margaret. It's seven o'clock in the morning. When was the last time you saw a mailman that time of day? I don't care if you live down the street or not, I mailed it…three days ago. The wrong address? I think I know the address, Margaret. I can see your house from my front porch. Yeah, that's right. It's my fault. I must have put the wrong address on it. Let me check and make sure I've got it right…Say, what's the zip code for Planet Bitch?" John jerked the phone away from his ear. "You too…right back at ya…no, I won't be sending them Federal Express…I'll use Pony Express. John slammed the phone and slumped into a chair.

"Pony Express?" Randolph laughed. "Nice touch."

"Eight grand a month. Some days I think it would be better if she just ran me over with her car and put me out of my misery."

"That ain't gonna happen." Randolph began scanning the business section. "She'd lose her annuity."

"I just wish she would get remarried."

3

Randolph raised an eyebrow. "Glad to see you're staying optimistic. Insane, but still optimistic."

2

Bertrand Wild straightened his lab coat and checked his appearance in the mirror. Satisfied with the blend of professionalism and business casual the long white coat and lavender golf shirt provided, he turned his attention back to his experiment. He flipped through a thick spiral notebook until he found the right page. He lit a Bunsen burner, adjusted the flame underneath a glass beaker and picked up a small vial and eyedropper. Bertrand again scanned the page and counted as four drops went into the beaker. He reviewed the formula, added six drops of a second liquid and waiting with folded arms. He lowered a thermometer and checked the temperature. He nodded, extracted the thermometer and removed the beaker from the heat. Leaning in, he sniffed and frowned.

"Too sweet."

He refocused on the formula. Bertrand added three drops of a third liquid and placed the beaker back on the flame. Moments later, he repeated the smell test.

"Better."

He turned the burner off and headed up the stairs to the kitchen. He emerged and found John and Randolph reading the paper.

"Morning," Bertrand said. "Is there coffee?"

Without waiting for a response, Bertrand headed for the coffeemaker. He opened the cupboard in search of a mug and found it empty. He turned his attention to the dirty dishes that filled both sinks and half the counter space. Bertrand stared at John.

John looked up from the paper. "What?"

"I hate to keep bringing this up…"

From behind the business section, Randolph said, "No, you don't."

Bertrand ignored Randolph and continued. "When are you going to hire a new housekeeper, John? It's been almost two weeks, and I don't know how much longer I can stand living in the middle of a garbage dump."

"She starts today," John put the paper down and got up for a refill. "Happy?"

Bertrand extracted a mug from the pile of dirty dishes, washed it, and held it up to the light to examine it. John poured, and Bertrand leaned against the counter and sipped.

"Yeah, that's great news. Where did you find her?" Bertrand said.

"She called about the ad I placed. She sounds nice."

"You didn't actually interview her?"

"Face to face? No."

"Why not?"

John shrugged his shoulders. "I was busy."

Bertrand and Randolph both frowned at the news.

"Didn't we learn anything from our last experience?"

Puzzled, John looked at Bertrand. "What? Are you talking about, Svetlana?"

"Of course, I'm talking about Svetlana."

"What was wrong with her?"

"She was 92, John. She was here three weeks and never made it off the first floor."

"The poor thing couldn't handle the stairs," John said.

"Of course, she couldn't handle the frigging stairs," Bertrand said. "Dragging that oxygen tank behind her walker kind of slowed her down."

"I thought she did a pretty good job," John said.

"John," Randolph said, putting the paper down. "She didn't cook, couldn't clean, and barely spoke English."

"But she was such a nice lady," John said.

Bertrand shook his head and sipped his coffee. He caught Randolph's stare. "What?"

"Who dresses you?" Randolph said. "Lab coat, plaid pants, purple shirt. Jesus, I thought black people all had a sense of style."

6

"It's business casual," Bertrand said. "And it's not purple...it's lavender."

"I guess it's what all the best-dressed...butcher-golfers are wearing these days. Hand me my seven iron, caddy. I've got to hack off a couple of veal cutlets."

Bertrand glared at Randolph. "Shouldn't you be out trashing someone's reputation?"

Randolph glanced at his Rolex and examined his manicure. "Not until ten."

"How's it going downstairs?" John said.

"Great. It's going to be a fantastic batch."

"You're going to have enough for the party?"

"That's the whole point," Bertrand said. "Don't worry. This is going to be the best Halloween party we've ever had."

"Boy, I don't know," Randolph said. "Pretty tough to top last year. I'm still getting hate mail."

The phone starting ringing again.

3

Randolph settled into the thick leather chair and studied the animal heads adorning the wall. He tugged the bottom of his cuffs until his gold cufflinks were visible then glanced back up at the collection of heads. A well-dressed man in his sixties with long white hair cleared his throat. Randolph looked across the desk and smiled despite the glare he was receiving.

"She's talking about buying a goddamn football team and moving it to Texas."

Randolph shrugged. "Well, she can certainly afford it."

"I'm glad you find it amusing."

"Senator, relax." Randolph draped one leg over a knee and brushed imaginary lint from his pants. "There's no way she can put an NFL franchise here in Austin. UT would go apoplectic."

"What about San Antonio?"

"Small market. But I guess it could work."

"You're supposed to make me feel better, Randolph."

"Senator, you've got nothing to worry about. She's a Democrat for chrissakes. Sure, she's closing a bit, but you've still got a huge lead."

"She's closed eight points in a week," the Senator said. "All of a sudden she decides to go positive…and it's working."

"It won't last," Randolph said. He turned his attention to his hair and patted it back in place with both hands.

"What? Her going positive or her bump in the polls?"

Randolph examined his hands and picked at a fingernail imperfection. "Yeah."

"What?"

Randolph looked up. "Huh?"

"Which one?"

"Right."

"Right? What are you talking about?"

Randolph, embarrassed, decided to spin. "I was just saying we need to make sure we get this right."

The Senator glared at him, picked up the remote and began channel surfing.

"Hold it," Randolph said. "You see her?"

The Senator paused to watch a few seconds of a shampoo commercial. "What about her?"

"I dated her," Randolph said. He leaned forward in his chair and bopped his head along with the music.

"Yeah? Not bad. She's cute." The Senator began swaying to the music.

"Farm girl turned model turned actress," Randolph said. "I think she's from...where the hell is it? Idaho...Iowa? I don't know. It's one of those other red states I can never remember the name of."

"Me neither," the Senator said. "What happened between the two of you?"

"The usual," Randolph said.

The Senator nodded and changed the channel. "Jesus Christ, there she is again." He tossed the remote aside and leaned back in his chair. A news conference was in progress and the Senator's opponent, Gloria Fontaine, an attractive woman in her forties, was answering questions from a captivated group of reporters.

Randolph watched the proceedings. "She is a good looking woman. You gotta give her that."

"Yeah," the Senator said. "I'm getting worried, Randolph."

Randolph placed both elbows on the desk. "I've got some good news for you, Senator."

"I could use good news. Is it dirty?"

"Very."

"Good. I'm tired of trying to run on my record."

"Just imagine how I feel running your campaign."

"What?"

"Nothing. Don't worry, Senator. Your record speaks for itself."

"That's what I'm afraid of."

"You'll love this," Randolph said. "One of our private investigators has uncovered something."

"Really? Which one?"

"Randy Van Swalo."

"Van Swalo? Isn't he a drunk?"

"Of course, he's a drunk. If you did what he does for a living, you'd drink too." Randolph leaned back in his chair. "Anyway, you know how Gloria is always putting herself out there as the champion of the American family?"

"Yeah, the bitch," the Senator said. "She's killing me with that family crap."

"Well, Van Swalo has pretty much put an end to that. It turns out that Gloria has a deaf mother who hasn't seen her in ten years."

"You're kidding."

Randolph shook his head and beamed at the Senator. "Nope," Randolph said. "Her mother hasn't seen her in ten years. Now I know why Gloria refuses to even acknowledge her. She's ashamed of her own mother."

"Holy shit," the Senator said. "This is big. Where's her mother?"

"She's in a nursing home outside of Waco."

"This is fantastic, Randolph. Well done."

Randolph waved away the compliment. "It's what I do. If this plays out the way I think it will, you just got yourself reelected for a third term, Senator."

"Let's not get ahead of ourselves, Randolph. We've got a long way to go yet."

"Hah," Randolph said. "Do you think Texans are going to vote for a politician who ignores the existence of her own mother? By this time next week, Gloria Fontaine will be a footnote in the history book of American politics."

The Senator got up from behind his desk and shook Randolph's hand.

"By the way, Senator," Randolph said. "Are you coming to the Halloween party this year?"

"I'm still working on it," he said. "After last year, my wife isn't a big fan of the hotel."

"I don't remember your wife being here last year."

"She wasn't. But she did see the tape."

Randolph grimaced. "Ouch. The tape. Bummer."

"Yes. The tape. I'm assuming that you won't be going as Cecil B. DeMille this year?"

Randolph, embarrassed, shook his head and waved as he left the office.

4

Bertrand closed his eyes as he inhaled and let the aroma wash over him. He opened one eye, squinted at the beaker he was holding and placed it on the table that ran the length of the picture window. Bertrand stared out the window at the large sign near the parking lot and smiled.

Harrison Hygiene - Helping America Smell Better: One Person at a Time.

Bertrand refocused on his work. He didn't hear Walter Harrison enter the office.

"Bertrand," Harrison said. "What's the progress on No Offense?"

Bertrand didn't look up. "Same as it was a half-hour ago, Walter."

Harrison twitched like an expectant father. "Yes, well, science is moving pretty fast these days. I don't want to miss anything."

Bertrand frowned and kept jotting notes on a yellow legal pad.

"I'm anxious to get it on the market," Harrison said. "When can I see it?"

Bertrand flipped the legal pad over. "You're the one who wanted the formula to be a secret."

"Yes, I did. But not from me. I own the place."

Bertrand stared out the window. "Well, in this business, you can't be too careful."

Harrison shook his head at the strange man who'd been his lead hygiologist for the past five years. Then he had an idea. He slid into a chair, put his feet up and casually announced, "Of course, as soon as No Offense is launched, I'll be awarding bonuses."

Bertrand wheeled from the window and smiled at Harrison.

"Yes, Bertrand. Bonuses. Big, fat bonuses."

"Define big. And while you're at it, define fat," Bertrand said. "As a scientist, I'm more comfortable dealing with specifics."

12

Harrison dodged. "It's too soon to say. But I'm sure you'll be more than satisfied when the time comes."

"I hope so, Walter. I've spent almost two years getting this product ready. And it's fantastic. In six months, you won't be able to step outside your house without getting a good whiff of No Offense." Bertrand frowned and looked at Harrison. "Hey, I just remembered. You still owe me a dollar, Walter."

"What?"

"Last week. The Coke machine. You borrowed a dollar from me."

Harrison shook his head but reached into his pocket and extracted a dollar from a large stack of bills. He handed it to Bertrand.

"Thanks." Bertrand slid the dollar into his wallet. "I don't like to let outstanding debts hang around for too long."

"Of course not." Harrison chuckled and headed for the door. "Keep me posted."

Bertrand put the wallet in his pocket and stared out the window, a big smile working its way to the corners of his mouth.

5

Emily Perkins parked her Jeep Cherokee in front of the large stone and wood building, got out and glanced up and down the street. Impressed by her surroundings, she looked up at the neon sign running across the front.

If love is hell, what does that make divorce?

"Good question." She rang the bell and waited. She knocked and continued to wait. Eventually, an impatient voice from inside called out.

"It's open. Just come on in."

Emily stepped inside and stared at the massive entranceway and staircase that led to the second floor. She frowned at the filth then focused on the two men on opposite sides of the registration counter. Both remained oblivious to her presence.

Behind the registration area, John was fumbling through a stack of papers while simultaneously trying to swipe a credit card through the reader. Several more unsuccessful attempts followed. "Goddamn technology. Whatever happened to a big stack of cash?"

"I think the stripe goes the other way," the man said.

John flipped the card over and swiped hard. The card registered, and he slid it across the counter. The man pursed his lips and returned the card to his wallet.

"There you go," John said, extracting the bill from the printer. "I hope you had an enjoyable and memorable stay with us, Mr. White."

The man grabbed the receipt and glared across the counter.

John flinched. "Well, given the fact that you're going through a divorce…maybe enjoyable isn't the best choice of words." John waited for a response but got nothing except the glare. "But I would say that the term memorable does indeed fit. I'm sure that the vast majority of our guests would say that spending time at our hotel is a very memorable event."

The man's glare deepened. John's face flushed with embarrassment. He glanced around the room and saw Emily for the first time. Silently, he begged for help.

"Oh, no," she said, laughing. "You're on your own."

John scowled at her and looked back at the man standing on the other side of the counter. "Perhaps a better word might be…tranquil. Yes, that's it. Tranquil. A wonderful tranquil week before you reenter the wonderful world of divorce." John forced a smile and tried cheerful. "You know, back to the world of rapid lawyers…venomous ex-spouses…bloody child custody battles…" Then John broke into song. And John shouldn't sing. "Memories… light the corners of my mind-"

The departing guest jammed the receipt into his pocket, grabbed his suitcase and slammed the door on his way out.

Emily watched him go then laughed. "Smooth."

"I need to work on that 'hope you had a nice stay' speech. You must be Emily Perkins. I'm John Germaine."

Emily returned the handshake. "It's nice to finally meet you."

"Likewise. And we're very glad you are here."

Emily glanced around at the mess. "I can see why."

"Yes, well," John said looking around the reception area. "Our last housekeeper left us on very short notice, and I'm afraid I've fallen a bit behind."

"Why did she leave?"

"Uh…she retired. Say, how about a tour of the place before you get started?"

"Sounds good," she said following him into the kitchen. "Oh, my God. How long ago did she leave?"

John thought for a moment. "A week? No, two, maybe three… close to a month."

Emily stared at the collection of dirty dishes, pizza boxes, and empty beer bottles. She frowned and glanced at John.

"Yeah, it's pretty bad," he said.

"I thought this was a hotel," she said. She opened one of the pizza boxes, saw what was inside and closed it.

15

"It is," John said. "But I guess it would be more accurate to call it a Bed and Breakfast."

"More like a Beer and Breakfast," she said, continuing to scan the mess. "Let me guess; it's a fraternity."

John forced a laugh. "It's not that bad. It just needs a good cleaning. I've gotten a bit behind. It's been hard to keep up all by myself."

Emily continued to scan the kitchen. She opened the refrigerator, shook her head and closed the door. "Leftoverville?"

John laughed. "It's threatening to walk on its own."

"I don't know, John," she said, still shaking her head. "It's not really what I'm looking for. Playing den mother."

"Let me show you the rest of the place before we get into that, okay?"

John ushered her out of the kitchen into a large entertainment room that contained six large screen televisions and an elaborate stereo system. Several recliners and two massive couches were positioned in front of the televisions, and Emily felt the thickness of the carpet beneath her feet.

"This is a nice room," she said. "Why all the big screens?"

John shrugged. "We watch a lot of football."

She smiled. "Good. Me too."

John was pleasantly surprised but said nothing.

"Tell me a bit more about this place." She sat down in one of the chairs. "What's the deal here?"

John sat down next to her. "Well, after my divorce several years ago, I bought this place as a fixer-upper. Everyone said I was crazy. I mean, why would a guy on his own need a nine bedroom, ten bathroom monstrosity, right?"

"Good question."

"I used to live down the street and every day I would drive by this abandoned house. It's such a beautiful piece of architecture, and it was wasting away from neglect. So when I filed for divorce from Margaret…remind me to warn you about her later since she still lives in our old house."

"Down the street?"

"Yup."

"How's that going?"

"Like the Hatfields and McCoys on acid."

Emily laughed.

"I'm not kidding. Just wait. You'll see. So I bought the place and moved right in even though nothing was working. Two years, and a couple hundred thousand later, it had been completely renovated."

"Did you do the work yourself?"

It was John's turn to laugh. "No. One thing you'll quickly discover is that physical labor and I don't often show up in the same time zone. I contracted it all out."

Emily glanced around at the quality of the workmanship. "The woodwork is incredible."

"Yeah," John said. He looked around the room and smiled. "There's something magical about this place. At least, I think there is. And being here helped me during my transition period. The first six months I would wake up in the morning surrounded by total squalor yet still feel peaceful. And that's when I hit on the idea for the hotel."

"Divorce Hotel," she said, nodding.

"Yes. A sanctuary for recently divorced men. A safe place to stay until they find their bearings and figure out what to do next."

"Pretty cool idea," she said. "How long do most of your guests stay?"

"Well, except for the Trilogy, usually a week of two."

"Trilogy?"

"They're the three permanent residents here besides me. They all came here right after their divorces and liked the place so much they decided to stay. That was fine by me since I needed the cash flow."

"Good guys?"

John considered the question. "Define good."

Emily started to laugh but stopped when she realized he wasn't joking.

"No, they're okay," John said. "Unique perhaps...but okay."

"What do they do?"

"Monty is a sports agent."

"Not Monty Mantooth?"

"The very one," John said.

"How about that? I used to follow him when he played for the Cowboys. What's one of the biggest agents in sports doing living here?"

"It's like I told you. He loves Austin and likes living here. But don't worry, he's got houses in Aspen and Maui, so it's not like he's wasting away."

Emily blushed. "No, I didn't mean that. I was only..."

John laughed. "Don't worry about it. A lot of people, especially all our ex-wives, have trouble with the idea that four adult men could prefer living together under the same roof. Once you get to know us and understand the central theme that bonds us, it'll become clear."

"Central theme?"

"We abhor all forms of personal growth," John said. "We avoid it like the plague."

Emily frowned. "Not exactly an enlightened point of view. I would have expected a bit more."

"That's precisely our point."

"You lost me."

"High, perhaps even unrealistic, expectations on the part of women," John said. "Each of us understands the type of man we are. And we've come to grips with it. In fact, we've discovered that we like ourselves just the way we are."

"Hence the attitude regarding personal growth?"

"Exactly. And when you're surrounded by people who are comfortable with themselves and like the way they live, they can get pretty protective in a hurry. Especially whenever someone tries to change them."

"What makes you think I would ever try to change any of you?"

"I don't know," John said, shrugging. "Life experience? Maybe it's genetic."

Emily glared at John and felt her anger build. John, prepared for her response, continued. "Please don't be offended. I have this conversation with everybody. Including the guests. I just want to make sure you understand what we're like. We yell and scream. We play stupid, often vicious, practical jokes on each other. We have outrageous parties. We tend to drink too much. At times, we can be lazy, even slothful. Childish, spoiled, sports-driven. You name every male stereotype and eventually you'll find it around here. We revel in our ability to be both grown men and adolescents simultaneously. That is if that combination can co-exist."

"I thought you were trying to sell me on this job."

"Oh, I am," John said. He stretched his legs and crossed them at the ankles. "It's a very good job. It's always interesting around here, and you're going to meet a ton of fascinating people. You'll be part of a family, a rather bizarre one at times I admit, but a very supportive, non-judgmental family. Once you're accepted, assuming you're able to pull that off, you'll have four new best friends for life. And you won't have to worry about getting hit on since we have a very strict hands-off policy when it comes to the housekeeper."

Emily laughed. "Don't worry. I can take care of myself."

"That's good. Because the weak get crushed around here."

6

John continued the tour. Emily paid close attention as he explained the architecture and layout of the massive house. She was impressed with the restoration and the painstaking attention to detail. On the third floor, John opened a door, climbed a flight of stairs and stepped out onto a huge balcony above the roofline that covered the back half of the house. Emily stared out at the expanse of hill country visible in all directions.

"Wow," she said. "Incredible view."

"Yeah, it's nice." John puffed with pride. "Smartest thing I ever did was buy this place. If I had waited, given the housing market today, I couldn't even get a sniff of it. This is where I come to relax."

"There's no railing," Emily said. She walked to the edge of the balcony and looked down. "Whoa. That's quite a drop."

"About sixty feet," John said. "I have a quote for the railing, but I'm having a bit of a cash flow problem at the moment."

"I know the problem." She admired the view and looked back at John. "How much did you say the salary was?"

"A thousand a week. It's not great, but your room, food, and utilities are all covered. Want to see your room?"

She followed him back down the stairs to the third floor. John walked a few steps and opened a door with a flourish. He gestured to her, and Emily stepped into a huge, fully-furnished bedroom suite that took her breath away.

"Our former housekeeper, actually, she was two housekeepers ago left it this way. Nice, huh?"

"It's amazing."

"Through that door is your bathroom. Walk-in shower and Jacuzzi."

Emily opened the bathroom door and peered in. "Fantastic. Why did your former housekeeper leave?"

"She got married," John said. "Fell in love with one of the guests and decided to take the plunge. We're still recovering. She'd been here since I opened."

"So I've got some big shoes to fill?"

"You'll be fine."

Emily sat down on the edge of the bed and took another look around the room. "How long have you been divorced?"

"Six years," John said. "It was a painful process."

"Yes, I know. I'm coming up on a year myself. The mental part is the toughest."

"Probably," John said. "But the physical pain was also tough."

"How so?"

"Margaret and I had an exotic parrot, and when I told her I was going to fight for custody, she hit me with his perch. Broke three ribs."

"Jesus."

"It worked out well, though. I told her if she gave me the parrot, I wouldn't press charges."

"That was smart," Emily said.

"Yeah. I was going to try the same strategy with the SUV, but I figured I'd better not press my luck."

Emily laughed. "So, she gave you the bird?"

"Constantly. But I did get the parrot. Then he ran away from home last year."

"Your parrot ran away?"

"Another long story."

Emily laughed again. "What does your ex-wife do for a living?"

"She's an actress. An aspiring, yet uninspiring actor."

"Really? My ex is also an actor. My mother said, 'Don't marry an actor. They're so self-absorbed they never have time for anyone but themselves.' She was right."

"Margaret spends all her time auditioning for film and television, but all she ever gets is the occasional commercial and summer stock theater."

"Is she unlucky or just not very good?"

"She sucks," John said. He caught the look Emily was giving him. "No, I'm not saying that because she's my ex-wife. She sucks."

"My ex isn't very good either," Emily said. "He did a Shakespeare festival two years ago, and one of the critics said if Shakespeare had known how bad my ex would be in the role of Romeo, he'd have gone into accounting."

"Ouch."

"It didn't slow him down a bit. He read the review and said, 'Those who can, do; those who can't, act.' He's not the sharpest tool in the shed." Emily laughed.

"So what do those who can't act do?"

"Act dumb."

John laughed and looked at Emily.

"What do you think? Want to give this job a shot?"

"Why not? What's the worst thing that could happen?"

"That's one of those questions we never ask around here."

7

John heard the door open and looked up from the stack of papers. A hunched bald man in his forties waddled through the door, two old suitcases in tow. John watched him repeat the same pattern; shuffle forward two steps, lower his head and sob, drag the suitcases forward.

Shuffle, sob, and drag.

Shuffle, sob, and drag.

John watched his turtle-like progress and shook his head in sympathy. "Hello. Welcome to Divorce Hotel."

The mention of the D word produced another sobbing spasm, and the man stopped dead in his tracks until it passed. He eventually reached the counter and handed John a folded piece of paper. His eyes never left the floor.

John accepted the paper and glanced at the writing. "What's this?" John said. "A note from your mother?"

Not looking up, the man nodded. John waited until the man's shoulders had stopped shaking and continued. "It says you need a room for a week. Is that right?"

Another nod.

"Let me guess," John said. "She threw you out, right?"

The man wept, and a puddle of tears began to collect on the floor.

"Going home to mom next week to get your life back in order," John said, reading from the note.

The man wailed. John wasn't sure if the latest outburst was driven by the divorce or the prospect of moving back in with his mother.

"A little of mama's home cooking, huh? Just what you need."

The man's wail turned into a wolf howl. John flinched. "Take it easy," John said. "The neighbors will think I'm running a zoo over here. And they've already got their suspicions."

The howl vanished, replaced by incessant sobbing. John shook his head and looked at the note. "Okay, we've got a very nice room for you on the third floor. I'll just need to see your driver's license and credit card."

Without looking up, the man reached into his pocket, extracted the two cards, and handed them across the counter.

"Mr. Willie Winkle," John said, reading from the driver's license. "Barton Creek, huh? Just up the road. Of course, I imagine you won't be spending much time there from now on will you, Willie?"

Emily entered, and John motioned for her to approach.

"What's up?" she said. She spied the wet spot on the floor. "Damn," she said, grabbing a handful of tissues. She knelt down in front of the man and wiped the area clean. She handed the remaining tissues to Willie. "You're dripping."

Willie silently accepted the tissues, wiped his eyes and blew his nose loudly. John and Emily waited for him to finish.

Emily placed a hand on his shoulder. "Are you okay?"

The man sighed then shrugged. He didn't know.

"Mr. Winkle will be spending a week with us, Emily," John said. "Let's put him in the Aquatic Suite."

Emily thought for a moment and frowned. "You mean right next to my room?"

John motioned her closer. "The Aquatic has special carpeting and linens designed for criers," he whispered. "The bed's got a rubber mattress cover. This guy's a mess so you should probably remove all sharp objects."

Emily stared at John. "Okay," she said. "Mr. Winkle. If you'll just follow me." She headed towards the stairs but stopped and looked back. And waited.

Shuffle, sob, and drag.

Shuffle, sob, and drag.

Shuffle, sob, and drag.

John smiled at Emily, followed their funeral-like procession up the stairs then refocused on the stack of papers.

Moments later the door opened again, and a tall man wearing a long flowing purple robe stepped inside. He had a long white ponytail and the tiniest of goatees that matched his hair. He closed the door and put both hands on his hip as he took in his surroundings.

"Magnificent," he said. "Absolutely magnificent."

"Thanks. Can I help you?"

"Indeed, my good man. You can. I am in need of a room."

"Going through a divorce are we?"

"Indeed I am," he said, striding towards the counter. "Those who cannot remember the past are condemned to repeat it." He stroked his goatee and pondered. "Was that Churchill? Perhaps, Santayana? Who said that?"

"Everyone who's been divorced more than once," John said.

The man laughed; a booming, hearty laugh that filled the room. John, although intimidated by the man's appearance and omnipresence, immediately liked him.

"I've heard many good things about your establishment. It's most impressive."

"Thanks," John said. "But how did you hear about us? I never advertise."

"In my business, information tends to just flow in my direction."

"And what business would that be?"

"The business of information."

John, overpowered by the intense stare, glanced down at the stack of papers. "Okay," he said. He looked up and received another blast. The eyes were neither judgmental nor welcoming, but John was certain they were seeing far beyond the physical and probing deep inside to places even John never visited.

"I know what you're thinking," the man said.

John squinted. "Do you now?"

"Indeed."

"You gonna share it with me?"

"What would be the point of that?" He smiled and squinted back. "Since we already both know what it is."

25

"Good point." John extended his hand. "I'm John Germaine. The owner."

The man reached across the counter and grabbed John's hand. "Nice to finally meet you, John. I'm Doctor Randle."

"Doctor?"

"Call me Doc."

"Okay…Doc." John handed him a registration card. "If you could just fill this out. And I'll need a credit card and driver's license."

"Of course." He filled out the card and slid it back across the counter along with the requested plastic.

John imprinted the credit card and made a photocopy of the license then handed both items back. "How long will you be staying with us?"

"I foresee…at least a week."

"Fine. Let me show you to your room."

"No, that won't be necessary. I'll find it."

"Okay," John said. "Dinner is served at seven sharp."

"I may take a nap. Can you give me a wakeup call?"

"Don't worry," John said. "You'll hear the bell."

"Fine. I'll see you at seven."

Dr. Randle broke eye contact, and John felt he was finally able to breathe again. The man with the flowing cape wheeled and strode across the room then up the stairs. John studied his exit and wondered about the circumstances of the strange man's divorce. He also caught himself wondering about the type of woman who would have married him in the first place. He decided she must have been someone comfortable having a spouse who could peer into her soul at any moment in time.

Or maybe she was blind.

8

John stirred a large pot on the stove that sparkled with a cleanliness it hadn't seen since being removed from its original packaging. He looked around the gleaming kitchen and smiled. He sampled the stew, added more garlic and a healthy crank of freshly ground pepper, and took another taste. Satisfied, he replaced the lid. He leaned against the counter and admired the kitchen.

Bertrand and Randolph burst through the door in the middle of a rapid-fire conversation.

"I told him to forget it. He'd never pull that one off," Randolph said.

"It doesn't matter," Bertrand said. "Your guy's going down."

"You just wait until-"

"Ain't gonna happen, Randolph."

"Bullshit."

"The Democrats have got this one in the bag."

"A Democrat from Texas in the Senate? Yeah, right."

"Wait and see."

"Yeah, I'll wait and see. You don't know what you're talking about."

"I'm only a voter, huh?"

"That's right. Leave elections to the professionals."

"You've got no platform. No ideas. What have you Republicans got? A campaign slogan."

"Fuck you."

Bertrand laughed and winked at John. "Fuck you. It's not much of a slogan, but at least it's honest."

"Fuck you," Randolph said. This time, he meant it. He looked around the kitchen. "Whoa. What happened here?"

"Wow," Bertrand said. He stared around the room and whistled. "I didn't even know the floor was that color. Who is this woman?"

John folded his arms across his chest and smiled. "Didn't I tell you I'd find a new housekeeper? Can I pick em or what?"

"Unbelievable," Bertrand said.

"What does she look like?" Randolph said.

John and Bertrand both frowned at the question.

"She's gorgeous. So stay away from her," John said.

"Hey," Randolph said. "I know the rules."

Randolph went to the refrigerator and returned with three beers.

"I love this Shiner Bock," Randolph said.

"Mine's better," Bertrand said. "Can't wait to unveil it at the party."

"Did we get any new arrivals today?"

"Only two," John said. "Some weird guy in a robe and a crier."

"Damn," Randolph said.

"Yeah," John said. "And he's going home to his mother in a week as soon as she finishes repainting his room."

"Not another momma's boy?"

"Yup. And leave him alone, okay? You had the last one in tears the entire week he was here."

"Hey, it wasn't my fault. I was trying to encourage him, lift his spirits. All I said was that a man is ultimately judged by his ability to rise during times of adversity." Randolph took a long pull on his beer. "How was I supposed to know he was impotent?"

Emily, showered and wearing a cotton dress, entered the kitchen. "I'm sorry I'm late getting down. I took a nap. I guess today wore me out more than I realized."

"Don't you worry about that," Bertrand said. "If John ever did that much in a day, he'd need the rest of the year off. I'm Bertrand."

Emily shook his hand and smiled. "Oh, the scientist. Nice to meet you. I'm Emily."

Randolph approached. "Hi, Emily. I'm Randolph Tut. I am so glad you're here."

"Nice to meet you, Randolph. You're the political consultant?"

"That's me. Making the world safe from democracy."

The others stared at Randolph.

"Did I say from?" he said, blushing. "I meant for, of course." He cleared his throat. "My, how Freudian of me."

Emily laughed and leaned against the counter next to John. "Is Monty here?" she said.

"No, he's up in the Bay Area with one of his clients. He's pretty high maintenance and Monty's trying to make sure he doesn't blow a bunch of endorsement deals he's got in the works."

"That's too bad," she said.

"Here we go," Randolph said, shaking his head. "Another woman drooling over Monty."

It was Emily's turn to blush. "What can I say? He's so good looking. And he's one tough son of a bitch. He doesn't know the meaning of the word fear."

Randolph said, "Of course, there aren't many words that Monty does know the meaning of."

"That's our Monty," Bertrand said. "The ladies love him."

"What's not to love?" Emily said. "And it wouldn't be the first time I've had to deal with dumb."

Bertrand finished his beer, placed it on the table but caught Emily's glare. He picked up the bottle and deposited it into the trash. Emily smiled with approval and turned to John. "This Doctor Randle. What kind of doctor is he?"

"I'm not sure. I didn't even check his registration card. Why?"

"There's salt all over his room," she said.

"Salt?"

"He's probably heard about your cooking," Randolph said.

John flipped a finger in Randolph's direction and crossed to the computer near the phone and retrieved the information.

"Let's see. Dr. Randle. Mantologist," John said, reading from the screen. "Bertrand, you're the resident genius around here. What's a Mantologist?"

"Mantologist?   The   science   of   Mantology.   He's   a fortuneteller."

"That's a first."

"Maybe he can predict how much your Senator is going to lose by," Bertrand said.

"All right, smart ass. A thousand buck says my guy wins and old Gloria gets dusted."

Bertrand didn't hesitate. "You're on." He pointed at John and Emily. "And you're both witnesses. A thousand it is."

"Okay, children," John said. "Enough. It's time for dinner."

John pushed a button next to the sink and the familiar ballpark organ rally-chant built and reverberated through the house. John, pleased with himself, smiled at Emily. "Catchy tune, huh?"

"Sure, if you're at Wrigley Field." Emily shook her head and started setting the table.

9

Dr. Randle accepted a bowl of the steaming stew from John and inhaled. "This smells fantastic. What is it?"

Before John could reply, Randolph interrupted. "We only have one rule at the dinner table, Doc. We never ask that question."

"Yeah, chances are you don't want to know." Bertrand nibbled on a small piece of meat. "Not bad. Is it a species I would at least recognize?"

"As long as it's not one I might have as a pet," Randolph said.

"Cooking is all about the spices." John sat down, served himself, and began eating.

"Tell us, Dr. Randle," Emily said. "What's it like being a fortune teller? It sounds so mysterious. You know, dark rooms, lots of candles and crystal balls."

Dr. Randle wiped his mouth and took a sip of wine. "For me, it's not like that at all these days. I've gone mainstream; some would say strictly commercial. And I've progressed to the point where I can use just about anything to predict someone's future."

"Would that explain the salt covering the floor in your room?" she said.

"Of course. Halomancy."

"Then I'm sure you were able to see the vacuum cleaner in your future," Emily said. "It's in the closet right outside your room."

"Fortune telling with salt?" Bertrand said. "What a joke."

"Not at all, Bertrand. Halomancy is one of the many techniques I've perfected over the years. When I first started out in the business, I used enoptromancy almost exclusively."

"En...op...tro...mancy?" Emily said.

"Yes. Fortune telling with mirrors. But over time, I moved away from it."

"Didn't like what you saw, huh?" Bertrand said.

31

Dr. Randle stared at Bertrand as he chewed a mouthful of salad. "How sad, another cynic. Tell me, Bertrand. What do you do for a living?"

Bertrand smiled. "You tell me."

"Bertrand's role in life is to make America smell better," John said.

"That's right," Bertrand said. "And it's a challenge I take seriously. I'm also a doctor."

"Really?" Dr. Randle said.

"Yes. I've got a Ph.D. in Hygiology. That's the science of hygiene. In the industry, they call me Aroma Man. And if I know anything....I know when something smells." He glared at Dr. Randle.

John leaned over and touched Bertrand's arm. "Bertrand...take it easy."

Bertrand flicked John's hand away and muttered under his breath.

"What did you say?" John said.

"I believe he said that I couldn't predict the future with a calendar," Dr. Randle said.

Bertrand stared at the man in the cape. "How did you hear that? I didn't even say it out loud."

Dr. Randle smiled. "Gastromancy. Fortune telling using ventriloquism." He glanced around the table. "Next time you're in Vegas, you should check out my lounge act."

Emily refilled the wine glasses. "I think it's fascinating. Do you do readings for people? Could you do one for me?"

"Certainly."

Bertrand leaned forward and smiled. "If you're so good at seeing the future, how come you're getting divorced?"

Dr. Randle leaned back and considered the question. "Well, Bertrand, each person's future holds many different potential paths, and one must choose wisely from the various alternatives. My occupation offers a wide variety of different choices which bring me into contact with a multitude of diverse and interesting people. Alas, that was the primary reason for my own marriage's ultimate demise."

John looked up from his bowl of stew. "Another woman?"

"Not in this lifetime. But I will have some more salad."

Willie Winkle shuffled into the dining room and stood nervously in the doorway. He sniffled but had stopped crying.

John motioned to him. "Mr. Winkle. Nice to see you up and about. Come join us."

Mr. Winkle glanced at the others around the table and shuffled forward.

"Here, Mr. Winkle," Emily said. "Sit next to me."

Winkle shuffled towards the table and slumped into a chair.

"He's aliiiive," Randolph said.

John glared at Randolph. "Knock it off." He refocused on Winkle. "I'm glad you could make it down. How do you like your room?"

Winkle looked up from his plate and took a deep breath before responding. "It's...fine." He stared down at the plate of food Emily put in front of him.

"At least you've found your voice," John said. "Why don't you try to eat something?"

"Okay." He picked up his fork and examined it, undecided whether to use it to eat or to poke out one of his eyes.

"I see a brighter future in store for you, Mr. Winkle," Dr. Randle said through a mouthful of salad.

"You do?" Winkle said.

"Indeed I do," Dr. Randle said.

"How?" Bertrand said. "Did his fork tell you something?"

Dr. Randle leaned over and whispered to Bertrand. "No. But the way I see it, this guy's got nowhere to go but up."

Even Bertrand couldn't argue with this one. He looked at Winkle struggling to get the fork to his mouth. His trembling hand shook the contents back onto his plate. He stared at the empty fork.

"Use your hands," Randolph said. "We do it all the time."

Winkle noticed everyone's stares, put his fork down and sighed. "I suppose you all think it's pretty strange that a man my age would be going home to his mother."

"Well-"

John cut Randolph off mid-sentence. "Not at all. We've all been there. We've all been divorced, and we know it's a very painful process."

"Everyone here has been divorced?" Winkle said.

"Absolutely," John said. "Some more than others."

Randolph held up two fingers. "Twice for me."

"Once," Emily said.

"Me too," Bertrand said.

"One for me," John said. "But I got double reward points for mine so…"

Winkle forced a smile and looked at Dr. Randle, gnawing on a chicken leg. He stopped chewing when he realized the rest of the group was waiting for his answer.

"Me?" Dr. Randle said. "This is my…fifth. No, sixth."

"Six? You've been divorced six times?" John said.

"Slow learner," Bertrand said.

Dr. Randle shrugged his shoulders. "What can I say? Just because I can predict the future doesn't mean I'm any good at believing it."

"I'd rather live in a cardboard box than go through that six times," Bertrand said.

"Unfortunately, that scenario could be in my future at some point." Dr. Randle eyed another piece of chicken. "As a scientist, I'm sure you understand the monetary implications of the half-life principle."

Bertrand laughed. "I certainly do."

Dr. Randle looked around the table. "If any of you don't understand the math of California divorces, take a million bucks, divide it in half and repeat five times."

John shuddered and spoke to Winkle. "You see, we've all been there. And we've all had to deal with it in different ways."

34

"That's right," Bertrand said. "I moved in here after a very difficult transition period. When my wife filed, I was shattered."

"Your wife didn't file," Randolph said. "She fled."

Bertrand glared at Randolph. "Whatever the circumstances were, I was devastated. And very angry. My life was turned upside down, and I was forced to deal with emotions and feelings I never wanted to confront. For the first three months, I was still carrying a torch."

"You were still in love with her?" Winkle said.

"No," Bertrand said, sipping his wine. "I tried to burn her house down."

Emily laughed but stopped when she realized that Bertrand wasn't joking.

"And I bought this place as a refuge for men, like you, who are going through a divorce and trying to put their lives back in order," John said. "Believe it or not, even Randolph went through a tough time."

"That's true," Randolph said. "Fortunately, I had my friends around to help me through the mourning period."

Winkle nodded. "And after that?"

"We had lunch." Randolph laughed.

John kicked Randolph under the table. Randolph winced. "Sorry. Bad joke. I was lost for a while. I couldn't get pleasure out of anything. Work became meaningless. You know the drill." He waved the memory away with one hand. "So I decided to travel the world. Eventually, I ended up in Tibet sitting in the mountains with some guru called the Grand Kahuna."

Dr. Randle, stunned by the news, said, "You studied with Kahuna?"

"Well, I bought his book, but I can't say I studied much," Randolph said.

"My God," Dr. Randle said. "I haven't heard from him in years."

"Who on earth is the Grand Kahuna?" Emily said.

"Why he's only the most famous practitioner of Gyromancy in the world," Dr. Randle said.

"Gyromancy," John said. He decided to try a guess. "Fortune telling with Greek food?"

"No, it's nothing like that," Dr. Randle said, shaking his head. "It's a fascinating technique. The mantologist, in this case, Kahuna, walks around in a circle until he's so dizzy he falls. The fortune is then told by the position of the body when he lands."

"You're joking, right?" Emily said.

"No, he's not," Randolph said. "What a weird fuck he was. I think he was a raging alcoholic and just using the old gyro-thing for cover."

"How is Kahuna?" Dr. Randle said.

"He's dead," Randolph said, refilling his wineglass.

"Oh, no. What happened?" Dr. Randle said.

"We were in the middle of an early morning training session when a thick fog rolled in, and he fell off a cliff."

Dr. Randle fell silent as he let the news sink in.

Randolph looked around the table. "Let me tell you something. You don't need gyromancy to predict the future of somebody who just dropped 8,000 feet."

Everyone around the table grimaced.

"Tragic," Dr. Randle said. He shook his head then brightened. "Oh well, he knew the risks."

Randolph, in total control of center stage, lit a cigar, leaned back, and blew a smoke ring that hovered over the table. "After he died, I stayed at the retreat for a few more weeks, but it began to lose its luster. It was barren and cold. They only gave us these thin robes that never kept you warm. There was hardly any food and what they did give you was inedible. They made us sleep on a board with a small blanket. One day I had this incredible breakthrough that just hit me right over the head."

"Spiritual rebirth?" Dr. Randle said.

"No. Tibet sucked."

A roar of laughter filled the room and Randolph, delighted with his storytelling, puffed on his cigar.

Winkle, mustering only a smile, returned to his sadness. "All I know is that I don't feel complete. It's like I'm missing an arm."

"I know the feeling," John said. "Only in my case, it wasn't an arm. Don't worry. In time it will pass and become ancient history."

"But how long will it take?" Winkle said.

John shrugged. "How long is a piece of string?"

10

Down in the basement, Bertrand continued to work his magic. He raced back and forth adding a dash of this, a dash of that to different beakers bubbling away atop Bunsen burners. His white coat flapped as John and Randolph watched with amused bewilderment.

Bertrand grabbed three plastic cups and poured from a large vat that filled one wall of the basement. He passed the cups out and raised his own in salute. "To the dawn of a new beer."

They touched cups and drained the contents.

"That's great," John said.

"Very good," Randolph said. "Tastes like an import."

"Thank you, thank you." Bertrand drained his cup, pulled on a glove and removed one of the beakers from the flame. "Now, take a whiff of this."

John and Randolph leaned in and smelled the aroma rising from the beaker.

"Wow," John said. "Fantastic. What is that? Jasmine?"

Bertrand nodded. "Very good. There is some Jasmine in there."

"I'm getting…what is that?" Randolph pondered, then frowned. "Patchouli?"

"Yes. Just a touch."

"Talk about your blast from the past," Randolph said. "I used to date this woman in college who I swear bathed in that stuff."

John laughed. "Bad memories?"

"No, great memories. Just a bad smell. But somehow it works in this stuff." He leaned closer and took another whiff. "Fantastic. So what's the deal? After the beer has finished brewing, you add in the scent?"

"That's right," Bertrand said. "It's going to be America's first great smelling beer. When it hits the market, I'm going to be a very rich man."

"And you're sure it's going to be ready in time for the Halloween party?"

"Don't worry, John. It'll be ready."

"I'm counting on it. And let's not forget, we've got our work cut out for us trying to top last year." He looked at Randolph. "ESPN's got college football on tonight. Wanna catch the second half?"

"I need to get online. But I will be down in time to catch the Lakers."

"Jesus," Bertrand said. "What is it with you two and sports? Can't you think of a better way to spend your time?"

"Doubtful," Randolph said. "What I can't understand is why you, of all people, would hate sports as much as you do."

Bertrand turned indignant. "What do you mean me, of all people?"

Randolph backtracked. "I didn't mean it that way, Bertrand. Relax."

"What? Just because I'm black, you think I was born with a basketball in my hand?"

"That's not what I meant, Bertrand. I'm sorry."

"You son of a bitch."

Randolph glared back at him. "You need help. I was talking about you living here in this environment. With us. That's all I meant."

Bertrand cooled off. "It's a stereotype that's only made worse by those pampered athletes."

"Then don't watch sports, Bertrand. Frankly, I don't give a shit." Randolph disappeared up the stairs.

"Sorry," Bertrand said. "I guess I overreacted."

"Probably. Don't worry about it. He's already forgotten it. But you should talk to somebody about your anger problem."

Bertrand's temper flared again. "What anger problem?"

"That one."

39

"I'm fine." Bertrand jammed both hands into the pockets of his lab coat.

"You okay?"

"I'm fine."

"We cool?"

"Yeah." Bertrand removed a hand from his pocket and gave John a lame thumbs up. "We're cool."

John turned towards the stairs. "Okay, I'm out of here."

"Say, John?"

John turned back. "Yeah?"

"You got that quarter you owe me?"

"What?"

"The quarter from last week," Bertrand said. "The parking meter. Remember?"

John shook his head. "Unbelievable. Yeah, I remember." He extracted a quarter from his pocket and flipped it across the room. Bertrand smiled, put the quarter in his pocket and refocused on his grand cervisial-science experiment.

11

Randolph puffed on the cigar lodged in the corner of his mouth and stared at the computer screen. He removed the cigar, took a long swallow of Remy Martin and savored. He reinserted the cigar and began typing.

"Sugarbuns? R U out there?"

He sat back in his chair and waited. He took another sip of Remy and stared at the screen.

"Yes, Big Dog. I'm here."

"Yes," Randolph said, leaning forward.

"How's my little Sugarbuns doing today?"

The reply came immediately.

"Great. I missed talking with U last night. Sorry...but I was busy."

Randolph thought for a moment and then typed.

"No problem. Me 2. Was wondering if you're going to be able to make the party."

"Yes. I've rearranged my schedule. I'll be there."

"Yes!" Randolph puffed on the cigar and clapped his hands once.

"Great news. The party starts at 9. When are U coming?"

"Hopefully, right after I meet U. LOL."

"You naughty girl. LOL."

Randolph wasn't laughing out loud, but he didn't know the correct acronym for hard as a rock.

"What's your costume?"

"I'm coming as Cat Woman. Sound good?"

"The Big Dog says Meeeoow."

"Okay, Big Dog. Back in your kennel. I'll see you at the party. Can't wait. XOXOXOXO."

"Sounds puuuuurfect. Bye."

Randolph logged off and headed downstairs with a huge smile on his face. He grabbed a beer from the fridge and headed to the entertainment room. John was simultaneously watching an NBA game, college football, and a boxing match. Bertrand, stretched out on a couch, was reading Trump's latest offering: The Best Hair a Billion Can Buy.

Randolph plopped down in an overstuffed chair, sipped his beer and sighed.

John glanced away from the big screens. "You're in a good mood."

"I've got a date for the party," Randolph said.

"The one you've been instant messaging with the past month?"

"That's the one. And she sounds hot."

"It's probably a man," Bertrand said, not looking up from his book.

Randolph grimaced. "Now why did you have to go and say something like that?"

Bertrand glanced up over the top of the book. "Because it's probably true. Latest research shows that over ninety percent of people use a false identity in chat rooms."

"Latest research shows," Randolph said. "You and your research."

"I think you touched a nerve, Bertrand." John laughed.

"What would you expect from the resident homophobe?" Bertrand closed the book and smiled at Randolph.

"I am not homophobic," Randolph said. "How many times do I have to tell you? I have no problems with homosexuals."

"Sure, Randolph," Bertrand said. "We believe you."

"I hope they all turn gay," Randolph said, sliding deeper into his chair.

"Less competition?" John said.

"Exactly."

"Well, I certainly wouldn't mind if one of the competitors would step up and get Margaret out of my hair," John said. "This alimony is killing me."

"Well, stop bitching about it and do something," Randolph said. "Let me put you in touch with this lawyer I know and see if he can't reopen your case."

"Listen to him, John," Bertrand said. "Six years of alimony at eight thousand a month is ridiculous. She's got no incentive to ever get remarried."

"You're getting screwed, John. Big time." Randolph finished his beer and stood. "Beers?"

"Sure."

"Yeah, thanks."

Randolph, deep in thought, leaned against the wall.

"What?" John said.

"I'm wondering," Randolph said. "What's the worst thing that could happen if you decided to take her back to court?"

"How about me catching a judge who ends up sympathizing with Margaret and she ends up getting half the hotel? Or all of it? Either one of you feel like having her as your landlady?"

Randolph caught Bertrand's eye, and they shook their heads. "Forget I brought it up."

"I'd rather follow in the footsteps of the Grand Kahuna," Bertrand said.

Randolph laughed and headed out of the room. He wheeled around the corner and bumped into Dr. Randle.

"Excuse me," Dr. Randle said.

"Sorry, Doc. I'm on a beer run and wasn't watching where I was going."

"No, it's my fault. I should have known you were coming."

"That's funny. You just hanging around tonight?"

"Yes," Dr. Randle said. "I guess I'm just hanging around."

"I see."

"Yes, well…I should head upstairs. I have some work I need to do."

"Right. Then I guess I'll be seeing you around."

"Yes. I'm sure you will."

Dr. Randle flipped his cape back and headed up the stairs. Randolph watched him go then headed off in search of beer.

12

John gulped the last of his milk and set the glass on the counter just as Emily raced through the kitchen on the way to her next task. She paused in the doorway and looked back. John caught red-handed, smiled then rinsed the glass and put it in the dishwasher. Emily flashed a quick smile and departed.

Dr. Randle wandered into the kitchen wearing pajamas and a fresh robe.

"Good morning, Doc," John said. "Coffee?"

"Please."

He sat down and flipped through the newspaper. John returned with two cups of coffee and sat down next to him.

"You know, John. I've been thinking," Dr. Randle said. "Perhaps one of the answers to your money problems is right in front of us."

"How do you know that I'm having money problems?"

Dr. Randle spread his arms and smiled. "It's what I do."

John frowned but said nothing.

"I've got a new book coming out soon that I'll be cross-promoting with a related seminar. I haven't had the chance to test out the seminar with a live audience yet, and I thought that perhaps this would be the perfect place."

"Here? In the hotel?"

"Yes. We could do one here. If it's successful, who knows, maybe it could become a regular event. I'll give you a cut."

"How many people are we talking about? I'm running a hotel here. The last thing I want is a bunch of people hanging around."

"Around 50. At 400 bucks a pop. I'll go fifty-fifty on the workshop fee plus 25 percent of merchandise. You're gonna love the T-shirts. You should net around nine, maybe ten grand for an afternoon."

"That works," John said. "A fortune telling seminar?"

"This one is more…therapy related. For the adult male."

"That could get ugly in a hurry."

"Let's hope so." Dr. Randle laughed. "Fortunately for me, dysfunction sells."

"What the hell…why not? When do you want to do it?"

"Soon. My publisher is getting anxious to get the book out but wants to see if the seminar has any legs before they finalize the marketing campaign."

"As long as you don't schedule it on Halloween, you got a deal. Nothing interferes with the party."

"Fantastic. I'll get back to you later today with a date."

"What's the book called anyway?"

"We're All Weenies Inside."

John thought for a moment and said, "Kind of a metrosexual meets Dr. Phil sort of thing?"

Dr. Randle smiled. "Hey, that's not bad. Mind if I use that?"

John laughed. "Consider it a gift."

13

Monty Mantooth, former king of the chop block and sports agent extraordinaire, had been reduced to an emotional pile of rubble and was frantically searching the room for an escape route. He looked around at the circle of men surrounding Dr. Randle, who was pacing back and forth and getting louder by the second. Seeing no path through the tight circle of straight-backed chairs, Monty hunched down behind the bald man sitting directly in front of him. The seminar, after a slow start, had kicked into high gear. The audience was now mesmerized by the dynamic presence of their speaker. Dr. Randle was on a roll.

"That's right. Each and every one of us." He pivoted on one foot and pointed. "You...and you...and you...and you. Deep inside those places where you're afraid to go, underneath your business suit, behind the designer sunglasses, inside your Calvin Klein underwear, beats the heart and soul of one, gigantic, frightened..."

On cue, the audience roared. "Weenie!"

"Exactly," Dr. Randle whispered. "We're all weenies inside."

Bertrand had had enough. He leaned towards Monty, who was still quivering from his recent bout with Dr. Randle. "This is fucking ridiculous. What on earth are we doing here? I've got beer brewing."

"Be quiet," Monty whispered. "He'll hear you. And I don't want him in my face again."

Dr. Randle spied their conversation out of the corner of his eye but kept speaking to the group. "And what do we do to hide our true nature?"

The group roared its answer. "We compensate!"

"Exactly." Dr. Randle wheeled on one foot and changed directions. "And what do we call that?"

"Weenie Compensation!"

46

"Exactly. Weenie Compensation." Dr. Randle spat the term out as if he'd swallowed poison. "We all do it. We all have it." He wheeled and headed slowly in Bertrand's direction. "We all have a phobia, one secret fear that drives the masks we face the public with. Even friends and family can be blind to the real motives that drive men's behavior. We've all got them."

He stopped directly in front of Bertrand's chair and pointed at him. "Take Bertrand for example."

Bertrand, caught not paying attention like a third-grader during math, glanced up from the shoelace he was retying. "What?" The combination of confusion and fear on his face only encouraged Dr. Randle.

Dr. Randle addressed the group without taking his eyes off Bertrand. "Bertrand obviously works hard and is a successful scientist. But is it enough for him?"

"No!" cried the group.

"And why not?" Dr. Randle said.

"Because he's a weenie!"

"Go fuck yourself," Bertrand said.

Dr. Randle continued. "Exactly. Because he's a weenie. Unable to be satisfied with his current lot in life, he invents things. Not so much for the sake of invention or creation, but to make money." Dr. Randle began to stalk the circle of men hanging on every word. "Perhaps he has seen many of his co-workers ravaged by downsizing. Perhaps he grew up in poverty. Perhaps his desire for money stems from his need to compensate for some physical shortcoming."

"Hey, watch it," Bertrand said.

Dr. Randle ignored him and continued. "Regardless, Bertrand is a man driven, even obsessed by the overpowering fear of being poor."

John leaned over and whispered to Randolph, "This guy's good."

"Be quiet," Randolph said. "He'll hear you."

Too late. Dr. Randle picked up the sidebar and stared at Randolph.

Randolph shook his head and glared at John. "Thanks a lot."

"Yes, Randolph," Dr. Randle said as he inched his way towards him. "Don't worry. Your attention seeking behavior has not gone unnoticed."

"Get away from me you quack."

Dr. Randle maintained his slow, interminable creep. "Just relax, Randolph."

"I'm warning you."

Dr. Randle was now standing directly in front of him. Randolph squirmed in his chair.

"We have a little secret don't we, Randolph?"

"I'm a political consultant. I've got lots of secrets."

"I'm sure you do," Dr. Randle said. "But you have one big secret fear. Don't you, Randolph?"

"I don't know what you're talking about."

Dr. Randle placed a hand on his shoulder and squeezed gently.

"Oh, I think you do. Maybe it was the lingering look of another boy in the shower after gym class. Perhaps something happened on a crowded train. Or maybe someone just rubbed you the wrong way."

Dr. Randle bent forward from the waist and kissed Randolph on the cheek. He slowly trailed a finger down Randolph's arm and winked. Randolph squirmed in his seat and shoved the hand away. Finally, unable to take any more, he jumped up out of his seat. "Get away from me." Randolph pleaded his case to the group. "Look, I am not homophobic."

The group wasn't buying it. "Weenie alert! Weenie alert!"

"I am not a weenie," Randolph shouted. "I'm one of the most successful political consultants in the country. I've got a contact list that every one of you would kill for."

"Compensator!" the group roared.

Randolph stood in the middle of the group and looked around the room desperately searching for a show of support. "This is unbelievable. I am not a homophobe."

Dr. Randle, having worked the room to perfection, beamed. "Well, I think that's a good note to finish on." He rubbed his hands together. "Let's see. We've got milk and cookies in the lobby. Also, I've got T-shirts, calendars, key chains and hats along with copies of my last bestseller; The Future: It's Not What It Used to Be. Of course, I will also be available for signings."

The crowd filed out amid a buzz of excitement and nervous energy. John approached Randolph and draped an arm around his shoulder. "You okay, big guy?"

Randolph shrugged John's arm away and straightened his sports coat. "Yeah," he said, glaring at Dr. Randle. "I'm fine."

14

John tugged at the white collar and eventually managed to loosen its stranglehold. He stared forlornly around the crowded room and tried tapping his foot to the lame music droning from the sound system. John glared at the DJ, who was oblivious to John's growing impatience as he chatted with a woman dressed as a hooker. John looked around at the bored conversations the partygoers were having. "This party sucks. Where the hell is Bertrand?"

Dr. Randle, wearing his usual attire, approached. "This is the famous party you've been talking about?" He flipped his robe back, placed his hands on his hips and surveyed the room with a sad shake of his head.

John scanned Dr. Randle's outfit. "It must be nice not to have to worry about deciding on a costume, huh?"

Not taking his eyes off the room, Dr. Randle nodded and said, "Yes, it's one of the perks of my profession."

"Where the hell is Bertrand?"

"I just saw him a few moments ago heading down to the basement."

"Good," John said. "This party is DOA."

"Is there some sort of message in your choice of costume?"

"What do you mean?"

"A priest? I wouldn't have pegged you for a religious type."

"By the time I got to the costume store, this was all they had left. It was either this or Sponge Bob Squarepants. Say, that was quite a session the other day. I'm still getting calls from people wondering when we're going to do another."

"It was memorable," Dr. Randle said. "But I'm not sure that Bertrand and Randolph have forgiven me."

"I wouldn't worry about it. How'd we end up doing?"

"Your cut's just over nine grand."

"Not bad for an afternoon. I guess there is money to be made in the self-improvement game, huh?"

"Yes, dysfunction is definitely a growth industry."

John nodded but then paused. "Hey, Doc, when dysfunction becomes as common throughout society as it is, couldn't normal behavior be accurately classified as dysfunctional?"

Dr. Randle was stunned. "That's fantastic, John. Can I use that?"

John laughed. "It's all yours. Think there's a book there?"

"The hell with the book. I'm thinking TV."

John laughed louder and caught a glimpse of Emily wearing a sexy French maid outfit. John looked away and stared down at his shoes.

Dr. Randle noticed. "You know, John, I didn't want to say anything during the seminar, but I know what's going on."

"What are you talking about?"

"Your deepest fear."

John chuckled nervously. "Me? The only thing I'm afraid of is my ex-wife, Margaret."

"Precisely."

John stared at him with a puzzled expression.

"We'll talk about it later," Dr. Randle said. "Right now, I think I have the perfect solution for this party."

Dr. Randle departed with a wave and John watched him disappear up the stairs. Moments later, Bertrand appeared wheeling a large keg of beer. He was wearing his white coat. His only concession to the costume was a wild, white-haired wig.

"It's about time," John said.

"Sorry," Bertrand said. "I had a hell of a time getting it up the stairs. This thing is heavy."

"How'd you finally get it up here?"

"Monty."

"He only needed one hand didn't he?"

"Yup," Bertrand said. "That is one strong son of a bitch."

"Okay, let's go," John said. "Let's get on with it. These people need to get several beers in them."

51

Bertrand moved to the center of the registration area and addressed the group. "Excuse me, people," he said. "Could I have your attention, please?" He waved to the DJ, who turned his attention away from the hooker long enough to turn the music off. Bertrand cleared his throat and patted the keg in front of him. "On behalf of John and the rest of us here at Divorce Hotel, we'd like to officially welcome you to our 5th annual Halloween party."

The crowd applauded loudly.

Bertrand laughed. "I can see that some of you have been with us before. Those of you who've attended in the past know that we take great pride in putting on this party. For all you first-timers in attendance, we only have one thing to say to you."

On cue, the group roared. "Fresh meat!"

Everyone laughed, and Bertrand rested one foot on top of the keg. "Tonight is a very special evening for another reason. For some time, I have been working diligently to perfect what I believe is a beer that will revolutionize the brewing industry."

Another round of applause ensued.

"Thank you. Thank you very much. Tonight…you will be the first people to taste what is destined to become America's first great-smelling beer."

Once again, applause interrupted Bertrand's speech. He bowed slightly, flushed with pride.

"John, Emily, if I could enlist your help." Bertrand removed his foot from the keg.

John and Emily went to work pouring several pitchers of the beer. Bertrand made his way up the stairs to the second-floor balcony where he stood staring down at the assembled crowd.

"If I could ask your patience until everyone gets a glass, I would like to propose a toast."

An excited buzz went through the room as John and Emily worked their way through the crowd.

"I call it," Bertrand said, holding up his glass, "Bertrand's Bouquet." He spread his arms and announced reverently, "As we work our way through the daily grind of life, I remind you to always take the time to stop and smell the beer. And now, let your nostrils partake."

He led the crowd through a group smell. A murmur of delight filled the room. Bertrand chortled and twitched, barely able to contain his delight. "Yes, it is wonderful isn't it?" He held up his glass in salute. "A toast. To me."

"To Bertrand!" shouted the group.

"And now, let's partake."

Bertrand beamed as he watched the crowd below taste his special concoction. Suddenly, his smile vanished as he bore witness to the largest spit-take in recorded history. Bertrand watched in horror and stared at his still untouched glass. He took a large gulp of beer, retched, felt his entire body spasm, and retched again. He vomited lunch off the balcony onto Mickey and Minnie Mouse, standing directly below clutching their stomachs.

"Jesus Christ," Bertrand said, gasping for air.

The crowd was thinning, and a long queue had formed outside the downstairs bathroom. Those unable to wait headed outside and the sound of coughing and gagging flowed back inside the hotel. John glared up at Bertrand on the balcony.

"Bertrand. Get your ass down here."

The sheepish Bertrand worked his way down the stairs. He approached John and burped. He wiped his mouth with the sleeve of his lab coat. "I don't know what could have happened."

"Did you ever taste it after you added the aromas?" John said.

"No, I wanted it to be a complete surprise."

"Well, mission accomplished."

Bertrand, fawn-like, stood silently.

John softened his tone. "Forget it. We just need to come up with something."

"What are we going to do?"

"Well, I'll tell you what you're going to do. You're going to do the fastest booze run in history while I try to figure out how to keep everyone from leaving."

Bertrand accepted his assignment without protest and nodded. "Okay." He started to walk away, then turned back to John. "You think it would be okay if I took up a collection?" John glared at him. Bertrand nodded. "Nah, probably not."

John watched him depart, transitioned into damage control mode and worked his way into the crowd.

15

Randolph gave Cat Woman the once over. Since he enjoyed it so much the first time, he repeated the process. She was standing next to Monty about ten feet away. Randolph admired the view. The tight black outfit could have been painted on, and he savored the long legs that didn't end. They evolved into the most magnificent posterior he had ever seen. Long black hair streamed down her back, and she tapped a six-inch stiletto to the pulsating dance mix.

Randolph, dressed as Zorro, adjusted his sword and sidled close from behind. Randolph cupped one hand and gently squeezed one of her buttocks. He quivered from its firmness.

"Legs like that should be illegal," he whispered.

Cat Woman turned, glanced at the hand clutching her ass, and looked at Randolph.

"That's what my coach says," said a diminutive black man in his early twenties. A trimmed goatee was on full display underneath the half-mask that covered his eyes.

Randolph, wide-eyed and looking like he'd been hit with a baseball bat, stared back. His hand was still clenching Cat Woman's right buttock. Monty, dressed in football uniform sans helmet, turned towards the two men.

"Hey, what's up? Have you two met?"

"God, I hope not," Randolph said.

Cat Woman gently removed Randolph's hand. "Do I know you?"

"God, I hope not."

"This is Dexter Clinchpoop."

"Dexter Clinchpoop? The rookie kick returner for the 49ers?"

"The very one," Monty said. "He's my most important client."

"I bet you say that to all the guys." Dexter laughed. "Nice to meet you. And you are?"

"Very confused," Randolph said.

55

He stared at Dexter's outstretched hand but eventually managed to return the handshake.

"That's quite a grip you've got there," Dexter said.

Randolph, sweating profusely, was torn between a hasty retreat or discovering if Dexter was his internet companion. He chose to stay. "Well, a guy like you must be busy, huh?'

Dexter frowned but nodded.

"What with practice, games, endorsement deals, and all that travel, you probably aren't left with a lot of free time. Yeah, you probably don't even have time for a hobby. Yeah, that's gotta be right. Spend much time on the internet, Sugarbuns? I mean, Dexter." Randolph wiped his brow. Dexter gave him a blank stare and glanced at Monty, who could only shrug back.

"Yeah, I spend some time on the Internet," Dexter said. "Why do you want to know? Are you a reporter?"

"No, nothing like that," Randolph said. "Well, gotta go. Nice meeting you." Randolph backed away, bowing slightly, and disappeared upstairs.

16

John gagged as he tossed the last handful of rancid paper towels into the plastic trash bag Emily was holding.

"Great party." Emily closed and tied the bag.

"It's still early." John glanced around the room. No one had departed, but he knew something needed to be done in a hurry.

"You want this outside?"

"Yeah…and you might want to double bag it."

Emily nodded and reached for another plastic bag. John, tugging at his collar, wandered off towards the reception area. He stood off in one corner of the room and observed the proceedings. Subdued small-talk continued to be the norm.

A woman, wearing an elaborate feather mask that covered the top half of her face and dressed in a very short skirt, was grinding herself up against a pirate with an eye patch and stuffed parrot on one shoulder.

Dr. Randle wandered over and stood next to John. They watched the woman and pirate continue their sexual gyrations. "That woman is demonstrating the classic signs of a frotteur," Dr. Randle said.

"A frot what?"

"A frotteur. The term used to describe someone who gets sexually aroused by rubbing up against others in crowded places. Judging from the looks of this party, she better hurry up and finish."

John continued to watch the amorous actions of the couple. "Something's not right here."

"You're telling me," Dr. Randle said. "I've seen more exciting funerals."

"What? Oh, the party. Yeah, it's a disaster. My reputation is going to be ruined."

"Have no fear, my good friend. Help is on the way."

John, still distracted by the couple, nodded without comprehension. "Yeah, whatever."

Randolph crept down the stairs, saw John and Dr. Randle, and made a beeline for them.

"Where have you been?" John said.

"I needed to get online for a few minutes."

"Is your date here yet?"

"I hope not," Randolph said. He glanced around and saw Monty chatting with Dexter in the kitchen. He then spied the couple doing the love-grind in the entertainment room. "That's quite a show."

"Indeed," Dr. Randle said, not taking his eyes off the couple.

All three stared as the couple turned up the heat. The pirate was standing behind the woman, and she leaned back and ground herself against him. She kept repeating the same movement; a slow, intense rocking that kept both of them tightly joined at the waist.

"You could sell tickets to this," Randolph said.

"Or at least rent them a room," Dr. Randle said.

The woman rocked against the pirate and slowly began to hike her already short skirt. John recoiled as the woman's upper thighs came into clear view. He looked around the room and decided, despite the crowd of people surrounding the couple, they were the only ones paying attention.

"Great legs," Randolph said. "I gotta give her that."

The pirate uttered a guttural Aarrrgh and smiled. The woman continued to inch her skirt up, and the bottom of her ass appeared.

"My god…they're going to go at it right here," Randolph said.

Stunned, the three men continued to stare, unable to take their eyes off the couple. The skirt, coaxed by her long, red fingernails, continued to climb.

Suddenly, it appeared out of nowhere.

John stared hard at the 666 tattooed on one of the woman's butt cheeks. "Margaret."

"Well, I'll be damned," Randolph said. "I can't believe I didn't recognize her. Has she been working out?"

John glared at Randolph then headed for the couple.

Randolph laughed as John strode off and then he saw Cat Woman standing a few feet away. He glanced into the kitchen and saw Monty still chatting with Dexter. He looked back at the second, almost identical, Cat Woman. He smiled, pulled down his Zorro-mask and walked towards her.

Dr. Randle pulled a small box from one of the pockets in his robe. He opened the lid and looked inside. Several large and furry black spiders scurried inside the box from the light and threatened escape. Dr. Randle closed the lid and inched his way through the crowd pausing to drop one of the spiders onto the floor every few steps. "Okay, my pretties," he said. "Go work your magic."

John approached Margaret, who now had her skirt bunched around her waist and was oblivious to everything except her own pleasure. She was quickly brought back to earth.

"Margaret, what the hell are you doing here?" John said.

Margaret opened her eyes, frowned at the voice, and pulled her skirt down. "Damn, I was so close. I guess some things never change. So nice to see you, John."

"I know this is the night for witches to appear, but did you have to do it here?"

"What can I say? It's always the best party of the year, and I didn't want to miss it. Plus, I have some good news for you. I thought you'd want to hear it from me before the rumor mill got it."

"That's a laugh. Good news and you don't ever show up in the same time zone let alone the same house."

"What did I tell you?" she said to the pirate. "A total asshole."

"Aarrrgh," the pirate said, adjusting his eye patch.

A nearby partygoer yelped in pain. "Ouch! What the hell was that?"

John, momentarily distracted, glanced at the man in a Dracula costume. Another guest, this one a large woman in a ballerina costume standing on the other side of Margaret cried out, "Damn. Something just bit me."

Randolph approached Cat Woman from behind. Cautiously, hands-free.

"Sugarbuns?"

Cat Woman turned around slowly. "Hey, Big Dog. Where you been?" She sidled up close and then jumped back in pain. "Ouch. That hurt. What is that?"

Randolph stared down at Cat Woman's bare wrist. "That's the biggest spider I've ever seen."

"Well, get it off me." She began to panic. "It's already bit me once."

Randolph's Zorro-like qualities only went as far as the costume. With shaking hands, he reached out and made a tentative grab for it. He was no match for the spider, and it jumped off Cat Woman and clamped down onto the fleshy part of Randolph's hand between the thumb and forefinger.

"Ow. Fuck that hurts." Randolph flung his arm out and the spider, like it was launched from a catapult, flew across the room and landed on Margaret's neck.

Margaret, broke eye contact with John, saw the spider and screamed. The scream snapped the spider out of its haze, and it began to scramble back and forth across Margaret's bare shoulders.

"Get this fucking thing off me."

The pirate slipped into role and drew his sword.

"Not the sword, you idiot," Margaret said.

John watched the spider doing shoulder laps with a perverse smile frozen on his face.

The pirate returned his sword to its scabbard, leaned closer and flicked a finger at the spider. Unfortunately, the finger landed a glancing blow which only served to piss the spider off. It stood its ground, planted all eight legs firmly on Margaret's shoulder and took a vicious bite of flesh.

"Ow. You son of a bitch." Margaret glanced down at the spider.

"Gee, that's too bad," John said.

"You furry motherfucker." She took dead aim and flicked her finger. The spider flew across the room and disappeared into the increasingly agitated crowd.

Cat Woman began shaking her shoulders in time to the music and smiled at Randolph. She tapped her right foot and the left soon joined in. "That's odd," she said. "But I suddenly feel like dancing."

"Go for it," Randolph said. "I don't dance."

"Me neither." She started swaying faster to the music.

Dr. Randle entered the room and observed the various dance moves breaking out around the room. He shook his head at the abysmal display of rhythm.

"This will never do."

He worked his way through the crowd towards the sound system. The DJ, before disappearing with the hooker, had put on a snoozy piano ballad normally reserved for corporate cocktail parties. Dr. Randle extracted a CD from his pocket, and soon an up-tempo, Italian tarantella blared from the speakers. Dr. Randle watched as both the number of dancers and the tempo of their movements increased.

Margaret began an erotic slither in time with the music. "John, I'd like you to meet someone." She grabbed the pirate by one arm and dragged him closer. "This is David."

"Nice to finally meet you, John," the pirate said. He pirouetted into a very bad Travolta-Stayin Alive and held the pose.

"Hi." John stared in disbelief. "Uh…nice costume."

"Thanks. It's from a Pirates of Penzance I did a couple of years ago." He made a production number out of drawing his sword and incorporating it into his dance. "I got great reviews."

Bertrand entered the room struggling under the weight of cases of beer and wine. He set the alcohol down on a table and surveyed the dancing.

"All right," David said, spotting the booze. "Supplies." He slid the sword back into its scabbard, extended an arm skyward and Travolta-ed his way through the crowd.

John watched him depart and turned to Margaret. "So that's what you've been spending my money on?"

"No. I spend your money on me." Margaret clamped a thumb and forefinger on her nose and slithered into the Swim.

John stared at her and turned his attention to the rest of the room: The party was beginning to rock. "What the hell is going on around here?"

"You're such a schmuck." Margaret transitioned into the Funky Chicken. "Just relax and enjoy the party."

"I'll relax as soon as you and your new boy toy are out of my house."

"He's not a boy toy. David and I are engaged."

John, certain she was playing a cruel joke, waited for the other shoe to drop.

"I told you I had some good news for you."

"Engaged? You mean I'm finally going to get rid...I mean...congratulations. He's a great guy."

"He's everything you never were," Margaret said, trying on the Charleston for size.

"You mean brain dead?"

"Keep it up, John, and you'll bear witness to the longest engagement on record."

"Sorry. Force of habit. When are you two going to tie the knot?"

"Soon. We're talking about starting a family. David says he's tired of being an only child."

Dr. Randle boogalooed his way towards them with a huge smile on his face. "Is this better?"

"Are you kidding? This is fantastic," John said. "I'd like you to meet Margaret Mayhem, my ex-wife. She's just told me she's getting married."

"Well, congratulations," Dr. Randle said. Without breaking his dance stride, he shook Margaret's hand. She held on longer than might be expected.

"My, my, my...aren't you an interesting specimen." She stared at Dr. Randle.

He broke free of Margaret's attempt at a full-body rub. "I told you I would take care of everything."

"What have you done?" John said.

Dr. Randle pulled John a few feet away from the crowd. He shook his shoulders and swayed to the music as he explained. "You're witnessing the early stages of a fascinating phenomenon that dates back to 14th century Italy."

"I am?"

"Indeed you are. It's called Tarantism. It began in the southern Italian city of Taranto, and there's a large, wolf-spider that's indigenous to the area. It's where the name tarantula originated. The bite of this spider is known to cause an energetic, almost uncontrollable urge to dance."

"You let loose a bunch of tarantulas? At my party?"

"Yes, and it seems to be working."

Both men stared at the throng of partygoers who, in some cases, were literally bouncing off the walls. The tarantella ended and was replaced by a loud Sympathy for the Devil.

"All right," Dr. Randle said. "The Stones."

"Spider-induced disco?"

"I wouldn't call it disco but, yes, it's very big in the clubs in Rome."

"How long is this going to last?"

"Historically, only a couple of days."

"A couple of days? Jesus, Doc, I'm trying to run a hotel here."

"Relax, John. Things should be pretty quiet by the morning."

"Are you sure?"

"Well, it's not an exact science."

Margaret shook her way over to Dr. Randle and dragged him away. They were soon involved in a strange exotic dance. Margaret shook provocatively and disappeared under his cape. She didn't come up for air for several minutes.

Randolph smiled at Cat Woman. "That's funny. I never dance."

"Yes," Cat Woman said. "I can see why."

"I guess we should probably take our masks off."

"Why not? Let's have a look at the Big Dog."

They removed their masks simultaneously. Still dancing, they glared at each other in disbelief. Courtship over.

"You?" Randolph found himself staring at the face of Gloria Fontaine, the woman running for Senate against Randolph's candidate.

"Randolph Tut? Ah, shit," Gloria said.

"Why the hell didn't you identify yourself when we were chatting on-line? You could have at least given me a clue."

"Yeah, that would be great," Gloria said. "A candidate for the U.S. Senate trolling for dates on the internet."

"Damn. I can't believe I called you Sugarbuns."

"Well, I can't believe I got sucked in by a dirtbag like you."

"Yeah? Look who's talking. How's your mother, Gloria?"

"Fuck you, Tut," she said, attempting to storm out of the room while doing the Texas two-step.

Randolph glared after her and waited until she had worked her way out the door before shuffling to the drink table.

Emily entered the room and approached John, who was staring at the goofy look on Dr. Randle's face. Moments later, Margaret emerged from under the cape, straightened her hair and blinked as she waited for her eyes to readjust to the light.

"Sorry, I'm late getting in here. I had to help Bertrand unload." She looked around the room. "Boy, when you said you threw great parties, you weren't joking."

"And who's this?" Margaret said.

"Margaret, this is Emily. My new housekeeper. Emily, this is my soon to be remarried, ex-wife, Margaret."

The two women shook hands and gave each other the once over.

"Nice to meet you, Margaret. Congratulations. You must be very happy."

"I'm ecstatic," John said.

"I was talking to her," Emily said.

"I know," John said. "I'm just so happy."

"Nice to meet you, Emily. John, you surprise me. She's adorable."

"When's the wedding?" Emily said.

"Soon," John said.

Margaret shook her head at John's blissful demeanor.

"I don't think I've ever seen you this happy before," she said.

"It's just the first time I've ever done it in your presence."

"You're such a dick," Margaret said.

Emily intervened. "So, is your fiancé here?"

"Yes, he's off getting drinks." Margaret glanced around the room. "He's on his way now."

"You're gonna love him," John said. "He's a great guy."

David, still doing Travolta, approached carrying two glasses of wine. He stopped short when he saw Emily. "Emily? What are you doing here?"

"I live here," she said. "What's your excuse?"

"You two know each other?" John said.

"Yeah, we know each other," Emily said. "We were married for four years."

"What?" Margaret sprang into action. "Married? You never told me you'd been married."

David downed one of the glasses of wine. "I guess it just slipped my mind." He glanced back and forth between Margaret and Emily and forced a smile.

"Slipped your mind?" Emily said. "That wasn't much of a trick since you don't have one."

"I'll handle this," Margaret said. She stepped closer to David and edged Emily back with a shoulder. "How long have you been divorced?"

"About a year," David whispered.

"A year?" Margaret flushed with anger and unable to stop her hippy-hippy-shake, lurched forward. "We've been dating for two."

This was news to Emily. "You cheating son of a bitch." She reared back her arm.

John grabbed her arm and inserted himself between the combatants. "Now, let's just enjoy the party."

"You were sleeping with me for a year while you were still married to her?"

"Margaret, just try and take it easy," David said, inching backward.

"Let me at the bastard," Emily said.

David looked back and forth between the two women and reached for his sword.

"You son of a bitch," Margaret said.

"Sleep around on me, will you?" Emily tried to reach around John and land a haymaker.

John grabbed Emily, and they waltzed away. Margaret, now with a clear shot, fired a punch at David that landed solidly on his jaw. David crumbled and collapsed in a half-dance, half-stagger onto the floor.

The music transitioned into a lively Russian folk dance. Flat on his back, semi-conscious, David gave Travolta the rest of the night off and transitioned into a Russian Cossack dance. Soon both feet were raised about a foot off the floor, thrusting back and forth.

"The wedding's off," Margaret said. She stared down at David then danced off with Dracula.

"No," John said.

Dr. Randle approached and stared down at the body that was going into spasms. John and Emily hovered over the body as did several other onlookers.

"Don't touch him," Dr. Randle said.

"Yeah, give him some air," John said.

Dr. Randle continued to stare down at David. "Here's a rare opportunity for me to practice a little spasmatomancy."

What the hell is that?" John said.

"Fortune telling by watching a twitching body."

Dr. Randle did a half-Twist, half-Limbo as he worked his way down for a closer look.

Margaret waltzed her partner close to the twitching body, delivered a crushing kick to the side of David's head and pirouetted away. David, his dance-card now officially punched,

66

groaned and managed only a soft tap with one foot in time with the music.

John stared down at the quivering body. Nasty welts and bruises were already forming on his face. "What do you see, Doc?"

"I see that eye patch coming in very handy."

A snappy Brazilian tune sprang from the speakers, and a conga line led by Randolph formed and worked its way out of the entertainment room, through the kitchen, and eventually up the stairs.

Bertrand, inconsolable, pounded beers and stayed in the corner.

John and Emily carried David to a couch and tucked him in with a blanket.

John stared up to the heavens, almost prayerful. Emily seized her opportunity and belted David with a quick right cross to the jaw.

David stayed quiet the rest of the evening.

17

Bertrand, snoring loudly from under the drink table, clutched an empty beer bottle in one hand and an unopened bottle of Bertrand's Bouquet in the other. The snoring was the only clue he wasn't in a coma. David, still dead to the world, remained in the same position John and Emily had left him. John, twitching from a bad dream, and Randolph were asleep in adjacent chairs. Emily, holding a large mug of coffee, surveyed the scene from the doorway. She noticed the two sole remaining partygoers gently swaying in the far corner of the room, slow-dancing without music. She tapped one of them on the shoulder and silently pointed towards the door.

The woman broke contact with her partner, then yawned and stretched. "Great party," she said.

Emily, her hangover roiling, managed to nod in agreement. She watched them leave and slumped into a chair near the sleeping Randolph. She sipped her coffee, coughed once, and grimaced as the pounding in her head increased.

Randolph opened one eye. "What time is it?"

"Around ten," Emily said.

"Day?"

"Saturday."

Randolph nodded, closed the eye and went back to sleep.

John opened his eyes and then squeezed them shut as the onslaught of light overpowered him. "Damn. Too bright. Turn off the light."

"It is off," Emily said.

"Damn."

"I know."

John tried a second time, and he blinked several times until Emily came into focus. "Is that coffee?"

"Want a cup?"

"Please. Anything to get the taste of Patchouli out of my mouth."

Emily shuffled to the kitchen and John, afraid to make any sudden movements, stayed frozen in the chair with a blank stare on his face. Emily returned with another mug and handed it to him.

"Thanks." He tested a small sip, waited, and decided it wasn't coming back. He took a bigger sip and set the mug down.

"How often do you have these parties?"

John burped loudly and waited. "Just once or twice a year."

"Good."

John frowned as his memory kicked in. He held up his thumb and index finger and adjusted them until only the smallest of spaces separated them. "I was this close." He shook his head. "I'm never going to get rid of that woman."

"How do you think I feel? Now I'm living under the same roof with my ex-husband." Emily glared at David, snoring softly on the couch.

John thought for a moment. "Well, I couldn't have sent him home with Margaret. She would have killed him."

"So? Mark my words, John. If he's going to be staying here, I quit."

John glanced around the disaster area. "Quit? You can't quit. You just got here."

Bertrand moaned loudly from under the table and rolled over.

"He's dreaming," Emily said.

John slowly turned his head in Bertrand's direction. "I hope it's a nightmare. Have you ever tasted anything like that in your life?"

Emily forced a smile. "It was pretty bad. I don't think he'll be quitting his job."

"What was he thinking?"

Bertrand's moaning increased, and he rolled back and forth underneath the blanket of his lab coat. The moaning turned into a scream. Bertrand woke and launched himself upright. Unfortunately, the bottom of the table halted his progress and the top of his head hammered against the hard wood. He collapsed into a fetal position and held his head with both hands. "Fuck me. That hurt."

"Good morning, Bertrand," John said.

Bertrand slowly maneuvered out from under the table and made his way to a couch. He collapsed face down into the leather. One leg dangled off the couch.

"Coffee, Bertrand?" Emily said.

"Asfunostu."

"I think that's a yes," John said.

"What time is it?" Randolph said.

"Five after ten," Emily said.

"Day?"

"Tuesday."

The answer generated a spark of life in Randolph. "What?" He sat up in his chair and looked around the room.

"Relax, Zorro," she said. "You want coffee?"

"Yes, please. I'll give you a thousand dollars."

Emily shuffled out of the room.

"I can't believe I danced," Randolph said.

"We couldn't either," John said.

"My legs are killing me."

"Mafuisto."

John looked at Bertrand and tried a laugh. It hurt.

"Tarantulas?" Randolph said, raising an eyebrow.

"I don't even want to think about the potential liability," John said. "But they certainly worked. Great party."

Emily returned with two more coffee mugs and handed one to Randolph. She went to the couch, helped Bertrand sit upright and watched as he clutched the mug with both hands.

"Thanks, Emily," Bertrand said.

Emily inspected the huge knot forming on the top of his head. "You're gonna have quite a bump there."

"It doesn't matter. I deserve it. I'm a total failure."

Emily patted him on the shoulder. "Don't beat yourself up."

"Yeah, don't," John said. "That's our job."

She picked up a small pillow from one end of the couch and fired it at David, sleeping peacefully a few feet away. The pillow bounced off his head onto the floor, and he slowly came to life. He groaned, lifted his head off the couch and, confused, looked around the room.

"Wake up, asshole," she said.

"Morning. Is their coffee?"

"No," Emily said. She retrieved the pillow, smoothed it out and returned it to its place on the couch.

David smiled wanly at John and felt the side of his face. Several purplish-blue welts had developed overnight. He winced and struggled into a sitting position. "How long have I been out?"

"You went down around 11," John said.

"Think I should call Margaret?"

"I'd give it a day or two."

David looked at Emily, who was sipping her coffee and not in the mood for conversation. He struggled to his feet. "I need a shower. Can I borrow a razor? I'll get some of my stuff later on."

"Use mine," John said. "Second floor, back corner."

David wrapped the blanket around his shoulders and trudged off.

"We need to talk about this, John," Emily said.

"Yeah, I know. Don't worry; we'll figure something out."

"Such as?"

John thought for a moment and sipped his coffee. "I guess we'll just have to figure out a way to get those two lovebirds back together."

"And how do you plan to do that?"

John looked at her and shrugged. He didn't have a clue.

18

John woke, let his eyes adjust, and put his hands behind his head as he stretched out in bed. Through the thick cloud of cigar smoke and candlelight, he could barely see the card table and the four players in various stages of undress. He blinked and tried to remember when he'd agreed to let them play strip poker in his room. He sat up and watched the hand play itself out.

"I'll raise," the shirtless Monty said.

Dr. Randle, down to his robe, said, "Call." He glanced at the naked Randolph, who was next to act.

"What are you looking at?" Randolph said. He tossed several chips into the pot.

"I'm missing a quarter," Bertrand said. He looked accusingly at the other players and scanned the floor around his chair.

"All my clothes are gone," Randolph said. "What happens next?"

"Who knows what your future holds?" Dr. Randle said. He smiled as he stared at Randolph.

"Cut it out."

Margaret, clad in skimpy leather, appeared in the doorway and posed provocatively. All four players paused to stare.

"Whoa," Randolph said. "I remember that outfit."

"Hey, boys," Margaret said. "Anybody want to see my tattoo?"

John squirmed under the sheets at the onset of a panic attack. He froze, hoping she wouldn't see him. It was too late.

"Are you ready to have some fun, John? It's been too long." Margaret held up ropes and a pair of handcuffs and dangled them in the air.

John pulled the covers over his head. Margaret slowly made her way towards the bed, pausing briefly at the table. She caressed the side of Dr. Randle's face with one hand and patted Randolph's stomach with the other.

"Randolph, you need to hit the gym."

"I've been busy."

"Oh, Johnny," she said.

"Get away from me."

"Oh, don't be like that. Especially now that I'm back on the market."

"Get away."

Emily, still dressed in her French maid's outfit, stepped into the room and glared at Margaret. "Leave him alone."

Margaret turned and glared back. "Mind your own business, House Girl."

"I said leave him alone."

"And I suppose you're going to stop me?"

Emily began to stalk Margaret and soon they were circling the table sizing each other up for battle.

Randolph looked at the other players and said, "Catfight."

Monty and Bertrand put their cards down and glanced back and forth between the two women. Dr. Randle smiled at Randolph.

"Cut it out," Randolph said.

Margaret, dragging the ropes behind her, made a beeline for the bed. Emily leaped over a startled Randolph and cut her off. Margaret grabbed Emily's hair and pulled. Emily cursed and flailed with both hands.

John peered out from under the covers and watched the action with a bewildered look on his face.

Emily and Margaret began to wrestle. They hissed, they slapped, they punched. They grunted and groaned, they quivered and quaked, they sweated and swore.

All four men at the table shifted uncomfortably in their seats.

Emily caught her breath, shifted into linebacker mode, and hurled herself at Margaret. She grabbed Margaret at the knees, lifted and drove her back and flipped her into the air. An airborne Margaret, still clutching the ropes, soared towards the bed.

John, flat on his back, stared up at the incoming leather-clad intruder and screamed in terror. Margaret landed, licked his ear, and tried to cuddle. He struggled against her weight and the mass of ropes now draped over his head and shoulders.

"No," he said. He continued his freedom struggle. "Not that. Please, Margaret. Not again. No…please…"

19

From the kitchen window, Emily stared outside. She rinsed the plate and handed it to Dr. Randle who was standing next to her and looking out the window. He dried the plate and added it to the stack on the counter.

"You were right, Doc. He's got himself stuck in the hammock again. Must be having another dream."

"Whose turn is it?" Dr. Randle said.

"You're up. I did it yesterday."

Dr. Randle dried his hands and headed outside. He approached the hammock that had ensnared the still dreaming John.

"No, not that. No." John's struggles had turned the hammock into a spider's web.

Dr. Randle studied the tangled mess and tapped John on the shoulder. "Hey, John. Wake up."

With a final glimpse of the sneering Margaret, John exited the dream and woke up sweating profusely and staring down at the lawn. He struggled against the hammock ropes, then gave up.

"Nice nap?" Dr. Randle said.

"Get me out of this thing."

"I think we should talk first. Now that I've got your undivided attention, so to speak." Dr. Randle laughed. John didn't find it quite so funny. "Are you finally ready to deal with your problem?"

"The only problem I have is with this goddamn hammock."

"I see. These dreams you're having aren't telling you anything?"

"Other than I shouldn't be eating spicy foods late at night? No."

"I see. Well…then I guess you don't need me after all." Dr. Randle turned and headed back towards the house.

"Hey," John said. "Get your ass back here and get me out of this thing."

75

Dr. Randle smiled and turned back. "Are you ready to start talking?"

John fumed and tried to extract himself one more time. Eventually, he gave up. "Okay. Let's talk."

Dr. Randle studied John and the hammock. He dropped to the ground, stretched out, and stared up at John whose face was only inches away. "That's better."

"Yeah, this is great."

Dr. Randle smiled. "Let's start with those dreams."

"The dreams...shit. I'm afraid to fall asleep."

"And they started right after the party, right?"

"Yeah, it's only been three days, but it feels like a month. I used to have similar ones all the time."

Dr. Randle flicked a bug from his nose. "I see. What are you dreaming about?"

"It's too weird to even talk about."

"Remember who you're talking to, John."

John laughed. "Well, everybody's in it...but Margaret's the major player."

"Bad memories?"

"When it comes to Margaret, that's the only kind I've got."

"How long have you had this phobia about sex, John?"

John was startled by the question. He stared down at Dr. Randle through the tangled ropes. "I wouldn't necessarily call it a phobia. That's a pretty strong word."

"Then what would you call it?"

"You're the doctor. You tell me."

"I just told you...but you disagreed."

John, swaying gently back and forth in the breeze, considered the comment. "Okay, I'll admit it. I'm afraid of it. Shows you what seven years of marriage will do for you, huh?"

"Don't you enjoy sex?"

"I used to...but it's been a while."

"Margaret is an adventurous type. Did some of her demands bring this on?"

"Demands? Jesus, Doc, she's psychotic."

"I agree that psychosis and intimacy can be a deadly combination." Dr. Randle smiled and drifted off to a memory. "But it sure does make for some hot sex, though."

"Doc, my circulation's getting cut off here. What are you proposing?"

"Therapy."

"Anything but that. Margaret and I tried that several years ago."

"How'd that work out?"

"She started banging the therapist. After that, the sessions went downhill."

"I'm serious, John. You and I start therapy sessions immediately. That's the deal."

"Can't do it, Doc. I've got a hotel to run, and I need to figure out a way to get Margaret and David back together. I don't have time to sit around and talk about my past." John paused and then shifted gears. "Hey, I thought you spent all your time dealing with the future."

"Over the years, I've had to moonlight from time to time. Do we have a deal or not?"

John considered his alternatives. "Okay, I'll try one session. After that, all bets are off."

"Fair enough," Dr. Randle said.

"Now get me out of this thing."

Dr. Randle crawled out from underneath the hammock and grabbed the side of the hammock. He spun it like a contestant on the Price is Right and watched as the hammock revolved three times and unraveled, depositing John face down on the ground.

20

John, steaming from their latest exchange, paced back and forth across his office and raked his fingers through his hair. Dr. Randle sprawled on a couch noted his patient's increasing agitation. Dr. Randle continued to observe John as he retraced his steps. Dr. Randle suppressed a yawn and cracked his neck.

"How can you say that?"

Dr. Randle peered over the top of his glasses. "All I said was that it takes two to tango."

"So now it's my fault? You sound like Margaret. For chrissakes, Doc, you've met her. Shit, she almost did you at the party in front of fifty people."

"Yes. Well, my work does lead me into some interesting research opportunities."

John scowled and sat down. His legs continued to jiggle, and soon he was back on his feet pacing.

"It appears to me that your fear of intimacy can be directly traced back to your marriage with Margaret."

"Brilliant deduction, Sherlock."

Dr. Randle waited until he made eye contact, then dropped the big one. "How long have you been afraid of sex?"

John grimaced. "Gee, Doc. Do you have to be that blunt? You make me sound like such a weenie."

Dr. Randle smiled and pointed a finger in John's direction. "Now that statement shows some real growth."

Dr. Randle got up and began pacing the office. John spied the empty couch, flopped down and struggled to get comfortable. Dr. Randle stroked his goatee, deep in thought.

"Most phobias set in gradually over time. They can stem from childhood experiences from things associated with parents, relatives, school, you name it. From what you tell me, that isn't the case with you. The starting point for your phobia is when Margaret entered your life. And the collections of experience, the mutual

78

interactions between you and Margaret, have combined to create a deep fear that prevents you from experiencing, let alone enjoying, one of our most basic human needs. Are you following me?"

"Yeah, I get it. I'm a weenie."

Dr. Randle chuckled. "Let's save that thought for another session. What we have here is a classic case of emotional baggage. You're carrying around extra emotional weight. And we need to get you on a diet. We need to alter the things coming into your brain and try to reshape your perceptions about doing the nasty. How does that sound?"

"Okay, I guess. As long as the treatment doesn't involve any actual field work."

"The manifestations of your current psychological and physiological underpinnings serve to undermine your primal instincts as a direct result of the unfortunate and unresolved questions surrounding basic conflicts and stresses stemming from attempts to destroy those physical characteristics central and essential to the higher primate's survival and happiness."

Dr. Randle smiled down with a look of pride at John. He received a blank stare in return.

"What the hell did you just say?"

Dr. Randle shook his head. "Well, to put it in terms you can understand, what I said was that your marriage to Margaret screwed you up early and often and it's continued long past the day when she left with your dick in her pocket."

"Oh," John said. He let the comment roll around in his head and then frowned. "Hey, that's not a very nice thing to say."

"I told you when we got started that my therapy approach involves tough love."

"If you think that's tough love, you should try spending a weekend with Margaret."

Dr. Randle cocked his head as he considered the prospect. "Yes. Well, the key to eliminating phobias is to start slowly and use a gradual reversing of the process that brought it on in the first place."

"Which means?"

"Desensitization therapy. We strip away your basic senses to the core, slowly start adding them back in and then build up from there."

"Build up to what?"

"Why sex, of course. Actual physical intimacy."

"With who?"

"Well, how the hell should I know? Jesus Christ, do I have to do everything around here?"

"Sorry."

Dr. Randle forced a smile in and sat down on the edge of the couch. He stroked his goatee. "How about Emily?"

"Emily?"

"Why not? She's attractive, unattached, and she does seem to be rather fond of you."

"Sex in the workplace? Gee, I don't know."

"Let's not worry about it right now. We've got lots of time to figure that out." Dr. Randle glanced at his watch, slapped his knees and jumped to his feet. "We've got some time left so why don't we get started." He searched his briefcase and removed a CD. He inserted it and grabbed the remote control. He sat back down on the edge of the couch. "I think we should start with a little aural stimulation."

John frowned and eyed Dr. Randle suspiciously.

"Not oral, you idiot. Aural."

"Just checking."

"Now I need to restrict some of your other senses so you can just focus on what you're hearing. I need you to get up off the couch so I can blindfold you."

"You sure you haven't been talking to Margaret?"

Dr. Randle paused. "She's into stuff like this?"

"You think I got this fucked up just by holding hands?"

"Hmmm." Dr. Randle refocused. "Okay, stand right there. That's good. And here comes the blindfold. How's that?"

"Dark."

"Good. I'm going to turn it on, and I just want you to listen. Try to shut down all your other senses and just hear what's going on. Forget everything else. Okay?"

"Got it."

Dr. Randle pushed a button on the remote and stretched out on the couch. He smiled and put his hands behind his head as the sounds of a couple making love filled the air.

John stood shaking at the knees in the center of the room, surrounded by darkness.

Dr. Randle cranked up the volume.

21

Randolph put the finishing touches to his hair, stared at himself in the mirror and adjusted his tie. Nodding at perfection, he left the admiring gaze in the mirror, grabbed his workbag and whistled as he left his room. In a good mood for a Monday and looking forward to the day, he headed down the hallway past John's room when the noises coming from inside caused him to stop short. He pressed his ear against the door and nodded in appreciation at the strenuous effort taking place on the other side.

"All right, John. Good for you. It's about time," Randolph said.

"No, wait. This isn't working," John said.

The sounds of passion stopped.

"Sounded pretty good to me," Randolph said. He pressed his ear tighter against the door.

"You're not even trying. Trust me. You can do this, John."

Randolph's head came off the door at the sound of Dr. Randle's voice.

"I must say that I'm a little surprised, John. You need to be more open," Dr. Randle said.

"That's easy for you to say," John said. "You're not the one blindfolded."

"Oh, my God," Randolph said. Stunned, yet unable to tear himself away, Randolph leaned back in against the door.

"Let's try something different then," Dr. Randle said.

"Okay, I'm in your hands," John said. "I can't believe I let you talk me into this."

"No shit," Randolph said.

The lovemaking sounds began to drift through the door again, this time, softer, less intense. Randolph blinked in disbelief.

"How's that? Better?" Dr. Randle said.

"Yeah, that's okay. I think I can deal with this," John said.

"Good. You just need to relax," Dr. Randle said. "Yes, that's much better. I knew you could do it."

Randolph scrambled down the hall and went down the stairs two at a time. He headed for the kitchen and continued, without pause, past Emily and Bertrand sitting at the table.

"Morning." Randolph quickly made his way towards the back door.

"Morning," Emily said. "There's fresh coffee."

"No," Randolph said, not breaking stride.

After a thirty minute bewildered drive to work, Randolph settled around a conference room table surrounded by Senator Toy's staff. As they chatted about their weekends and the upcoming election, Randolph stared silently out the window.

Senator Toy entered and approached Randolph from behind. He placed a hand on Randolph's shoulder and jumped back from the reaction he received. "Jesus, Randolph," the Senator said. "You're a little jumpy today."

Embarrassed, Randolph forced a smile and said, "Sorry. You startled me."

"Are you ready?" the Senator said.

"Huh?"

"Don't you have something to show me?"

"What?"

"Our new campaign spot?" The Senator continued to stare at Randolph as he sat down at the table.

"Oh, yeah. The new spot."

Randolph nodded at one of the staffers who picked up a remote control and pushed a button. A large screen descended from the ceiling and the lights dimmed. Randolph focused on the screen.

An elderly woman, sitting in a rocking chair in a barren apartment, appeared on the screen. The forlorn woman slowly rocked back and forth. Through the sound system, a gentle female voice was heard against the backdrop of the solitary old lady.

"Where would we be without our mother? Our mom."

The image shifted to a Hallmark moment of a young mother running through a park with two young children.

Good ole Mom. Mom, who fed you, who taught you the difference between right and wrong, and who took care of you when you were sick. Or frightened. Mom. Who was always there when you needed her? Good ole Mom, that's who.

The image on the screen shifted back to the old lady in the rocker.

We all know just how special our mothers are.

A close up focused on a single tear sliding down the old lady's face.

But Gloria Fontaine doesn't. Gloria's mother, the woman who did everything a mother could ever be expected to do, is deaf. And Gloria Fontaine's deaf mother hasn't seen her daughter Gloria in ten years.

The old lady held a cupped hand up to her ear.

"I can't hear you, Gloria. I can't hear you," she said to the camera. The camera pulled back until the viewers were left with a long shot of the old lady slowly rocking in the barren room. "

Maybe she can't hear you, Gloria. But we can. We can hear you loud and clear."

The commercial ended and the lights came up. Several staffers choked back tears, and Senator Toy coughed before being able to speak.

"That's beautiful, Randolph."

"Thank you, Senator."

"But there's no way I can use that as part of my campaign."

"No need to worry about that, Senator," Randolph said. "I've got a new non-profit set up that we're using. It won't be part of your campaign."

"But they'll know where it came from," one of the Senator's staff said.

Randolph glanced at the staffer and shrugged. "What they know is one thing. What they can prove is something else altogether."

"What's the name of this non-profit?" the Senator said.

"Stopping Crimes Against Motherhood," Randolph said.

The Senator thought for a moment and smiled at the acronym. "SCAM."

Randolph returned the smile. "It's got a nice ring to it, doesn't it?"

"Randolph, you're a genius."

22

John, standing on the rooftop verandah, fired a dart and heard the loud whack as it struck its target. A villainous smile appeared on his face as he reached for another dart. Emily, sitting nearby in a lawn chair, sipped a beer and watched John launch another missile.

"I'm running out of patience, John. I ran into David four times today. I didn't see him that much when we were married."

John fired another dart. This one missed the target and whizzed away into the open air. John strode to the other side of the rooftop and peered over the edge.

"Sorry," he said, calling down to the street below.

On his way back he extracted several darts from the dartboard, a custom job that featured a large autographed photo of Margaret. John took a few seconds to admire his handiwork.

"So what's this big plan you've come up with?"

John sat down next to Emily and sipped his beer. "It's simple. We use Margaret's shallowness to our advantage. We buy her affection back."

"That's your plan?"

"Yeah. Remember who we're dealing with here."

"Think it'll work?"

"Sure. She loves that stuff. Flowers. Maybe some artwork. Jewelry. A piece of cake."

"Cake?"

"No, I meant that it will be a piece of cake. Margaret's a total sucker for that sort of crap."

"You're such a romantic," Emily said. "How much is this going to cost me?"

"Think of it an as investment."

"I don't know if David can pull it off. He never bought me anything when we were married."

"Really?"

"Never. He always said that he, by himself, was more than enough for any woman."

"We have to get these two back together. Talk about two people being perfect for each other."

"Plus, he can be stubborn. I'm not sure he's going to play along."

"Then I guess we just won't tell him about what we're doing for a while."

Emily finished her beer and considered the idea. "I'm not that thrilled with your plan, John."

John stood and turned his attention back to the dartboard. "You got a better idea?"

Emily shook her head and grabbed another beer from the cooler. Bertrand stepped out onto the verandah and veered away to one side as he noticed John's arsenal of darts.

"Hey, bud," John said. He fired a dart and smiled at the result.

"Evening," Bertrand said. He helped himself to John's chair and a beer. "There's somebody downstairs who wants to check in."

"I'll take care of it," Emily said. She departed and John darts in hand sat down in her chair.

"Good day?" John said.

"Great day. We closed the deal on that new deodorant I developed. We're doing a big marketing campaign that's going national. It could be huge. And with the end of year bonuses coming up, the timing couldn't be better."

"That's great, Bertrand. Not that you need the money."

"What are you talking about? Don't need the money."

"You don't. You just think you do."

Bertrand thought for a moment and shrugged. "Maybe. But I certainly would like more. I'm tired of watching all these morons get rich for the wrong reasons."

"Welcome to America," John said.

23

Dr. Randle kept repeating the same pattern. Randolph, standing next to him, looked on with a mixture of bemusement and fascination. Dr. Randle scooped up a handful of leaves from one of several raked piles that dotted the backyard. He stared at the handful, tossed them into the breeze, and darted after them as they fluttered through the air.

Randolph laughed. "John's gonna be pissed. It's only taken him a month to get them raked."

"Shhh," Dr. Randle said. "Say, don't you have an election tomorrow?"

"Yeah. What about it?"

"Shouldn't you be working instead of watching football?"

"I'm working the phones. I can do that from anywhere."

Dr. Randle nodded and grabbed another handful of leaves, flicked them away and studied their short flight.

"C'mon, Doc. I only asked you to pick me a winner, not play in the leaves."

"What do you think I'm doing?" Dr. Randle, annoyed by the interruption, glanced over his shoulder at Randolph. Randolph rolled his eyes and stuffed his hands in the pocket of his coat.

"I need your pick, Doc. It's almost time for kickoff."

"Shhh. You're ruining my concentration."

"Sorry."

Dr. Randle launched another handful into the air and watched the leaves tumble and drift.

"What are you doing?"

"Austromancy. Fortune telling by observing and interpreting the wind."

Randolph shrugged. "Well, I guess it's as good as anything else for picking football."

"Shhh."

"C'mon, Doc. It's ten minutes to kickoff."

Dr. Randle scribbled on a pad of paper and flipped through several other pages filled with his notes. He sat down on the ground, glanced around in several directions and fell silent. Randolph looked at his watch but forced himself to remain quiet.

"49ers," Dr. Randle said.

"The 49ers? They're only getting three points, and they suck on the road. You gotta be kidding me."

"Not at all. That's the reading I'm getting. Take the points. The 49ers will fly today."

"You sure about this?"

Dr. Randle glared at Randolph.

"Okay, okay, relax. You're the fortune teller around here."

They headed inside and found the gang already assembled around the big screens. John was behind the bar putting the final touches on the food and drink. Monty and Emily were sitting next to each other on one couch rapidly working their way through their first Bloody Mary. Bertrand, a reluctant viewer, was sitting at the bar taking full advantage of the feast that Monday nights in the fall always brought to the hotel. Dr. Randle spied an empty chair and settled in. Randolph made a beeline for a couch. He removed the Post-It note with his name written on it and sprawled.

"When you said that couch had your name written on it, I thought you were joking," Emily said.

"I never joke about watching football," Randolph said.

John headed for his couch, grabbed the remote, and settled in with a plate of food and a fresh beer. "Game time. Life begins again."

"Hey, Monty," Randolph said. "Remember that five grand I owe you from the New England game yesterday?"

"Even coming from you, Randolph, that's a pretty dumb question. Of course, I remember."

"Feel like going double or nothing?"

Monty considered the idea. "Sure, why not? The way you pick football? Who have you got in mind?"

Randolph winked at Dr. Randle. "I like the 49ers. In fact, I like the 49ers a lot."

"You do, huh?" Monty laughed and looked around the room. "Usually, I try not to bet against the teams my clients play for, but with what's been going on up in the Bay Area this week, what the hell, okay. I'll take the Cowboys. The line's still three, right?"

"Hah," Randolph said. He clapped his hands and wiggled his feet.

"I don't know, Randolph. Dexter's been shooting his mouth off all week," John said.

"He's just trying to fire up his teammates," Randolph said.

The opening to Monday Night Football appeared and soon the announcers took over.

"Welcome to Monday Night Football. Tonight, we have two teams going in opposite directions. The Cowboys, coming in at 6 and 2, have been hot the last month and are gearing up for a playoff run while the 49ers, at 4 and 4, have been struggling. But the big story tonight is the comments made all week by the 49ers talented rookie kick returner, Dexter Clinchpoop."

Monty nodded in approval at the mention of Dexter. "Our clients love it when they mention him early in the broadcast."

"Clinchpoop has repeatedly called the Cowboys, and I'm quoting here, an overrated bunch of pansies. I have a feeling that the Cowboys are going to be on the lookout tonight for Dexter the Dangerous."

"Yeah, Al. I'm sure you're right about that one. During warm-ups, I had a chance to talk with Clinchpoop's therapist who said, that once Dexter overcomes his death wish, he's going to be a real force in this league."

"Damn," Monty said. "Why did they have to mention his therapy?"

Dexter appeared onscreen standing at the goal line doing similar dance steps to those he showed off during the recent party.

"C'mon Dexter. Take it all the way back," Randolph said.

"And here's the kick. It's high and long, and Clinchpoop takes it eight yards deep in the end zone. He'll take a knee...no, wait, he's coming out. He's at the five, ten, fifteen-"

A series of sickening pops and thuds filled the room. John and the others grimaced as they stared at the television.

"Fummmble. And the Cowboys scoop up the loose ball, and it's a touchdown. Six seconds in and the Cowboys are already on the board. Wow. That was quite a hit Clinchpoop took there."

"I felt it up here. And it hurt."

Onscreen, Dexter staggered to his feet. Dazed, he began walking around in small circles.

"Well, Clinchpoop is up. But he's very groggy."

"Look," Emily said. "He's walking around in circles. Hey, Doc, think he's hurt or is he just practicing a little Gyromancy?"

"Hard to say," Dr. Randle said, staring at the TV. "Let's see where he goes with it."

Dexter continued to stagger and then collapsed face down, arms and legs spread wide apart.

Emily looked away from the TV to Dr. Randle. "What's that tell you?"

"That he should probably double up on his therapy sessions," Dr. Randle said.

"Maybe you should try another one. Like the ventriloquism thing," Emily said.

"Well, you certainly wouldn't be able to see his lips move," John said.

A concerned Monty interjected. "Hey, cut it out. He might be hurt. No, he's sitting up. He's okay. Now that is one tough son of a bitch." He leaned back and relaxed.

"I can't believe you people are enjoying that poor man's misery," Bertrand said.

"That poor man, as you put it, Bertrand, is making three million bucks a year," John said.

"What?" Bertrand said.

"Yeah," Monty said. "Not counting endorsements. All up, he's gonna pull down around seven million this year."

"Are you shitting me? The only thing this guy is good at is getting knocked unconscious, and he makes seven million dollars?"

"Is this a great country or what?" Monty said.

"This country should carry a Surgeon General's warning," Bertrand said.

"And Monty, as his agent, gets somewhere around ten percent," John said.

Bertrand's eyes narrowed, and his face took on a light purple tone. He screamed at the TV. "Get up you bastard. Get up so they can hit you again."

The commercials ended, and a woozy Dexter came into view.

"We're back. And so is Clinchpoop. I must say I'm a little surprised to see him back in after that last hit."

"For his sake, I hope they kick it out of the end zone."

"Here it comes. No such luck. Clinchpoop takes it at the two. He's at ten, the fifteen, the twenty. What the hell? He's back at the fifteen, the ten, and he's heading... straight left?"

"I think he's hoping to get out of bounds, Al."

Another round of pops and thuds filled the room. They watched Dexter get bent in several directions and collapse under a ton of weight. The ball popped in the air and was soon in the end zone tucked safely in the arms of one of the Cowboys.

"Oh, my God," Randolph said.

"Dexter," Monty said. "I warned you to think about our future."

"Touchdown Cowboys. Two touchdowns in fifteen seconds. That's gotta be some kind of record. Clinchpoop got hit by nine...no, ten guys that time.

"Yeah, Al. Everyone but the kicker got in on that one."

"It wasn't lack of effort on his part. There just wasn't enough room for him to get in there."

Monty shook his head at the TV and held his breath until he watched Dexter crawl towards and finally reach the sidelines under his own power.

"Jesus," Randolph said. "Nice pick, Doc."

Dr. Randle shrugged. "Long way to go."

"That's what I'm afraid of."

The rest of the first half provided little relief to Randolph's mood.

24

Randolph downed the last half of his fifth beer and cracked open a fresh one. He stared sullenly at the commercials then brightened as his new campaign ad appeared on the screen. "Shhh," he said. "You guys have gotta see this."

The group fell silent and watched along with Randolph. At the end of the ad, Randolph glanced up from the screen beaming.

"Not bad, huh?"

"Jesus, Randolph," John said. "It's pretty brutal. Did you have to bring her mother into it?"

"Bad form, Randolph," Bertrand said. He shook his head dismissively and grabbed a sandwich.

"What are you talking about? We need a bump in the polls."

"This is how you spend your days?" Emily said.

"How would you like it if she was talking about your mother?" Monty said.

"Hey, it's politics," Randolph said. "She's fair game. He looked around the room for a show of support and received several disgusted looks in return.

"Amateurs," Randolph said. He turned back to the screen as the game reappeared.

"We're back, and with a half-time score of 54 to 3, we hope some of you viewers are too. We're going down to the field, and I see that Michelle has a very special guest with her."

The camera cut to a woman standing on the sideline, holding a microphone.

"Thanks, Al. With me is someone who is very well known, especially throughout Texas. I'd like to welcome U.S. Senate candidate, and potential NFL owner, Gloria Fontaine."

Gloria came into view and Randolph sat forward in his seat.

"Hey, Randolph, you gonna pay me my ten grand now or do I have to wait until the game's over?" Monty said.

Randolph waved him away and focused on the screen. "Damn, how'd she manage to pull this interview off?"

"You must be one busy woman these days. The election is tomorrow, and we understand that you're also entering final negotiations on a deal that would bring another NFL team to Texas. How is your bid for a franchise shaping up?"

"It's looking very good, Michelle. And I would like to take this opportunity to thank the countless number of Texans who have written or called to voice their support for this long overdue initiative. Football is almost a religion in Texas and two NFL teams simply aren't enough."

"What a suck up," Randolph said.

"She seems fine to me," Emily said.

"She looks great. And the camera loves her," Monty said.

"Bah," Randolph said.

"So when can we expect to hear some news about your bid?"

"We should have an announcement sometime around the middle of November. I'm very excited about it."

"Mid-November. Conveniently timed for just after the election. What a cheap stunt," Randolph said. "C'mon…get to the real news. Ask her about her mother."

"From the latest polls, it looks like the gap has narrowed between you and your opponent Senator Toy. Three weeks ago you were down eleven points, but the latest Gallup has you trailing by only two points."

"The polls, as usual, are all over the place, Michelle. But we're very confident about the outcome."

"C'mon, cut the crap. Ask her about her mother," Randolph said.

"Of course, I would be remiss if I didn't ask you about a very controversial campaign ad that began running the other day. It deals your relationship with your mother."

"Yes, sadly, it's just one more unfortunate example of how depraved some of our political campaigns have become."

"So can you answer the questions raised in the ad, along with the widely reported news stories, that say your mother hasn't seen you in ten years?"

"Ah, yes. The story. Another classic example of the sickness demonstrated throughout the campaign by my opponent and his chief political consultant, the amazingly sleazy, Randolph Tut. Please excuse the language I'm using to describe Mr. Tut. It's the nicest term I could come up with."

"National name-drop," Monty said. "Way to go, Randolph."

"Reduced to name calling," Randolph said. "She's toast."

"So what can you tell us about the story, Gloria?"

Randolph knelt in front of the television like a lion ready to pounce.

Gloria smiled and turned coy.

"Oh, the story."

"Yeah, that's right, Gloria. The story."

The camera cut to an extreme close-up of Gloria. She stared directly into the camera. Randolph, about to burst, leaned even closer towards the screen.

"The story is... absolutely true."

Randolph leapt to his feet. "Yes. Touchdown. Put it on the board."

"My mother, bless her heart, hasn't seen me in ten years. And that's because she lost her sight ten years ago. My mother's not deaf. She's blind."

Randolph's touchdown dance was cut short. "What did she say? She's blind? Did she say blind?" Randolph scrambled back in front of the TV.

"Hold on." John laughed. "I think there's a flag on the play."

"Yeah," Emily said. "This one's definitely coming back."

"Your mother is blind. I see."

"Yes, but she is doing very well. She currently lives in a very modern assisted living community in Houston but, if I should be fortunate enough to be selected as the next Senator from the great state of Texas, she will be moving with me to Washington."

"How sweet."

"Would you like to meet her?"

"I would love to meet her."

"No," Randolph said. "Not the mother."

"Nice touch," Monty said.

"Beautiful," John said. He stared at the TV and did his best not to laugh.

Gloria stepped out of camera and reappeared holding an elderly woman's hand.

"Mom. This is Michelle."

"It's so nice to meet you, Michelle."

"Are you excited about the upcoming election?"

"Oh, yes. But I just wish those awful people would stop saying those terrible and completely untrue things about my daughter."

"I have a good feeling they might stop very soon, Mrs. Fontaine. Back to you, Al."

Randolph collapsed onto the floor and held his head with both hands. His cell phone rang, and he answered it on the second ring. "Hi, Senator...Yes, I saw it...I know...He's a drunk, what can I say? Senator, you can't do that. You'd go to jail...Oh, I see. You expect me to do it. Yes, I'll be there."

25

Randolph pulled into his parking space, checked his hair in the mirror, then got out and locked the car. He walked towards the converted storefront that he had dubbed Mind Meld Central a mere four months ago. Several people exiting the building were hidden behind large boxes they were carrying on their way to the parking lot. He moved to the edge of the sidewalk to let several of Senator Toy's staff members get past him.

"Hey, Bob," Randolph said.

"Fuck you," said the box.

Randolph flinched but bit his lip and turned his attention to another person struggling under the weight of a large box.

"Need a hand, Mary?" Randolph said.

A solitary finger popped up from the side of the box as it went by. Randolph watched the line of former staff and volunteers make their way to their cars. He gave them a small, unreturned wave and headed inside. Randolph approached a woman standing behind the reception desk packing up the phone system. She glanced up at Randolph. "He's in there," she said, nodding at the conference room.

"Thanks," Randolph said.

He walked towards the conference room but stopped when the woman called after him.

"Hey, Randolph?"

"Yeah?"

"What the hell happened to you?"

The woman stared at him with both hands on her hips as he considered the question.

"What do you mean?"

"You? You used to be so sharp. What happened?"

Randolph looked down at the floor then smiled at her. "That's funny. I haven't heard that question from you in a long time."

"No, this isn't about that, Randolph. This is about him," she said, nodding her head in the direction of the conference room. "He should have won this thing."

"No, he was gonna lose. He's been beaten for about a month. This latest thing just gives him a good excuse."

The woman shook her head in disgust but remained silent.

"As for what's happened to me…you tell me. You're the one who married me."

The woman laughed. "Poor old, Randolph…petulant to the end."

"Well, you would know better than most. So what are you going to do now?"

"I've got an offer in St. Louis I'm thinking of taking."

"Politics?"

"God, no. No more of this shit. Accounting. Boring, but very stable."

Randolph studied the woman he'd spent three years married to and realized he barely knew her. "That's right. You're an accountant."

The woman brushed her hair back from her face. "You forgot that, didn't you?"

Randolph shrugged and gave her a weak smile.

"What are you going to do?"

"Take a break I guess. And then start looking for work. But I doubt if anybody is going to be lining up to hire me."

"No, probably not." She turned back to her packing. "Take care of yourself, Randolph."

"Yeah, thanks. You too."

Randolph took a final look at her and headed towards the conference room. He stuck his head through the open door and saw Senator Toy sitting in a leather chair with his cowboy boots up on the windowsill. He was staring outside and either didn't hear or care about Randolph's arrival. Although it was still early in the day, the Senator was working his way through a large glass of Jack Daniels and ice. Apparently, ice was in short supply.

"Morning, Senator."

The Senator flinched but didn't turn around. "Randolph. Thanks for stopping by."

Randolph sat down at the conference room table and stared at the back of Senator Toy's head.

"Where you been, Randolph?"

"Oh, just getting the preliminary bouts out of the way."

"Ah, yes. Your ex-wife."

"Yeah."

"She's a good woman. I'm going to miss her. Very organized."

"Yeah."

"And she doesn't tolerate fools. That's a very good quality for a woman to have wouldn't you say?"

"Well, I'd say it's a fine quality for an ex-wife to have."

The Senator chuckled and sipped his Jack and ice. He continued to stare out the window. "You know why I called you here don't you, Randolph."

"Well, Senator, I doubt if it's to write your victory speech."

The Senator set his glass down on the windowsill and reached for the bottle of Jack. He refilled the glass. "I dropped thirty points in the polls overnight."

"Yeah, I saw that," Randolph said.

"That must be some kind of record don't you think?"

"I'm not sure if they keep track of stuff like that, Senator. But, yes, I'd say it's one for the books."

"Her mother hasn't seen her in ten years?"

Randolph flinched and waited.

"I warned you about using that drunk. Why on earth didn't you feel the need to check the accuracy of his findings?"

"Because I was busy doing other things? Like trying to keep your ass in the Senate for another six years."

The Senator laughed and took a large sip from his drink. "It doesn't matter. I was already beat."

Randolph nodded in agreement.

"But this sure does give me one hell of an excuse," the Senator said. "I guess I should thank you for that."

"You're welcome, Senator."

"Go to hell, Randolph. I said I should thank you. I didn't say I was going to."

"Yes, Senator."

"You're fired, Randolph."

Randolph drummed his fingers on the tabletop. "Actually, Senator...not that it matters. My contract ends on Election Day. So you can't fire me since, technically, I don't work for you anymore."

"Randolph," the Senator said. "If you ever want to work in politics again, today, of all days, you should avoid playing your usual game of semantics with me. Got it?"

"Yeah, I got it. Sorry."

"Want a drink?"

"No, thanks. I've gotta go vote."

"And you need to be sober for that?"

"Yeah, why not?"

"You know, it's funny." The Senator raised the glass to his lips and downed another third. "But being half-hammered has always improved the voting process for me. Somehow it always makes bad choices easier."

Randolph stood and cleared his throat. "I guess I'll be going, Senator."

"Fine. Go."

"What are you planning on doing next?"

"I've got a book deal lined up."

"Already? That was fast."

"What can I tell you, I'm hot at the moment. America loves the fallen leader."

"You'll be back, Senator."

"Fuck it. Fuck it all."

Randolph thought for a moment. "Fuck it all. That would make a good campaign slogan. Good crossover appeal to the disenfranchised and malcontents. "

"Up to this point, it's always worked for me."

"You're a man of true vision, Senator."

"I'm sure you can let yourself out, Randolph."

26

John stared in disbelief across the table then got up and grabbed three beers from the fridge. He slid two down the table in opposite directions and forced himself to concentrate on David's unrelenting discourse. Emily stretched out with her feet on a chair and stared up at the ceiling.

"But the real key to any actor's success is his ability to listen. To stay completely in the moment and just be there." David smiled at his insight and took a sip of beer.

"Fascinating," John said. Giving up all hope of finding an entry point into the conversation, he decided to jump in with both feet. "Now about this situation with Margaret."

"I remember a couple of years ago when I was doing this beer commercial…"

Emily sighed and began hitting herself on the head with a fist.

"The director tried to bring his personal biases into the shoot. When I tried to confront him about his total lack of perspective about what my character was attempting to accomplish in the scene, which was a demonstration of my complete empathy for the beer itself…you know, this cold liquid, stuffed in a can, tucked away on a shelf, just waiting, hoping to be selected as the chosen one." David picked up his beer and gazed at it. "For me, the beer was like the lonely girl of sixteen waiting by the phone hoping the star quarterback would call and ask her to the prom."

"Fascinating," John said.

"And do you know what this so called director had the audacity to say?"

"It's only a fucking beer commercial?" Emily said.

"He said it's only a fucking beer commercial. Can you believe that?"

"Unbelievable," John said. "And I'm sure only Margaret understood what you were going through."

"Fifteen hundred for the day and the only thing this guy wants me to do is to sit there and enjoy the beer. What a waste of my talents." David took a long sip. "This is good."

"Your check's in the mail," Emily said.

"What's that, Em?" David said.

Emily, still staring up at the ceiling, sighed again.

"David," John said. "Are you with me, David?" He waited until he made eye contact. "Emily and I have come up with a plan for you and Margaret."

"Plans are good," David said.

"Yes, but we need to follow it closely. We need perfect execution."

"Execution? Isn't that a bit extreme?"

John considered the question. "Perhaps. Let's make that Plan B."

"Ooh, backup plan. Good thinking." David said.

"But you have to want it, David. You've got to sell yourself to Margaret," John said.

"Oh, I want it," David said. He glanced at Emily, then leaned across the table and whispered to John. "Lately, I'm getting pretty…twitchy. If you know what I mean."

John blushed.

"We get it, David," Emily said.

"Sorry, Em. But you know how I get when I don't get my tires rotated on a regular basis."

"Still the hopeless romantic." Emily got up from the table and walked to the sink.

"Think of this as an acting role," John said.

David gave John his undivided attention. "Cool."

"Yes, David. It's way cool. In this particular scene, you're playing the part of the heartbroken lover. Not jilted, mind you. But somehow torn apart from the woman you love. She's blaming you for the breakup and you need to be the bigger person this time. You need to subjugate your real feelings for the good of the relationship."

"My real feelings?"

"Yes."

"And what would they be?"

John blinked, scratched his head and looked to Emily for some help. She stood with her back against the sink shaking her head. John nodded and turned back to David.

"Well, let's see. You're hurting... somewhat angry."

"Should I be taking notes?" David said.

"Jesus Christ," John muttered, under his breath. "No, I'm pretty confident that a man with your talents will be able to identify his real feelings."

"Yeah, probably," David said.

"You're lonely, feeling isolated, and the only thing that will rescue you from the depths of despair is the return of the woman you love."

"Got it," David said. "Do I get a love scene?"

"What?"

"The love scene. You know, when we finally reconnect. The big payoff. I love the love scenes. Especially with Margaret. She's an animal."

"Well, I'll leave that up to you. Maybe you can improvise when the time is right."

"I hate improvising," David said. "Like I always say, if it ain't written down, why bother saying it?"

"I'm sure you'll figure it out."

"Couldn't I at least get some notes?" David said.

"From me?"

"You used to be married to her. Why not?"

Finally, John snapped. "Because the only ones I wrote back then were suicide notes."

David stared wide-eyed at John.

"Sorry," John said. "Look, David. Just think hot, think sweaty, think...I don't know, think naked."

"And wet?"

"Wet? Yeah, I guess wet works," John said.

"And doggie."

"Excuse me?" John said.

103

"I love doggie. Remember that weekend up in Palm Springs, Em?"

"All right," Emily said. "That's enough." Emily flushed with embarrassment and turned her back to both men and focused on the dirty dishes.

"I think I'm gonna playing like this part," David said. "So what's the plan?"

"You will be bestowing gifts on Margaret as an expression of your love and affection."

David frowned. "Bestowing? Gee, I don't know, John. That sounds like it could get expensive."

"You leave that to us," John said. "All you need to do is show up and follow the script. In no time, Margaret will be eating out of the palm of your hand. Or some other body part of your choosing."

"Sounds great."

John jumped to his feet. "Now go…practice. Learn your lines. Get to know your character inside and out. Go out there and become the man you already are."

David considered John's instructions. "Go become the man I already am. Wow. What a concept."

"It's a fantastic part. The role of and for a lifetime."

"Of and for a lifetime." David shook his head in admiration. "Man, you're good." David thrust his chest, gave them a wave and strode out of the kitchen.

John collapsed back into his chair. "What I am is exhausted."

Emily sat back down at the table. "He tends to have that effect on people."

"How on earth did you two ever hook up?"

"I was young. And overly impressed by…certain physical characteristics."

John thought for a moment and glanced up at her. "You mean?"

"Yeah."

"That was the basis for the relationship?"

"Pretty much," Emily said. "Certainly at the start."

John felt his face flush with embarrassment. "I see. Well, I guess we all have our reasons for doing some of the things we do, huh? What can one say?"

"Woof?"

27

Monty entered the registration area the same way he always entered a room; on an impeccably well-dressed mission. Emily, standing behind the desk, looked up from her wood polishing and beamed at him.

"Good morning, Monty."

"Hi, Emily."

"You look nice today."

"Thanks."

"Where are you off to today?"

"Flying to LA. I'm working on a new endorsement deal for Dexter."

"How's he doing by the way?"

"Well, yesterday he was able to walk to the bathroom on his own and eat solid food. He's listed as probable for Sunday."

"He's gonna play? I thought he was supposed to be out for a month."

"Nah. Dexter's like the Black Knight in that Python movie."

Emily remembered the scene and laughed. "It is but a flesh wound."

Monty laughed back. "That's the one." He turned towards the rattling newspaper on his right. "Hey, John. Have you seen Randolph?"

John lowered the sports page, looked at Monty and shook his head.

"The son of a bitch still hasn't paid me. He owes me ten grand."

"Good luck getting it," John said. He disappeared back behind the paper.

"He never pays his gambling debts," Monty said. "And it's starting to piss me off. Sometimes I can't tell who the bigger miser is. Him or Bertrand."

"Bertrand," John and Emily said simultaneously.

106

John put the paper down and tossed it on the floor. Emily glared at him, and he leaned over, picked it up and carefully folded it. He placed it on the coffee table in front of him, smoothed out the rough edges and smiled at her.

"Was that so hard?"

The front door slowly opened, and a very small man of Indian descent entered. He set the two small suitcases he was holding down in front of him and looked around the room.

"Can I help you?" Emily said.

"Oh...yes, please." The man shuffled his way towards the registration desk and smiled at the three people who were doing their best not to stare. He stopped in front of the registration counter and Emily, no long drink of water herself, looked down at the top of the head that barely reached past the top of the registration counter.

"Do you need a room?"

"Yes, a room. That would be good."

"Welcome to Divorce Hotel," Emily said. "Do you have a reservation?"

"No, I'm so sorry, I don't. I'm here on short notice."

She slid a registration card across the freshly polished wood and watched the pen overwhelm his small fingers. He rose on tiptoes and began writing down the requisite information. John stared at the man and glanced at Monty, who was also dumbfounded by the new arrival. The man set the pen down, slid the card back towards Emily, and lowered himself back to the floor.

"Even after all this time," the man said, glancing around. "It's still hard getting used to how big everything is in this country."

"Jockey, right?" Monty said.

"Jockey? Me? Oh, my no," the man said. "I'm afraid horses frighten me."

The tiny man winked at Monty. Monty frowned but said nothing.

"Mister...Duh...harna?" Emily said.

"Close," the tiny man said with a smile. "It's Dar...nuh."

"Thanks," Emily said. "The H threw me for a loop."

She glanced down at the card. "Mr. Dharna."

"Please, just call me Dharna. Or The Dharna if you prefer."

Monty extended his hand. "Nice to meet you, Dharna. I'm Monty Mantooth."

"Nice to meet you, Monty."

Dharna extended his hand, and it disappeared from view. "Quite a grip you have there, Monty."

Monty stared down at the tiny hand he was holding. He squeezed gently, and Dharna winced. Fascinated by the size of the man, Monty placed his thumb and forefinger around Dharna's wrist. Monty held up his handiwork for the others to see. He slid his finger-thumb bracelet up and down the man's lower arm with ease. "Would you look at that? How the hell did you get so small?"

Dharna removed his hand from Monty's and winked. Monty wasn't about to let it pass a second time.

"Hey, Dharna. I need to tell you that it's probably not a good idea for you to be winking at men around here."

"I'm so sorry," Dharna said. "Whenever I get nervous it just happens. It's called Involuntary Winking Syndrome. Or IWS for short. It's very troublesome, and I wish I could control it, but I'm having great difficulty. My doctor says it is stress-related. And lately, undoubtedly due to my pending divorce, it has gotten worse."

"IWS, huh?" Monty said. "Never heard of that one." He glanced at Emily and John. "Unbelievable. If two people happen to sneeze at the same time, next day there's a syndrome named for it."

"You learn to live with it," Dharna said.

"Dharna, I think you made a small mistake filling out this card," Emily said. "You've listed Dharna as your occupation. You wrote your name down twice by mistake."

"No, that's not a mistake," Dharna said. "That is correct. My occupation is Dharna."

"That's a little strange," Emily said.

"I come from a long line of Dharna."

Emily, Monty, and John glanced at each other. Eventually, it silently fell to John to ask. "Okay, I'll bite. What's a Dharna?"

"In my country, India, a Dharna is what you would call a debt collector."

Monty did his best to control himself but still burst into laughter. Dharna stiffened, offended by the laughter.

"I'm sorry. But the thought of you muscling somebody to pay up is funny," Monty said.

"I must tell you that I am one of the most successful Dharna's in recent history."

Monty stopped laughing but was unable to wipe away the smile.

John interceded. "It's funny you mention debt collection, Dharna. We were just talking about it before you came in."

"Well, I'm sure you weren't talking about this particular form of collection," Dharna said. He forced a smile and winked again.

"Damn, that wink bothers me," Monty said. "Look, Dharna, I'm sorry I upset you. Over here, people who don't pay up often end up getting their legs broken. And you're, well, instead of a leg breaker, you seem more of an ankle biter."

"Violence isn't part of my profession at all," Dharna said.

"Well, don't keep us in suspense." Monty laughed. "Why don't you tell us how little old you gets people to pay up."

Dharna shuffled towards a large chair and was soon completely wrapped in leather. "In my country, India, debtors are viewed in a very poor light. And it is the job of the Dharna to not only shed light on the debtor in question, to make the situation public if you will but also to get the individual to pay off the debt in question."

"Makes sense," Monty said.

"So, the Dharna's job is to shame the debtor into paying up."

"Shame?" Emily said.

"Yes," Dharna said, nodding.

"Still waiting," Monty said. He glanced at his watch and shook his head.

"Yes, of course," Dharna said. "Sorry, my thoughts are somewhat jumbled these days. In my country-"

"India," Monty said.

"Yes, thank you. India. The Dharna's job is to camp out at the debtor's place of residence or workplace. As you would say in your country…"

"America?" Monty said.

Dharna smiled. John and Emily laughed. Eventually, Monty got the joke.

"You were just fucking with me, weren't you? You little devil." Monty looked at John and Emily. "This little fella's all right."

"Yes, I was just fucking with you, Monty. So, as I was saying, the Dharna's responsibility is to hang around and eventually shame the debtor into paying by refusing to eat."

"What?" Emily said.

John sat forward in his chair. "You starve yourself?"

"Yes. Historically, it has always been seen as a very bad thing for the debtor if the Dharna dies in the performance of his duties."

"Probably not the best outcome for the Dharna either," John said.

"Tragically, no. But we all know the risks," Dharna said. "If a Dharna does die on the job, it is said that his spirit will haunt the debtor and his house and family forever. It is, how you say, bad mojo."

"You're shitting me. Aren't you?"

"No, I would not shit you, Monty."

"And you've made a career out of this?" Emily said.

"Oh, most definitely," Dharna said. "I have taken my profession to new heights with some of my contributions to the field. In addition to hanging around the debtor's home, I have developed a variety of facial expressions and gestures in the hope of eliciting a combination of sympathy and shame to help expedite what can be a lengthy process."

"Sympathy and shame, huh? Sounds great," Monty said. "Show me one of your faces."

Dharna contorted his face and transformed himself into a cross between a lost puppy and an orphaned child. All three observers were impressed.

"Wow," Monty said. "That's good. Lay another one on me."

Dharna opened with mouth wide and somehow managed to elongate his face until he bore a striking resemblance to the tortured individual in Edward Munch's painting, The Scream.

"Whoa," Monty said. He patted his chest and looked at Emily and John. "That one gets you right here."

"Yes, indeed," Dharna said. "Some of the debtors I have worked on have developed nightmares as a direct result of that particular one. It's my showcase piece."

"That's amazing," Emily said.

"Thank you," Dharna said. "But business has been bad lately. I'm afraid technology is starting to take over my profession."

John frowned. "Computers?"

"No. Big guns."

Randolph, unshaven and still in his robe, stormed down the stairs, through the reception area and into the kitchen, oblivious to the group and cursing non-stop. "Son of a bitch…goddamn, soulless sonofabitch."

The Dharna started winking rapidly. Monty turned to John and smiled. They both landed on the idea at the same time.

"You wouldn't?" John said.

"Of course, I would." Monty roared with laughter.

"What?" Emily said. The light bulb went off. She started to giggle.

"Dharna," Monty said. "I think I have a business opportunity for you."

"A business opportunity?"

"Indeed. That man who just went past owes me ten thousand dollars. And I'd like you to get it from him."

"Oh, Monty, I'm not sure if my techniques will work on an American very well. Given your culture, it could take a very long time."

"Take your time, Dharna," Monty said. "The longer, the better."

"Really?"

"Absolutely," Monty said. "How much is this going to cost me?"

"I get four hundred a day plus 25 percent of the recovered amount," Dharna said.

Monty slipped into negotiating mode. "Three hundred a day and 20 percent of what you're able to collect. But I'll cover the cost of your stay here."

Dharna considered Monty's counteroffer. "Deal. When would you like me to get started?"

"Right after lunch," Monty said. "And if I were you, I'd eat well."

28

As the delivery van pulled into the driveway, John crouched further down behind the row purple sage bushes separating Margaret's front yard from the street. He tapped Emily on the shoulder, and she followed suit. Sufficiently hidden, they used their hands to open lines of sight through the thick foliage. They peered through the bushes as the driver hopped out, opened the back of the van and extracted a huge plant. He staggered under the weight and slowly worked his way towards the front door.

"That thing is huge," Emily said.

"Yeah," John said. "I told the florist to go all out."

"What is it anyway?"

"Venus flytrap."

"How romantic."

"It's perfect for her. She'll love it."

The delivery man rang the doorbell and stood on the front steps smiling, unwarned and unaware about the address's occupant.

"Yeah? What do you want?"

The delivery man looked around for a person to put with the voice.

"Up here, moron."

The delivery man looked up at a second-floor window and saw a flushed, disheveled Margaret staring down at him. She was wearing a loose T-shirt that ended mid-stomach with the saying: Objects Under This Shirt Are Larger Than They Appear. Margaret yawned and stretched to prove her point.

The delivery man walked to the edge of the steps and peered up. "I've, wow, I've got a delivery for you."

"What is it?" Margaret said.

"It's a plant."

"Plant? I didn't order any plant."

The delivery man hopped off the steps and moved directly under the window. He stared up and smiled.

"Maybe it's a gift. There's a card."

"Read it."

The delivery man trotted off and returned with the envelope. He ripped it open and read from the card.

"To my darling Margaret," he said. "Is that you?"

"Yeah, that's me. Read."

"I am so very sorry. So, so, so, so very sorry," the delivery man said. He stopped and looked up. Margaret frowned but nodded for him to continue.

"Nice job on the note. It's so David," Emily said.

"No, he wanted to write it himself," John said.

"That was a mistake." Emily shook her head and peered through the bushes.

The delivery man continued reading. "Let's not fight, nor take offense. Let's go to bed, because I'm too tense. I'll be waiting, just you wait and see. Have to go now, I need to pee."

"The man is incapable of having an unexpressed thought," Emily said.

The delivery man looked up from the card with a confused look. He stared up at Margaret: Truth be told, he was staring at the bottom half of her breasts that had worked their way out of the T-shirt into the morning sunlight.

"Is that it?" Margaret said.

The delivery man glanced at the back of the card and nodded.

"That fucker," Margaret said.

"Uh-oh," John said, ducking into a lower crouch.

"What?" Emily said.

"Mood swing. Get ready to duck."

"You want me to bring it inside?"

Margaret gave him the once over, then shook her head. "No, just leave it on the steps. I'll get it later."

The delivery man continued to stare up at her.

"What are you looking at?" Margaret said.

"Haven't we met before?"

Margaret glared down. "Yeah, I'm the receptionist at the local VD clinic."

The delivery man missed his opportunity for escape. "No, I'm serious. You look very familiar. Have we gone out before? "

"Doubtful," Margaret said. "I don't date outside my species."

"He better get out while he can," John said. "She's getting dark."

"How can you tell?" Emily said.

"Her temples are pulsating."

Emily stared up at the window. "You're right. What's that mean?"

"He's got about twenty seconds before she blows."

Unabated and severely misguided, the delivery man decided to go for broke. "It's just that you look so sexy up there in that T-shirt." He took a step towards the window.

"You think I put this on because I knew you were stopping by?" Margaret's eyes narrowed, and she laughed; a dangerous, guttural growl.

"You never know," the delivery man said. "From what I've seen so far, if I was ever able to see you naked, I know that I'd die happy."

"I'm sure of that," Margaret said. "But if I ever saw you naked, I'd die laughing."

"Hey, that's not necessary," the delivery man. "You don't have to get mean about it."

"Oh, I'm so sorry," Margaret said. "Let me try again. I would love to come back to your place, but I don't think there's enough room for two people under that rock."

Margaret picked up a glass of water and dumped it out the window. It splashed into the delivery man's face. He sputtered and wiped his eyes. "What's the matter with you?"

"Oh, you'd go to the end of the world for me? How nice," Margaret said. "The only problem is you wouldn't stay there." Margaret fired the glass out the window.

Boink.

The glass bounced off his forehead, and he began to stagger in small circles.

"Look. Gyromancy," Emily said.

John did his best to stifle a laugh.

Margaret heard the laughter and scanned the front yard. John and Emily ducked further down behind the purple sage. Margaret disappeared from view but returned a few moments later, rearmed.

"What's that you say? You'd like to get in my pants? Sorry, but I'm afraid there's already one asshole in there." She fired a volley of large candles out the window. All of them hit their mark. The delivery man raised both arms to protect his face and dropped to his knees.

Margaret side armed an ashtray that caught him in the chest.

She dropped a copy of War and Peace, unopened since purchase eight years ago, onto the top of his head. "You should try reading something a bit lighter, sugar."

A small reading lamp glanced off his left shoulder. "I'm sorry, sweetie. I didn't quite get that one. Oh, how do I like my eggs in the morning? Unfertilized."

A baseball bat, followed by a still humming vibrator, bounced off his head.

"I think that's the Turbo Commando 7. Good choice," Emily said.

John was pretty sure she wasn't talking about the bat.

The delivery man crumbled face down onto the lawn as the sprinklers came on.

"So, sweetie. You still wanna see me naked?" Margaret stared down at the trembling mess of humanity on the ground directly below her.

"Ahfufishu," the delivery man said.

"That's what I thought," Margaret said. "Next time, you stop here, on your rounds, remember this. I'm one of those bad things that happen to good people." Margaret slammed the window shut.

"We should probably get out of here," John said.

"Okay," Emily said. "Let's go."

John started to rise out of his crouch then stopped. "Wait. She's coming out."

They dropped back down behind the bushes and watched Margaret, barefoot in T-shirt and panties, step outside, tiptoe past

116

the Venus flytrap, and hop over the delivery man. She grabbed the vibrator, shook the water off, and bounced her way back inside the house.

"She doesn't lose focus easily," John said. "I'll give her that."

Emily nodded and led him out from behind the bushes and down the street towards their car.

29

John slowly turned the page, glanced at the photo, then looked up at Dr. Randle and shook his head. "Nothing."

Dr. Randle scribbled on the pad in front of him. "Okay," he said. "Try the next one."

John took a bite of his sandwich, flipped the plastic sheet containing a color photo, and stared at the naked woman. He stuffed a handful of potato chips into his mouth and looked up from the photo. "Nuffin."

"Odd," Dr. Randle said. "Most men are extremely visual."

"She's cute," John said. "Don't get me wrong, but as far as excitement goes…nah."

"Amazing. You don't have even the slightest loin tingling?"

John pushed the binder away and focused his full attention on the other half of his sandwich. "Just what are you trying to accomplish here, Doc?"

"We've entered the next phase of our desensitization therapy. You've made excellent progress throughout the auditory phase, so I thought we'd move on to visualization."

"I'm going to have to sit here and look at pictures of naked women?"

"Yes."

"Jesus, Doc. Do I have to?"

"For chrissakes, John. You'd think I was asking you to sleep with your ex-wife."

"Yeah, right, like that's gonna happen. Hell would have to freeze over first." John chewed a mouthful of roast beef. "Of course, if anyone could pull that off, it would be Margaret."

Dr. Randle grabbed the binder and flipped through several pages until he found the photo he was looking for. He pushed the binder back in front of John.

"Look at her," Dr. Randle said. "Penthouse Pet of the Year a couple of years ago."

John grimaced and put his sandwich down. "Jesus, Doc. Do we have to do this now? I'm trying to eat here."

Dr. Randle flipped to another page and pointed. "Playboy. Miss August. Anything?"

"What can I tell you? Yeah, she's cute."

Dr. Randle sat back in his chair deep in thought. "This is going to be harder than I imagined."

"It's like I told you, Doc. It just doesn't interest me anymore. Are we done? I've got some shopping to take care of."

"Yeah, we're done," Dr. Randle said. "But I want you studying later. I'll leave this on the counter for you."

John stood, put his plate in the dishwasher, stuffed the remainder of the sandwich in his mouth and left the kitchen with a wave.

Dr. Randle began flipping through the binder. Bertrand and Monty entered and headed straight for the refrigerator.

"Hey, Doc," Bertrand said.

"How's it going, Doc?"

"Gentlemen," Dr. Randle said.

Bertrand and Monty returned to the table armed with beers and snacks. They plopped down at the table.

"Whatcha got there?" Bertrand said, spying the binder. "Whoa. A little light reading, Doc?"

"It's part of John's therapy," Dr. Randle said.

Bertrand quickly thumbed his way through several pages occasionally pausing to show Monty a photo. "How's he doing making his way back to the land of the libido?"

"He's got a way to go yet."

"So you've got him looking at pictures of naked women?" Monty said.

"Indeed."

"Now there's a therapy session even I would pay for," Bertrand said. Monty snickered.

"Gentlemen, this is not funny. John has a real problem that needs to be addressed."

119

"C'mon, Doc," Bertrand said. "So the guy doesn't like sex anymore. What's the big deal? I go without it for months myself sometimes."

"Yeah, but not from lack of trying," Monty said.

"Look who's talking. I haven't seen you scoring much lately, Mr. Touchdown."

"I've been busy," Monty said. "What's your excuse?"

"Gentlemen, your banter is most amusing, but I would like to get back to the matter at hand."

"Where does this go next?" Monty said. "The therapy?"

"Well, after the visualization phase, we'll progress to video. After that, a live encounter."

"And that would consist of what?" Bertrand said.

"Strip club," Dr. Randle said. Dr. Randle closed the binder and got up from the table. "If you'll excuse me, I have a few things to take care of."

"See you, Doc," Bertrand said.

Monty waved and sipped his beer. He caught the evil grin on Bertrand's face. "What are you up to? You've got that look."

Bertrand smiled. "I just thought that we should insert ourselves into John's therapy. See if we can spice things up a bit."

Randolph, unshaven and wearing his robe, shuffled into the kitchen, nodded at both men and dropped into a chair.

"My, how the mighty have fallen," Bertrand said.

"God, Randolph," Monty said, grimacing. "You stink. Take a shower."

Randolph ignored them as his eyes wandered without purpose around the kitchen. Eventually, they landed on the binder. He pulled it closer and glanced down at the nondescript cover.

"What's this?" he said.

"Part of John's sex therapy," Bertrand said. "Dr. Randle has got him looking at pictures of naked women."

Randolph flipped through several pages of the photos. His mood improved slightly. "Nice," he said. "Oh, I like her." He continued scanning the photos. "When's that quack leaving?"

"The Doc? Not for a while, I don't imagine. What's wrong with him?" Monty said.

"It's just getting weird around here. Besides him, now there's some bug-eyed troll hanging around."

"Dharna," Monty said. He smiled at Bertrand. "Have you talked with him yet?"

"Nah, why bother," Randolph said. "I just want to be left alone."

"Probably a bad time to bring this up, but when are planning on paying me?"

Randolph shook his head. "You'll get your money when I'm ready, Monty. Jesus, isn't that four million a year you pull down enough?"

Bertrand whipped around in his chair. "What? Four million a year?"

Monty glared at Randolph then turned back to the flushed Bertrand. "Relax, Bertrand. He's exaggerating."

"No, I'm not," Randolph said. "Do the math."

"You're making four million a year? For what? Helping those cretins of privilege you represent find the signature line on a contract?"

Bertrand got up from his chair and started pacing.

"Randolph, you know the rule," Monty whispered. "No talking salaries in front of him. It's not good for his blood pressure."

"Well, then stop hassling me about a lousy ten grand," Randolph said.

Bertrand picked up his pace. "I can't believe you make that much. And for what? I bust my ass each and every day developing quality products that benefit society and promote the health and wellbeing of people throughout the world."

"Let's not get carried away, Bertrand," Monty said. "You make scents for a fucking deodorant company."

"Well, it sure beats pandering to a collection of overpaid athletes whose only role in life is to tell me which beer to drink."

"Yeah, maybe." Monty laughed. "But it sure doesn't pay as well."

Bertrand slammed his hand down on the counter. "You son of a bitch."

"Relax, Bertrand. I'm only joking. Lighten up."

"Don't tell me what to do. I am not one of your goddamn clients." Bertrand rubbed his forehead with both hands. "I can't believe this. I spent nine years in college to get where I am today."

"Show's how smart you are," Monty said. "It only took me six."

Randolph laughed. "And he's got the associates degree to prove it."

Monty laughed along. Bertrand failed to find the humor.

"I have a Ph.D.," Bertrand said. "I am a Doctor of Hygiology."

"Nobody cares, Bertrand," Monty said. "Everything is market driven. You know that. More than anybody, you should know that."

"It's not right," Bertrand said. He stopped pacing and sat back down at the table.

"Well, boo-fucking-hoo," Monty said. "You're gonna drive yourself crazy. Some people are born to have initials after their name. Others are destined to have a bunch of zeros on their checks."

"It's just not fair. Do you realize that I make less than five percent of what you do in a year?"

"That sounds about right." Monty chuckled but stopped when he saw the murderous glare on Bertrand's face. "I'm kidding. Jesus. What do you expect me to do about it? I don't make the rules. If Pepsi wants to pay one of my clients a million bucks to sip and say yummy, who gives a shit? And my client would be nuts not to do it."

Bertrand stewed in silence.

Monty stood and patted him on the shoulder. "I gotta go. Try not to think about this stuff. It's not good for you."

Bertrand stared blankly at the wall.

"Later." Monty waved and departed through the backdoor.

Soon, the roar of his Porsche filled the kitchen. Bertrand continued to stare at the wall while Randolph returned to the binder.

"Now she could help me out of my funk," he said. Randolph pointed to a photo. Bertrand was still a million miles away, his mind definitely not on naked.

30

"What was wrong with the note?"

Emily rolled her eyes. "Have to go now, I need to pee? What on earth were you thinking?"

"I did have to pee," David said. "Hey, you were the one who was always on my case about the importance of truth in a relationship."

Emily's eyes narrowed. "Yeah, and obviously you listened well since, unknown to me, you were cheating on me for a year."

"You weren't meeting my needs," David said.

"You son of a bitch." Emily jumped out of her chair and launched herself at David. "What you need is a punch in the mouth."

John jumped between them and pulled Emily back a safe distance. "Hey, hey, hey," he said. "Focus people. Let's try to remember why we're here."

"Good question," David said. "Why are we here?"

John sighed and stared at David. "We're here to figure out the next step in our plan to get you and Margaret back together. Remember?"

"Got it."

"Obviously," John said. "We need to do a bit better this time. Something more personal. Perhaps direct contact between the two of you."

"Do you think that's a good idea?" David said.

"I think it's a great idea," Emily said. "Put him in a UPS uniform and turn him loose."

"I could handle that. I played the delivery guy in an off-Broadway production of The Tale of Two Envelopes. I got great reviews."

"Off-Broadway?" Emily said. "You were in fucking Cleveland."

"Cleveland is off-Broadway."

"Focus people," John said. "No more deliveries. David has to be the one to pull this off. More personal, more sophisticated. I'm thinking tuxedo, champagne, something very romantic."

"I can do my Bond. The Connery Bond," David said. "Shaken, not stirred."

"Oh, god," Emily said. "This is hopeless."

"No, wait a second, Emily," John said. "He might be on to something here. Not necessarily Connery, but let's stay with that idea. What actor does Margaret respond to?"

"That's easy," David said. "Leonard Nimoy."

Emily laughed. "Leonard Nimoy? Spock? You gotta be joking."

"That's right," John said. "I completely forgot. She loves Leonard Nimoy."

"You got that right," David said. "Man, the first thing I do every week is TiVo the original Star Trek reruns. Whenever Margaret sees Spock in uniform, she goes off like a firecracker. I mean, she gets so hot, she..." David caught Emily's glare and trailed off. "Sorry," he said. "Just trying to make a point."

"I could never figure that one out," John said. "I always used to leave the house every time it came on. Talk about hoping to get beamed up."

"It's the ears," David said. "She equates big ears with...well, you know."

"So, you think you can handle this one?" John said.

"I was born to play Spock." David stood at attention and gave them the Vulcan salute. "Logic is the beginning of wisdom; not the end," David said, doing a bad Spock. "That's from Star Trek capital V, capital I."

"It's Star Trek six, you idiot," Emily said.

David smirked at Emily. "Right. Like you know Star Trek."

John held up both hands and tried several unsuccessful attempts of the Vulcan salute. "Damn," he said. "I could never get my fingers to work that way."

"Yeah, I know. Margaret told me. Maybe I'll do something from Wrath of Khan." He began pacing, deep in thought. He

125

snapped his fingers. "No, I've got it. I'll go back to the original TV series. What was that episode called? Oh, yeah, Spock's Brain." He wheeled around to face John and Emily. "Spock's brain disappears, and it's up to Kirk to find it within 24 hours, or Spock dies."

"You've managed to last a lifetime without yours," Emily said. "Twenty-four hours shouldn't be too much of a stretch."

David smiled and nodded. "Thanks, Em. Yeah, I can do this one."

"David," John said. "Let's not get carried away with this one. A couple of well-timed quotes and Spock references should do the trick. Let's not make it too big of a production number, okay?"

"Huh? What's that? Oh, sure. No problem." David fell silent and stroked his chin. "I'll need ears. Gotta have the ears."

"And the gift. Don't forget the gift," John said.

"The gift? Oh yeah, that's right. A little token of my Vulcan-affliction."

"Lord, just take me now," Emily said. "Affection, you moron."

"Well, sure. That goes without saying."

John removed his wallet and counted out five one hundred dollar bills. He handed them to David and rested a hand on his shoulder. "Now it should be something tasteful. Something nice, but not too gaudy. Maybe a nice piece of jewelry."

"Yes, David," Emily said. "Maybe a bracelet, pair of earrings."

"Or a choke collar with matching leash," John said.

Emily laughed.

"It's just a thought."

"This is gonna be good," David said.

"Remember, David. Choose wisely. We need to make sure this comes across as real."

"That's right, David," Emily said. "Real life. You do remember what that's like, don't you?"

David, already preparing for his role, broke concentration long enough for a quick smile in their direction. He gave them a perfect

Vulcan salute and said, "Captain, life is not a dream." David puffed his chest out as he stared off into the distance.

"Star Trek. Capital V."

31

John glanced at the setting sun disappearing behind the house and focused the binoculars on the second story window. "Where the hell is he?"

"Typical," Emily said. "What's she doing in there?"

"No sign of life, but her car's in the garage, so I'm pretty sure she's home. No, wait." John squatted further down behind the purple sage. "Uh, oh."

"What?"

"She's got company." John lowered the binoculars and looked at Emily. "Horizontal company."

He handed her the binoculars and Emily peered up at the window. "Woo, I'll say she does. That's gotta hurt."

Emily offered the binoculars back, but John shook his head and waved them away. Emily took one more look then sat down with her back against the hedge.

"What do we do? If David finds out she's got someone up there; we're screwed."

John sat down next to her. "Well, as long as we can get her to come to the window, we should be okay. Once she sees David, I'm betting she'll figure out a way to get rid of whoever's up there."

"You sure?"

"Yeah. One thing about Margaret, she's very comfortable doing the wrong thing, but she sure hates to get caught doing it."

Emily nodded and caught a glimpse of the figure striding down the street in their direction. "Oh, Jesus."

John followed her stare.

David, dressed in a full-blown Spock uniform, complete with ears, smiled and gave them the Vulcan salute. "Requesting permission to come aboard."

"Get over here," John said, making room for him behind the hedges.

"Pretty cool, huh?" David said. He knelt down and turned his head sideways. "Check out the ears."

"Very nice," John said. He exhaled loudly and looked at Emily.

"Don't look at me," she said. "I'm speechless."

"Thanks, Em," David said. He got to his feet and studied the house. "So, is this the planet we're exploring today, Captain?"

"It is indeed," John said. "Did you remember the gift?"

David pulled out a small box and handed it to John. John opened it and nodded.

"Wow. Nice job, David."

"Please, call me Spock."

Emily examined the elaborate bracelet covered in diamonds. Even against the backdrop of the early evening sky, it sparkled.

"You got this for five hundred bucks?" she said.

"Nope."

"Didn't think so." She continued to examine the bracelet.

"Nineteen, ninety-five," David said. "Plus shipping and handling."

"What? You bought her costume jewelry?" John said. "Are you crazy? She'll sniff that out in two seconds."

"Nah," David said. "The woman at the Home Shopping Network said that only one in a hundred people could tell the difference."

"Margaret's hobby is diamond cutting," John said. "Why do you think she vacations in South Africa?"

"For the beers," David said.

"What are you talking about?"

"The beers. She told me she likes going to South Africa for the beers."

"Not the beers, you cretin. DeBeers."

David stared blankly at John.

"Forget it," John said. "We'll just have to roll the dice." John had a thought. "Hey, what happened to the rest of the five hundred I gave you?"

"Expenses, man," David said. "Costume rental, ear molds...plus I needed a full-body wax...and beer...and cigarettes."

"Welcome to my nightmare." Emily continued to stare at her ex-husband.

"Hey, check this out," David said. He removed a small metal object from his belt. "My phaser."

"What is that?" John said.

"Well, it's not a real Star Trek phaser, but pretty close. It's a Taser."

"Be careful with that thing," Emily said. "I hear they give you a pretty good jolt."

"That's right...Spock. They're nasty."

"Ah, don't worry," David said. "It doesn't work. Watch."

David jammed the Taser into his chest.

Zzzzzzt.

David staggered backward, bounced off the hedge and collapsed. He quivered and gazed at a distant planet through a vacant stare.

"Jesus Christ, David," John said.

"Call...me...Sp...ock."

Emily, convulsing with laughter, rolled on the ground.

"Hey," John said, "It's not funny." John glanced at Emily and then down at David quivering on the sidewalk. John smiled, started to chuckle and eventually broke into a belly laugh.

John and Emily regained their composure and leaned over the body.

"Hey, Goober," Emily said. "Wake up." She kicked him in the shoulder.

"Vulcans do not approve of violence," David said.

"He's fine," Emily said. "Walk it off."

"I'm needed on the bridge."

John leaned close and slapped him on the cheek.

"I'm tired, Margaret," David said. "Go get one of your toys."

John held up a hand in front of his face and performed a perfect Vulcan salute. "Hey, check it out," John looked at Emily.

"I finally got it." John, still holding up the salute, glanced down. "Hey, Spock. I'm up here. How many fingers do you see?"

"Two."

"Close enough." John pulled David up to a sitting position.

David shook his head. "Woo. Talk about your Vulcan mind-meld."

"C'mon, you've got work to do," John said.

Emily and John helped him up on his feet. He staggered for a few seconds then found his bearings.

"You better let me hold that," John said.

David shook his head and returned the Taser to its holster.

"No, I need it for my character."

"All right," John said. "But at least be careful."

David nodded, took a deep breath, and slid back into character.

"Okay, Spock. You ready?"

David nodded.

"You're sure?"

David nodded.

"Go get her. Go rescue your beloved princess from the clutches of your dreaded rival."

"Who?"

"Never mind," John said. "And let's keep it outside. Don't go in the house."

"Why not?"

John, reluctant to mention Margaret's visitor, fell silent.

"Because…outside you can add a touch of Romeo and Juliet," Emily said.

"Good one," John said. "Go summon your princess from yonder window."

"Romeo and Juliet? I thought I was Spock."

"You are Spock. But Spock with a romantic side."

"Don't over-direct. You're confusing me."

"Just play it from outside the window, okay?"

David nodded and headed down the driveway towards the front door in more or less a straight line. John and Emily returned to their position behind the bushes and watched David ring the doorbell. John peered through the binoculars up at the window. Margaret appeared then turned her head back towards the bed. The window slid open, and Margaret peered out. "Yeah, who is it?"

"Doesn't the woman ever wear clothes?" Emily said.

David left the front steps, approached the window and stared up.

"What the hell are you supposed to be?" Margaret said.

"It is I. Spock." He flashed the salute.

Margaret stared down in disbelief but smiled. "Spock, huh? Isn't that sweet. My little Leonard."

"Yes, my princess. I have come to rescue you from the clutches of my enemy."

Margaret glanced back at the bed. "Nobody here who meets that description," she said. "And look at the ears. You did this all for me?"

"Beautiful," John said.

"I can't believe this is working," Emily said.

"I would go to the end of the galaxy for my beloved," David said. "Now, let us put our difficulties behind us. Let us move forward together intertwined towards a new horizon where we'll remember our past, and reconnect with a brighter, more intense, future."

"What?"

"Beam me up and let's get naked. I got a two-day rental on the costume."

Margaret, in fact, did beam. "Two days huh, Spocky? Hang on a sec." Margaret left the window.

John picked up the binoculars and watched the proceedings. "Yeah, she's booting him out. I bet he's going out the back door."

"Man," Emily said. "I gotta start watching that show. I must have missed something."

Margaret reappeared in the window, ready to play. "And who am I again?" she said.

"My beloved princess."

"Princess Margaret," she said. "I like that."

132

"Yes," David said, bowing slightly. "Your royal majesty." He extracted the box containing the bracelet and held it up. "Please accept this gift as a small token of my love and affection."

Margaret cooed at the sight of the box. "Jewelry? Lenny, you shouldn't have."

"It is the least that I can do," David said.

"For your sake, let's hope not," Margaret said.

He opened the box. The bracelet sparkled.

"Ooh, nice," Margaret said. "Let's have a look at it. Throw it up."

David closed the box and tossed it skyward. It fell short and landed on the ground under the window. "Damn," he said.

Margaret frowned. David, embarrassed, retrieved the box and hurled it towards the window. Margaret snatched it out of the air. She turned away from the window. "What? No, use the back door. Yeah, call me in a couple of days."

"What's that, my princess?"

"Nothing," Margaret said, once again giving David her undivided attention. "Now let's have a look at this." She opened the box and draped the bracelet across her wrist. Her smile vanished.

"Uh-oh," John said, staring up at the window through the binoculars.

"She figured it out already?" Emily said.

"Does a dog know the difference between a steak bone and celery?"

Margaret disappeared from the window and returned wearing a jeweler's eyepiece. She examined the bracelet.

David looked up at the window nervously. "Is there a problem, m'lady?"

"And from which part of the galaxy were you able to procure this fine piece of contraband from?"

David thought for a moment, scuffed a boot tip into the ground, and looked back up. "Planet Zirconia?"

"I see," Margaret said.

"This isn't going to end well is it?" Emily said.

"No, he's hosed," John said.

"Too bad," Emily said. "Well, at least he's got his phaser with him."

Margaret disappeared from the window again but returned shortly carrying the bracelet in one hand and a hammer in the other. She smiled down at David, placed the bracelet on the windowsill, and attacked it with the hammer. Thousands of tiny, sparkling objects floated to the ground.

"You son of a bitch," she said. "How dare you come around here trying to pass this shit off on me."

David ducked as the hammer whizzed past his ear and disappeared into the hedge. "Now, Margaret. Just relax. I come in peace." David flashed the Vulcan salute. Margaret returned the salute, minus a few fingers.

"Get out of here."

"Now, Margaret. Just let me come inside and I'll explain."

"Don't make me come down there."

"Margaret, please. Be reasonable."

Margaret growled; one part wolf, two parts bear.

"Wow," Emily said. "Did you hear that?"

John cringed. "Now there's a memory."

Margaret glared down at David. She had his undivided attention, and he began to shake in his boots. He took a small step backward and removed the Taser from his holster. He held it up with a shaking hand.

"It that supposed to scare me?" Margaret chuckled. "That dinky little thing. You wanna see a stun-gun? I'll show you a stun-gun." Margaret again stepped away from the window.

John waited until she was out of sight and popped up from behind the purple sage. "C'mon, David. Now's your chance."

David, frozen in his tracks, looked at John helplessly.

"Run, Forrest, run," Emily said.

David's legs told him he wasn't going anywhere. He stood trembling and holding the Taser out at arm's length. Margaret returned.

"Point that thing at me, will you?"

"Shit," John said. "I can't believe it. What doesn't she spend my money on?"

"What is that?" Emily stared up at the window. "A squirt gun?"

"No, that's the latest in personal safety technology. The liquid stun-gun."

John peered up at the apparatus Margaret was holding. It resembled a Super Soaker and did shoot water, but was much deadlier due to water's ability to conduct electricity. And judging from the size of the backpack filled with water, Margaret had more than enough ammunition to handle her upcoming intergalactic battle. Margaret pumped the weapon and fired a few tracers over David's head. The early evening sky momentarily brightened.

"Holy shit," Emily said. "She's gonna kill him."

"I don't think it's deadly. At least in small doses," John said. "But it will definitely get his attention."

David got down on one knee and looked up at the window. "Darling...my princess...Margaret, I thought the bracelet was real. Honestly, I would never try to-"

Zzzzztttt.

The stream of water, zinc, and salt designed to maximize conductivity caught David in the thigh.

"Yowser," David screamed and rolled to his left.

Margaret flashed an evil smile that sent chills down John's spine. She fired another blast. It glanced off David's shoulder and one of his ears melted. The ricochet hit the hedge. Smoke and a small fire ensued.

"Margaret, please."

"She does adapt well to new technology," John said. "I gotta give her that."

Emily nodded and focused on David, who was struggling to his feet. Margaret seized her opportunity and fired a long, continuous blast that hit David in the groin. A bluish light flickered back and forth as the charge bounced from one testicle to the other.

"Ooooooohhhh. B-b-b-beam me up. Th...that...hu...hurts."

135

"It's supposed to hurt," Margaret said. She lowered her weapon and surveyed the battle scene below. She nodded in satisfaction and disappeared from the window. Moments later, the garage door opened. Margaret backed out of the driveway and squealed her tires as she drove away. John and Emily jumped up from behind the bushes and raced over to David.

"What have you got to say for yourself now, Spock?" she said, nudging him with her foot.

"I have noted that the healthy release of emotion is frequently very unhealthy for those closest to you," David said, staring blankly up at the sky.

"I know this one," John said. "It's from the Plato's Stepchildren episode."

"Emotional, isn't she? Yes, she has always been so," David said, reciting from memory.

Emily glanced at John. He thought for a moment. "Journey to Babel episode where Spock is talking to his father about his mother."

"Well, he still remembers his lines," Emily said. "That might be good news."

David continued. "It seemed like the logical thing to do at the time."

"No, forget it, he's out of it," Emily said.

"There are many aspects of human irrationality I do not yet comprehend," David said. His eyes rolled back further in his head.

John slapped David's cheek. David smiled up weakly.

"Live long and prosper," he whispered.

John placed a hand on his shoulder and tried to shake him back to life.

David, semi-comatose, turned coy. "Please, Margaret, not in front of the Klingons."

32

John opened the grill and flipped the steaks. He closed the lid and wiped his hands on his apron then sat down next to Emily.

"I blame myself," John said.

"I blame you too," Emily said. "How much have we got sunk in this supposed reconciliation?"

"About fifteen hundred each."

Emily frowned and looked around the backyard. The picnic table was set, and Dr. Randle was busy working his way through a bowl of corn chips and guacamole. Randolph, still in his robe despite the approaching dinner hour, was asleep in the hammock. Dharna, dog-like, salivated while glancing back and forth between the guacamole and Dr. Randle's energetic crunching. Dr. Randle stared at Dharna, grabbed another handful of chips and waited. Dharna eventually got the 'no-begging' message and wandered away. He settled on the lawn near the hammock and stared at the napping Randolph.

Bertrand and Monty bounced through the back door, down the steps and headed for the others. Bertrand was carrying John's three-ring binder under one arm, and both of them giggled like schoolboys. Bertrand headed straight for the appetizers. Monty paused long enough to grab two beers from a cooler next to the table. Bertrand dropped the binder on the table, glanced in John's direction, then winked at Monty.

"You're bad," Monty laughed. "Like the guy doesn't have enough problems already."

"This is gonna be great."

Monty opened the binder and flipped through the first few pages. "Jesus, that could make a guy feel downright inadequate."

"Yeah, I know," Bertrand said.

"Where on earth did you find those magazines? You got a secret you want to share, Bertrand?"

"Go screw yourself," Bertrand said. "I got them from one of my co-workers."

Monty laughed and headed towards the barbecue. "You're a sick man, Bertrand."

Randolph opened his eyes and came face to face with Dharna. "You. Everywhere I go, you're there staring at me."

Dharna's shoulders slumped, and he transitioned into his puppy face. Randolph frowned, tightened his robe and sat upright in the hammock. Dharna extended both his hands out towards Randolph.

"What on earth is the matter with you?"

He got out of the hammock and headed for the cooler. He glanced over his shoulder and noticed Dharna following him. Randolph opened a beer and sat down at the picnic table next to Bertrand. Dharna sat down on the other end of the table and stared at Randolph.

"What the hell is this guy's story anyway?" Randolph whispered to Bertrand.

"Who? Dharna?" Bertrand said. "What's wrong with him?"

"He keeps following me around."

Bertrand smiled and said, "Maybe he just likes you. I think I'll go check on how the steaks are doing."

Randolph watched Bertrand depart then looked down the table at Dharna, who was flipping through the binder.

"Oh, my," Dharna said. "What is this?"

Randolph remembered the women he'd seen in the binder earlier. "I think my favorite is the one on page six."

Dharna glanced at Randolph and flipped to the page. Two naked men were engaged in an erotic version of Greco-Roman wrestling. Dharna fought back against the onset of nervous tension.

"Yeah, that's pretty hot stuff, huh?" Randolph said. He took a long swig of beer and glanced skyward again with a look of contentment.

"I beg your pardon," Dharna said.

"That," Randolph said, pointing to the binder. "Hot stuff. Yeah, a man could get lost for days in that."

Dharna slammed the binder shut and pushed it away. He twitched in his seat looking for something to do with his hands.

"What's the matter?" Randolph said. "Don't tell me you don't like what you see there?"

"I, uh, don't know what to say."

"Well, I know what I say," Randolph drained his beer as he stood. "I'd crawl through the frigging desert for a crack at that."

Dharna, speechless, stared at Randolph. Randolph cracked a fresh beer and smiled at Dharna. "Yeah, I'd crawl on my belly through the desert. And my dick would be so hard; I'd leave a trail in the sand."

Dharna's twitching increased.

"What the hell is wrong with you?" Randolph said.

Dharna concentrated on controlling his spasms, but the nervous energy found another escape route. Dharna winked at Randolph.

"Hey. Who are you winking at, pal?"

Dharna winked again.

"Cut it out," Randolph said.

John and Emily approached carrying trays of steaks and everyone settled around the table. David appeared at the back door, and John waved. David slowly made his way towards the table.

"Here comes Sparky," Emily said.

"The guy's a walking light show. What the hell happened to him?" Bertrand said, through a bite of steak.

"He's fine," John said. "He just needs a few days to settle down."

"What he needs is a surge protector," Bertrand said. "He walked in my room yesterday, and the lights flickered."

David approached the table and gingerly settled down on the bench. "Hi, folks."

"Hey, Edison," Bertrand said. "Don't forget; you owe me two bucks for the blown light bulb."

David nodded and grabbed a plate. He reached for a fork, poked it with a finger then picked it up.

"How you doing?" John said.

"Well, I'm not conductive anymore," David said. "So that's good."

"Planning session tomorrow," John said. "Don't forget."

David filled his plate with salad and shook his head. "I don't know, John. I'm beginning to wonder if this is worth the effort."

"What are you talking about? You and Margaret are perfect for each other."

"I'm going to be six feet under at the rate we're going now," David said.

"It's a start," Emily said.

John glared at her before turning back to David. "Relax. It's just a little lover's tiff," John said. "Trust me; she'll get over it."

"I don't know. Maybe I should just move on," David said. He turned his attention to his steak and chewed slowly.

"There'll be none of that talk at this table, young man," John said. He waved his knife to emphasize his point. David cowered in his seat.

"I just can't see us getting back together. After what she did to me."

"That? That was nothing," John said. "She's not even warmed up yet. I mean, she'll get over it. She's very close to coming back to you."

"She burned a hole right through my costume. The costume shop's policy is 'you burn it; you bought it' so now we're out another three hundred. I suppose a crotchless Spock costume could come in handy at some point, but I don't know if I can take all this humiliation."

"Will you listen to yourself? Are you going to give up that easily? Is this the same man who saved the entire town from the psycho gardener in the classic, Evil Hedges?"

"I got great reviews," David said.

"Or the father of the self-absorbed, autistic child in the off-Broadway smash, Birth of a Salesman?"

"I was good. But that damn kid kept stepping on my lines."

"And who could ever forget you as the eunuch cop in the erotic thriller, Empty Holster?

"That part was a real stretch," David said. "Because I'm so…well, you know."

Randolph, polishing off his beer, obviously didn't know. "What? You're so what?"

David glanced at Randolph and looked around the table. "Endowed," he said, shrugging.

"You? You don't say," Randolph said.

"Yeah," David glanced at Emily, who continued eating her salad.

"How big?" Randolph said.

"Do we really need to talk about this?" Emily said.

Randolph grabbed a fresh beer and staggered as he returned to the table. "Why not? Everybody is always making references to size and whether or not it matters. I, for one, would like to know. So, David, enlighten us. Tell us how big it is. Give us your definition of endowed."

David looked around the table and said, without a trace of self-consciousness, "It's about a foot."

Randolph sp beer across the table.

Monty whistled.

Randolph grabbed a handful of paper towels and reached across the table. He spied Dharna, who twitched, then winked at him.

"Cut it out," Randolph said.

Bertrand wiped his mouth with a napkin. "Statistically, David…you're what we call an outlier."

"Outlier? No way, man. I almost never take it out in public," David said.

John looked at Emily who stared down at her plate as she chewed salad.

"It's just a number," David said.

"No," Bertrand said. "Six is a number. Seven's a number. I don't even know what twelve is."

"If I remember my math, it's almost a foot," David said.

"Jesus," Randolph said. "Emily…?"

"What?" Emily said, not looking up.

"But you're so tiny," Randolph said.

"Don't let that fool you," David said. "Em's a real trooper."

"Drop it," she said.

"No, I'm serious. I mean, twelve? That has to make a difference. Doesn't it?"

Emily glared at Randolph. "Let's say it gets your attention and leave it at that, okay?"

David smiled.

"Well, there you go," John said. "Question answered. Now back to what we were discussing, David. As I was saying, you're the man. You're the star, the hero, of this show. And the hero always has to overcome adversity before he gets the girl. So stay focused."

"You're right," David said. "We're still only in the second act."

"Absolutely," John said. "So I want you to prepare. Go focus on our planning session tomorrow. Can you do it?"

"I can do it," David said, rising to his feet.

"Who's the man?"

"I'm the man," David said, thrusting his chest forward.

"He's got my vote," Randolph said.

"That's more like it," John said. "Now go to your room and prepare."

David pumped a fist in the air and headed towards the house. John watched him go and shook his head as he returned to his steak. "Sometimes," he said. "I think I'm the only one who cares about this relationship."

John reached across the table for the bottle of Tabasco and knocked the three-ring binder off the table. He leaned down to retrieve it, saw one of the photos staring up at him, and turned his attention to Bertrand. "Is this supposed to be funny?"

Bertrand feigned innocence but smiled sheepishly.

"How'd you know it was me?"

John looked around the table at the others, then back at Bertrand. "Process of simple elimination."

33

Randolph opened his bedroom door and peered out through the tiniest of cracks. Encouraged by what he saw, or rather what he didn't see, he opened the door further and stuck his head out. He looked up the hallway to his right. Not a soul in sight. Randolph smiled and looked left. A Dharna sighting. Randolph, startled and cranky, looked down at the tiny man who was sitting in the lotus position with a blank expression on his face.

"You. Again?"

"It is I," Dharna said. He morphed into his puppy-dog expression and stared up at Randolph.

"How many times do I have to tell you? I'm not interested in what you're selling."

"Give it time. You will be. I tend to wear people down."

Dharna spread his arms and gave Randolph another puppy-dog.

"Hey. I'm warning you. Cut it out."

"Don't try to fight it, Randolph. You know it's the right thing to do," Dharna said.

"I'll tell you what I'm going to do. I'm gonna kick the crap out of you if you don't stop following me around."

"Oh, I won't stop, Randolph. Not until we settle this."

Randolph took a step out the door and glared at Dharna. Dharna began to fidget and twitch. Then he winked.

"Stop with the winking, will you? Jesus. Look, I know I'm a real catch, but...hey, what's up with your face?"

Dharna began transitioning into his showcase expression. He slowly rotated his head and his face became to elongate. His eyes sunk back, his cheeks hollowed, his face began to pale. Randolph knelt and stared at the transformation occurring directly in front of him. Dharna fully morphed into The Scream and thrust himself forward until his face was only inches from Randolph. Randolph jerked backward, banged his head against the door, and scrambled back inside his bedroom. Randolph stretched out on the floor and felt the knot forming on the back of his head.

Out of options, he dragged himself towards the shower and lingered until he sparkled. Randolph rinsed away the last trace of shampoo and turned off the water. Soap dripped into his eyes, and he blinked back against the sting and blindly stretched one arm out towards the towel rack. He came up empty, cursed, stepped out of the shower, and tried to locate a towel. His hand came to rest on plush cotton, and he grabbed the towel. He pressed it hard against his eyes and dabbed at them until his eyes stopped stinging. He tossed the towel back in the general direction it came from and opened his eyes. Randolph jumped backward immediately.

"Jesus," Randolph said. "You?"

Dharna, holding Randolph's towel, gave him the puppy-dog expression. "Yes, me again."

"Get out of my bathroom."

"Not until you give me what I want," Dharna said, leaning closer.

Randolph, remembering he was naked, pulled the shower curtain around his body. "Never. You will never get that from me."

Dharna fought back the nervous tension and tried to maintain his composure. But the sight of the frantic, naked Randolph was making things difficult. He twitched and sat down on the toilet. "You have directly challenged my abilities," Dharna said. "This matter has now become a question of character."

"It's a question of choice, pal," Randolph said. "And I choose not to play."

"Is that right? You don't have a choice. You need to take care of this." Dharna leaned forward and blasted Randolph with The Scream. Randolph slunk backward and cowered behind the shower curtain. Dharna's face relaxed, and he smiled at Randolph. "I'll be seeing you around, Randolph."

Dharna tossed the towel in Randolph's direction and left the bathroom.

34

Bertrand glanced at his watch then up at Gina, Walter Harrison's stern, yet efficient, assistant. Seemingly oblivious to his presence, she continued to work the phones and pound her keyboard into submission. Bertrand leaned forward in his chair and prepared to speak. Gina, without looking up, beat him to the punch. "He won't be long, Bertrand."

Bertrand sat back in his chair wondering where her sixth-sense came from. "What sort of mood is he in today?"

"Oh, the usual. He's been doing performance appraisals all day if that tells you anything."

"That's why I'm here," Bertrand said. He tapped the large folder he was holding in his lap.

Gina glanced up, flashed a smile and returned to her world. The door behind her desk opened and two men stepped out.

"Thanks, Walt, I appreciate it," said a marketing executive whose name Bertrand could never remember.

"Anytime," Harrison said. He chuckled. "Well, at least once a year, right?"

The marketing man laughed along, waved goodbye to Gina, and left with a quick nod in Bertrand's direction.

"Come on in, Bertrand," Harrison said.

Bertrand stood, smoothed out the imaginary wrinkles in his white lab coat and followed him into the office. He sat down at a small table and opened the folder.

"Thanks for stopping by, Bertrand. I hate these things, but human resources say they're mandatory. What can you do, huh?"

"What can you do?" Bertrand began organizing the contents of the folder into several stacks.

"What have you got there?"

"Oh, just a little supporting documentation I've pulled together about my performance over the last year. I thought it might come in handy."

Harrison frowned at the stacks and glanced back at Bertrand. "I'm not going to have to read all that shit, am I?"

"Only if you think it will help," Bertrand said.

Harrison grabbed a folder of his own. He removed the lone piece of paper it contained and closed the folder. He quickly scanned the paper and nodded. "That sounds about right," Harrison said. "So, let's get started."

Bertrand selected the first piece of paper from the stack to his left and cleared his throat. "Okay, I began last year by instituting a new process to streamline and reduce the amount of time it took management to review submissions of new ideas for improvements and enhancements to the effectiveness and efficiency of our internal operations."

Harrison, confused, said, "You did what?"

Bertrand began rereading, but Harrison cut him off. "English, please, Bertrand."

"You remember, Walter. The improvements I made to our corporate improvement initiative program."

"You're talking about the suggestion box?"

Bertrand, embarrassed, mumbled down at the table.

"I suppose that's another name for it."

"Jesus Christ, Bertrand. You painted the box."

"In the official corporate colors," Bertrand said. "And don't forget I incorporated our logo."

Harrison shook his head and glanced down at Bertrand's stacks of paper. "Let's just stick with the basics, shall we?" Harrison said. "Your role as lead hygiologist."

Bertrand folded his arms in front of him and stared down at the table. "Fine."

Harrison placed the sheet of paper he was holding on the table and slid it in Bertrand's direction. "Read it. It's all good."

Bertrand studied the completed appraisal form.

"It's an outstanding review," Harrison said. "You've had a great year."

"In the comments section, it says I have a zealous attitude. What's that supposed to mean?"

"Diligent, tenacious."

"Opinionated?"

Harrison thought for a moment and nodded in agreement.

"Sometimes. Yes."

"Quick to anger?" Bertrand said.

"I think we both know that to be true, Bertrand."

Bertrand flared.

"And what's this 'has a strong adherence to his principles' comment? Stubborn?"

"It means you stick to your guns, Bertrand. That's all it means. Look at the overall rating, for chrissakes. It says outstanding. You're one of our stars around here."

Bertrand relaxed and smiled.

"And that's what makes this next bit somewhat…tricky," Harrison said.

Bertrand went on point.

"Your amazing creation of No Offense, which looks like it could revolutionize the deodorant market, has generated enormous interest throughout the industry."

"Yeah, I know. I read the trades," Bertrand said. His eyes narrowed, and he stared at Harrison. "Continue."

"Well, you know our joint venture partners are hooked in with some of the big guys."

"Yeah."

"And a couple of days ago, one of the big guys, I'm not at liberty to say which one at this point, made an offer to buy Harrison Hygiene."

"Wow," Bertrand said. "That is big news."

"Yes," Harrison said. "As a family-owned business, it's an extremely difficult decision, but it could happen."

Bertrand remained silent as he pondered the potential impact on him.

"But this potential buyer is in the middle of several other transactions and has asked that we postpone certain planned funding operations and initiatives to help preserve their current and projected cash flow position."

Bertrand raised an eyebrow in Harrison's direction. "English, please, Walter."

"All salary increases and bonuses are on hold for the foreseeable future," Harrison said.

"What?"

"Now, Bertrand. I know this is not what you were expecting to hear."

"You're right, Walter. It isn't. I was expecting to hear you say 'Thanks for making me another several million, Bertrand. Here's a nice salary bump and a big bonus for the effort.'"

"I'm sorry, Bertrand. I'm hoping to be able to free up some bonus money after we close the final No Offense deals. All I can ask is your patience."

"The hell with patience."

"Now hold on, Bertrand. At some point, I see a big bonus in your future."

"And I suppose you used enoptromancy to come up with the prediction?"

"What?"

"You certainly spend enough time in front of the mirror?"

"What the hell are you talking about?"

"Just find me some more money, Walter. Let's leave the fortune telling to the professionals, shall we?"

35

John swiped the credit card through the reader and smiled at Mr. Winkle as he waited for the transaction to process. Emily waved at Mr. Winkle and slipped back behind the newspaper. David, sitting in a chair next to Emily, casually flipped through a magazine. He took a sip of coffee and lit a cigarette. Emily shook the newspaper in the direction of the drifting smoke but said nothing.

"Okay, Mr. Winkle," John said. "You're all set. Hope you enjoyed your stay."

"Thank you, John. I must say, you operate quite an interesting place here."

"We do our best. Is your mother here yet?"

"Yes, she's parked out by the curb," Winkle said. "I guess I should be going."

"You take care of yourself," John said. "And remember what I told you. All divorce lawyers are scared of one thing."

"Attack dogs. Got it."

"I just wish I had discovered that in time to save myself. You call that number I gave you and tell them I sent you. They breed a cross between a Rottweiler and a Dingo I think you'll find very useful."

"Got it," Winkle said. "Goodbye, all."

He waved and strolled towards the door in good spirits. John watched him go out the door. "And they said it couldn't be done."

"What's that?" David said.

"A satisfied customer." John turned all business. "All right. We got work to do." John sat down and leaned forward in his seat. "Why don't we start with some brainstorming. You know, just kick some ideas around."

"Okay," Emily said. "How about we spring for a surprise vacation for the two of them? Maybe a week in Belize."

"That could get expensive," John said.

150

"I don't like it," David said. "If she goes off on me while we're in a foreign country, I might never get out. I could end up in a Mexican prison."

"Hmmm, interesting," Emily said. "Maybe we should make it two weeks. That would have to increase the odds."

"A Mexican prison?" John said.

"Yeah," David said. "Belize is in Mexico."

John gave David a blank stare.

"Okay, good point. Scratch international travel. Well, we certainly don't want to try the jewelry angle again."

"How about I do a different role?" David said. "Maybe Rhett Butler. 'Frankly, Scarlett, I don't give a damn.' Or how about Brando? 'Stella! Stella!' What do you think?"

"The horror…the horror," Emily said.

"Hey, I'm just trying to help," David said.

"Do us a favor, don't."

"Somebody getting a visit from her friend is she?" David said.

"Yeah, every time you open your mouth, my eggs catch the first train out."

"Okay, enough," John said. "I'm not running a day care program here."

"We're supposed to be brainstorming. That means you don't criticize every suggestion when it's made," David said.

"He's right," John said to Emily.

David smiled and stuck out his tongue at her. She gave him the finger. John got up from his chair and paced, deep in thought. "What can we give her? What would get her attention? Come on, David. This should be right up your alley."

"I usually just wait until she cools off and then swoop in for a big round of make-up sex."

"That could take forever," John said.

"It won't this time," David said. "I'm ready to pop. I won't last five minutes."

"He's talking about her, moron," Emily said.

"Oh."

"We need to wrap this up," John said. "She's bleeding me dry. I mean, we need to get you two back together as soon as possible."

"You're such a good friend," David said.

"What?" John said. "Oh, yeah. Well, that's what friends do. Come on, think. We need ideas."

"What does she do in her spare time?" Emily said.

"Well, she works on her body," David said.

"The gym?"

"Occasionally," David said. "But Margaret hates to wait. She usually goes the other route."

"That's right." John snapped his fingers and sat down. "Plastic surgery. She's a junkie for that stuff."

"She's had a bunch, that's for sure," David said.

"Wow," Emily said. "I hadn't even noticed."

"Well, it's pretty hard to tell these days where the real Margaret begins and ends," John said.

David nodded in agreement.

"What has she had done?" Emily said.

"Well, lately, I'm not sure," John said. "But when we were married she had her boobs done twice, a tummy tuck, multiple liposuctions, and a nose job."

"Just last year, she had her left nipple enlarged and her ears done," David said.

"What the hell was wrong with her ears?" John said.

"She says they've been stretched out of shape." David tugged at his ears. "What do you think? Should I get mine done?"

"Unbelievable," Emily said.

"No, hang on, Em," John said. "I think we're onto something here."

"It sounds like there's nothing left to be worked on."

"Trust me, she'll think of something," John said. "But there's no way we could suggest anything specific. Not and live to tell about it."

"I don't know," David said. "We might be able to come up with something she'd like."

152

John stared at David in disbelief. "We're talking about Margaret. The same woman who nuked your Johnson a few days ago."

"I'll think of something," David said.

Emily said, "Gift certificate? Do they have those for plastic surgery?"

"Fantastic, Em," John said. "We'll get her a gift certificate for the procedure of her choice."

"Cool," David said. "I'll start working on the card."

John and Emily watched him head for the registration counter where he began jotting down ideas.

"Don't worry," John said. "We'll do quality control on it."

"How much?"

"Gee, I don't know," John said. "Five grand? Maybe ten."

"Ten grand? John, I think you're getting a little carried away with this thing."

"That's only about one month of alimony. If it works, it'll be more than worth it."

"You're on your own with this one," Emily said. "I can't afford it."

"Okay," John said. "But it better work."

David walked out from behind the counter holding a piece of paper. "Check this out." He cleared his throat and slipped into his best James Earl Jones voice. "Here's something you don't need, cuz you're my little movie star…"

"Not bad," John said.

"But your butt could use some tuckin', so make sure they hide the scar." David beamed but frowned when he saw their stares of disbelief. "What?"

"Are you insane?" Emily said.

"It could use a little nip and tuck," David said. "She's not eighteen anymore. John, you know what I'm talking about."

"Have you got a death wish?" John said.

"What's wrong with it? It rhymes and everything."

"Never tell any woman, especially Margaret, that her butt is anything less than perfect," John said.

153

"It's just a note," David said.

"Yeah," John said. "And Gettysburg was just a place for a bunch of gun owners to hang out."

David crumpled the note and tossed it behind the counter. He sat down petulantly in his chair. "You write it then."

John looked at Emily. "You got any ideas?"

"Let me think." Moments later, she nodded. "I think I got something that might work." She glanced at David and shook her head. "Let's replace the 'your butt needs a tuckin' reference with…this gift shouldn't even be given because you're perfect as you are."

John considered the line and looked at David, who nodded back.

"Great," John said. "That should do it."

"What do we do next?" David said.

"Well, I'll call it in to her doctor and make sure it gets delivered with the note," John said. "You lay low for a couple of days. After that, hopefully, Margaret will show up professing her undying love for you. And as soon as she takes the bait, I mean, when she finally comes to her senses, we set the wedding date."

"Cool," David said. He slipped back into his James Earl Jones voice. "I have news for you, Luke. This is CNN." He hopped to his feet, thrust his chest out, and wandered out of the room bowing to silent, imaginary applause.

"It must be a nice place to live," Emily said, watching David's departure.

"Oblivionville?"

"Yeah. Well, I need to get back to work."

"I've got some homework I've been putting off."

"How's that going?"

"I'm having some trouble with the visual, but I passed the auditory and verbalization portions. Got an 82 on the final."

"Good for you." Emily laughed. "So you're able to talk about it, huh?"

"As long as it's not too graphic, I'm okay," John said.

Emily laughed and got up from her chair. "Well, let's see how you handle this one." She swayed her way towards the kitchen; butt pressed tightly against denim. "And what do you have to say about this?"

John thought for a moment and smiled. "Perfect."

"Good answer."

36

Margaret wheeled her 500SL into the parking lot and came to a screeching stop in a handicapped space. A security guard sitting outside the front door hopped up from his stool and adjusted his belt. He took a couple of quick steps towards the car. Margaret, hands on hips and wearing micro-shorts and a T-shirt emblazoned with Remember my name because you'll be screaming it later stared defiantly at the approaching guard. The man stopped short when he recognized her, waved nervously, and scurried off. Margaret smiled and bounced towards the door. She nodded at another security guard sitting behind a large desk and walked down the hall. She opened a door, stepped inside and approached a young woman working reception. Margaret drummed her fingers on the top of the desk. The young woman glanced at the fingers and glared up at Margaret.

"I'll call you back." The woman hung up the phone and flicked the hair back from her face. "Can I help you?" she said, examining her manicure.

Margaret's eyes narrowed. "I need to see Sidney."

"The doctor is booked solid today," the young woman said. "Do you have an appointment?"

A small smile appeared on Margaret's face. She chewed on her gum and stared down at the receptionist. "You're new, aren't you?"

"I beg your pardon," the receptionist said.

"You. Here. New. Try to keep up. I tend to move pretty fast."

The woman cocked her head to one side and gave Margaret a petulant smile.

"Don't give me that go fuck yourself look, sweetie," Margaret said. "I invented it."

"Excuse me?"

Margaret leaned over the counter. "Here's what you're going to do, Bambi. You're going to call Sidney on that intercom and have him come out."

"Not without an appointment. That's the rule. Now, if you'd like to make an appointment..." She looked at the screen and typed without her nails touching the keyboard. "The doctor can see you a week from Friday. How does eleven-thirty work for you?" She glanced up and fluttered her eyelids at Margaret.

"We're a few fries short of a Happy Meal, aren't we?"

"Well, at least I'm not like...rude."

Margaret leaned closer.

"I should probably warn you; I don't handle no very well."

"Like I care."

Margaret rubbed her palms together. "I see. Okay, princess, I don't care what village you're currently depriving of their idiot, but you've got five seconds to get him on the phone, or we're gonna need some real medical expertise around here very soon."

"Huh?"

"I'm going to have to ask Sidney about making sure you have a window..."

"A window would be nice."

"...just so you can ask people if they'd like fries with that."

"Look, maaaaam. I'm sorry. No appointment, no doctor. Now, if you'll excuse me. Some of us have work to do."

Margaret's temples quivered.

"What happened, dear? Flunk out of makeup design school?"

"Yeah, and it's too bad. You sure could use some help."

Margaret popped. "Sidney!" She said it quick, sharp, loud. "Get your ass out here." And she only had to say it once.

A balding, middle-aged man's head appeared around a corner. "Margaret. So nice of you to stop by. Why didn't you tell me Margaret was here, Tiffany?"

"She doesn't have an appointment."

"Margaret doesn't need an appointment, Tiffany. She's a very special patient."

"Yeah?" Tiffany said. "Since when?"

"Since I put his last kid through Stanford," Margaret said.

Sidney gestured for Margaret to follow him. "Come, come, come…please. No, after you."

Margaret strolled past the receptionist and glared at her. To her credit, Tiffany hung tough and gave it right back. Sidney led Margaret into an office, and they both settled down on a large couch.

"Is it time for your tune up already?" Sidney said.

"No, I got a gift certificate from my fiancé."

"Oh, yes, now I remember. How sweet? How is David?"

"He's in the doghouse, but I'm about to let him out. He's been punished enough."

"Been a bad boy has he?"

"You're all bad, Sidney. You know that better than anyone. Tiffany? Really, Sidney. What is she? Nineteen?"

"Twenty. So, when I do finally get to meet this David? If you've agreed to marry him, he must have many fine qualities."

Margaret smiled.

"He's got about a dozen."

Sidney stared at the strange smile on her face.

"No way."

"Yup." Margaret's smile broadened.

"Wow. Well done. So, what can I do for you?"

"Are you sure you can work me in today?"

"Oh, I'm fine. At noon, we're having a little graduation ceremony for a fifty-year-old who has hit silicone saturation. I told her the new boobs would max her levels out, but do they ever listen to me? I've got to move her out of the Advanced Gravity Resistance Program, so she's a little down. But I've hooked her up with a new therapist so she'll be fine. It's nothing big, just champagne and cake. You should come. And at two, I've got a set of collagen-dependent twins coming in for their weekly. Other than that, I'm all yours." Sidney clapped his hands together once and jumped up out of his chair. "Okay, let's get started."

In a flash, Margaret was out of her shorts and T-shirt. Sidney stared at her naked body with pride. "Ah, Margaret. You are my masterpiece. My Mona Lisa."

"Don't bullshit me, Sidney. Is my butt dropping on the left side?"

"Let's have a look."

Sidney moved behind her, leaned in for a close inspection and gently patted her butt cheeks. He paused to catch his breath then said, "It seems fine to me, Margaret. In fact, it's magnificent."

"I don't know," she said. "It just feels like it's slipping a bit."

"Margaret, what can I tell you? Have you ever heard me turn down work before? I'm telling you; you've got the ass of a teenage goddess."

Margaret cooed and pinched his cheek.

"You're so sweet. What about my breasts?"

Sidney reached out and gently grabbed two handfuls.

"They're perfect," he said. "Best money can buy." He continued to work his way around her body with gentle touches complementing his comments. "All the work we did on your face has paid off. You look magnificent. Stomach's great. I'm really happy with the way that six-pack implant is holding up. And your thighs look like they could crack walnuts."

"Yeah, I work them out a lot."

"So I hear," he said. Sidney smiled and worked his way around her various body parts. "Your back is strong and very supple. Calves are still perfect. Arms are great." He faced her again. "Margaret, I must say. I'm stumped. I wouldn't know where to begin. Unless… "

"Unless, what?"

"Well, I just thought that there's only one part we haven't worked on."

Margaret squinted, deep in thought. She scratched her left breast and held out her hands and shrugged her shoulders. "I give up, Sidney. You lost me."

"Your...vagina. We've never done anything down there."

"My vagina? What's wrong with it?"

Sidney, senses honed from years of experience with Margaret, deflected the question. "Relax, Margaret. I'm not saying that. I'm only talking about your options."

"Okay." Margaret watched him closely.

"More and more women are having things done down there," Sidney said. "After childbirth, for example, some women are coming in for vaginal rejuvenation."

"Rejuvenation? You make it sound like it's the fucking fountain of youth."

Sidney considered the comment and said, "Well, it's the closest thing I've ever found. But that's beside the point. It's nothing major, just a general tightening."

"You're saying I've got a loose pussy? Who you been talking to, Sidney?"

"Margaret, please. Just try and relax. I haven't been talking to anyone." Sidney drifted off for a moment and allowed himself a memory. "In fact, if I remember correctly, you're quite tight down there. That little rippling thing you do with your-"

"Drop it, Sidney. That was one afternoon a long time ago. And I still think you overdid it with the anesthesia. I wasn't thinking straight."

"Whatever you say, Margaret."

"What are some of my other options?" she said.

"Well, they run the gamut from total reconstruction, which is completely out of the question here, to more minor alterations to your labia."

"What are you talking about? A little off the back and sides? Jesus Christ, Sidney, you're my plastic surgeon, not my fucking stylist."

"I'm just explaining your options, Margaret."

Margaret sat down in a chair and began examining herself. "It looks fine to me," she said. "But maybe I'm missing something."

"No, Margaret," Sidney said. "Trust me; it's just fine. Besides, if you were to have such a procedure done, you couldn't have intercourse for at least six to eight weeks."

"Deal breaker," Margaret said. "That ain't gonna happen."

"No, of course not," Sidney said. He sat down behind his desk and put his hands behind his head. "I don't know what to say, Margaret. I'm stumped."

"Tell you what," she said. "Just whack a few of the trouble spots with some Botox and we'll carry the balance as a credit."

"Deal," Sidney said. "Where would you like it?"

"Anywhere above the waist, Sidney."

37

Margaret slowly pushed the front door open with her foot and stepped inside. She removed her sunglasses and baseball cap and flicked her hair back away from her face with a toss of her head. "It is a nice little clubhouse you boys have going here," she said, glancing around the room.

John peered over his newspaper. "Uh-oh."

"Hello, John."

"Margaret."

"So nice to see you."

"Full moon already?"

Margaret strolled across the room with a twisted smile on her face. John got up from his chair and headed for the registration area. Margaret rested her elbows on the counter and stared at him. "You should be nice to me."

"What do you call eight grand a month?"

"Penance." She widened her grin and held it.

"New teeth?"

Margaret snapped her mouth shut, her expression now a plump-lipped grimace. "I'm looking for David."

"Look, Margaret, if you're planning something nasty, take it outside. I don't allow violence in my hotel."

"Relax, John. I've come to collect him."

John's eyes widened. "Really? You're taking him back?"

"Yes, I think the poor boy has suffered enough, don't you?"

"Well, he's been with you for two years, so I guess that's a rhetorical question, right?"

"Go fuck yourself."

"Right back at ya."

"Just tell me where he is."

"He's in his room. Second floor, third door on the left."

Margaret wheeled and headed for the stairs.

"Hey, Margaret."

162

Margaret stopped and turned. "What?"

"Be gentle with him. He's pretty bruised at the moment."

"Just the way I like them."

"Just go easy, huh?"

"You know me, John." She flashed a smile and headed up the stairs.

John watched her go and drummed his fingers on the counter. "Yeah, that's what I was afraid of."

Margaret bounced up the stairs and headed down the hallway past a small, emaciated man sitting on the floor and making faces.

"You need to get some protein in you," she said.

Dharna flashed the puppy dog and extended his arms up at her. She reached into her jeans and flipped a quarter through the air. Dharna nodded thanks and slipped the quarter into his pocket.

Margaret knocked firmly on the door.

"Come on in."

She stepped inside and closed the door behind her.

"Margaret," David said. He closed the book he was reading and hopped up off the bed. He cowered slightly. "You're not here to hurt me, are you?"

"No, David. I've come to take you home. That is if you think you've learned your lesson."

"Of course, I have." He frowned. "Which lesson is that again?"

Margaret shook her head and chewed her bottom lip. "The lesson about what happens when you lie to me."

"Oh, yeah, that one. Yeah, I learned it. Can I really come home?"

"If you're ready to behave."

"I'm more than ready to behave, my darling," he said.

"And I'm not through punishing you either."

David's shoulders sagged. "I know. I've been bad."

"Yes, you have," Margaret said. "But I've forgiven you."

"So the wedding is back on?"

"Yes, it is."

163

Margaret and David were startled by the loud cry of joy from the other side of the door. Margaret pulled the door open and John, on his knees, looked up sheepishly.

"Congratulations."

38

John downed the last of his champagne, looked around the entertainment room and realized his efforts to get everyone's attention had failed miserably. He refilled his glass, waited for the initial burst of bubbles to subside and poured some more. He turned off the televisions and waited.

"Hey," Randolph said. "We were watching those."

"The sooner we get through this, the sooner they go back on. Now pay attention."

The gang focused their attention on John, who wheeled a white board directly in front of the big screens. John sipped his champagne and beamed. "Thanks for coming," he said.

"Like we had a choice," Monty said.

John ignored the comment and continued. "I am pleased to confirm that David and Margaret have reunited."

Sporadic golf claps broke out.

"Thank you, thank you. As the proud ex-husband and soon to be ex-alimony provider, I'm sure I don't have to tell you how much this means to me."

"And to your bank account," Bertrand said.

"Precisely. Now, I've called you here because I need your assistance in organizing David's bachelor party which will be held here in the hotel tomorrow night."

"That soon?" Bertrand said. "Why so sudden? Margaret isn't pregnant is she?"

"No, despite David's protests about being an only child, Margaret is not pregnant. But hope springs eternal."

"Where is David?" Bertrand said.

"He's upstairs packing, and he doesn't know about the party so let's keep it to ourselves. Now, let's go over some ground rules." John held his pointer up to the whiteboard. "As you can see, I've taken the liberty of jotting down a few of the most important categories. First on the list, is the booze. After the disaster at the Halloween party, I'll take care of that one myself."

"Jesus, man," Bertrand said. "Let it go."

"In good time, Bertrand, all in good time," John said. "And since I'll be out anyway, I'll pick up the food as well."

An emaciated Dharna stared longingly at a nearby tray of snacks and raised his hand.

"I can help you with the food, John," Dharna said.

"Nice try, Dharna," Monty said. "No food for you."

Dharna tried his puppy dog on Monty. Monty laughed and shook his head, and Dharna slumped back in his chair.

"Just make sure you don't assign him and me to the same task," Randolph said. He glared at Dharna, who dropped the puppy dog and fired The Scream back at Randolph.

"Jesus," Randolph said, recoiling in his seat. "Will you cut that out?"

"Settle down. Let's try and stay focused here," John said. "Next is the music. A live band is out of the question, but I think we can do just as well with the sound system here. Randolph, I'd like you to handle that."

Randolph opened his robe and scratched his stomach. He drained the last half of his beer and belched loudly. "Got it."

"And take a shower sometime before the party," John said.

"I just took one." Randolph stood and grabbed a fresh beer.

"It's been five days, Randolph."

"Who cares? I'm only going to get dirty again."

"And Doc," John said, turning to Dr. Randle. "No tarantulas, okay? I don't want to run the risk of injury. If David ended up breaking a leg or something, who knows what could happen?"

Dr. Randle nodded in agreement.

"This brings me to our next item." John tapped the pointer several times on the whiteboard. "Security."

"Security? It's a frigging bachelor party, John. What could possibly happen?" Bertrand said.

"Nothing's going to happen, Bertrand, because I'm making sure nothing happens. Hence the need for tight security. Monty, I need you to handle this one."

"What am I supposed to do?"

"Just stick to him like glue. If he gets so much as a hangnail, I want to know about it."

"I think you're overreacting a bit here, John," Monty said. "Margaret's already taken him back."

"I'll relax when the ring's on her finger. Until then, protect him like you would your quarterback."

Monty shook his head. "This oughta be a fun party."

"Let me know if you think you'll need any backup. I can make a few calls," John said.

"I think I can handle it," Monty said.

"Good. Now, the last item, and I'm way out of my league on this one, is entertainment. Bertrand, I thought you and Dr. Randle might be able to take care of that."

"Love too," Dr. Randle said.

"How much is this going to cost?" Bertrand said.

"Bertrand…," John said, his voice rising in warning.

"Well, the last party ended up costing me almost 500 bucks."

"And whose fault was that?" Randolph said.

"Don't start with me," Bertrand said.

"People, focus please," John said. "Bertrand, if you'd like to handle the food and booze, I'd be more than happy-"

"No, forget it," Bertrand said. "What do we need in the way of entertainment?"

"Don't worry, John," Dr. Randle said. "We'll take care of everything."

"Okay," John said. He reviewed the board while he sipped his champagne. His smile returned. "Let's do everything we can to make sure David gets a safe sendoff. No more screw-ups with this relationship. That's our mission."

"What do we do about Emily?" Randolph said. "We can't have her hanging around."

167

"It's already taken of," John said. "She's going to be babysitting Margaret."

"You're joking, right?" Bertrand said.

"No, I'm not. I needed to make sure we didn't have any surprise pop-ins during the party, so I asked Emily to hang out with Margaret for the night."

"And she agreed?"

"Eventually," John said.

"Those two locked up in the same house?" Bertrand said. "Now that's entertainment."

39

Bertrand clicked the button on his key chain, waited until the car beeped back at him, and headed towards the front door. He paused at the curb and looked up at the garish pink and lime green neon sign that blinked back at him.

Sinful Pleasures: Come on in and see what's in store.

Dr. Randle stopped next to Bertrand and looked up at the flashing sign. "Catchy," he said. "And how about that, you match."

"What?" Bertrand said.

"You. Your clothes. With the sign."

Bertrand glanced at his pink golf shirt and the lime green sweater he had draped over his shoulders. He glared at Dr. Randle and looked around the nondescript mini-mall. Bertrand hitched up his white Dockers, relaxed fit, and shook his head in disgust. "Let's get this over with," he said. "I still can't believe I'm doing this."

"I thought you liked watching porn," Dr. Randle said.

"I do," Bertrand said, starting towards the door. "I just don't like paying for it."

Dr. Randle followed Bertrand inside. The door closed behind them, and both men stood still and waited until their eyes adjusted to the light. Various items, all adult, began to take shape in front of them. Bertrand whistled when he caught sight of the leather section that filled one entire wall.

"Interesting," Dr. Randle said.

Bertrand eyed him suspiciously.

"Speaking strictly as a scientist, of course."

"Sure, Doc. I believe you." Bertrand laughed. He looked around the room and frowned. "Does anybody work here?"

"Bertrand, you need to relax," Dr. Randle said. "That temper is not good for you."

"I don't have a temper." Bertrand looked around the room again. "I said, does anybody fucking work here?"

169

Dr. Randle draped an arm around Bertrand's shoulder. "Let me work with you, Bertrand. I know I can help."

"Just leave me alone."

A large man in his fifties appeared through a doorway draped with strings of colored beads that stretched to the floor. The beads rattled as he entered carrying a large female doll. He posed the doll provocatively in a chair and wiped his hands. "Sorry. Didn't hear you come in," he said. "The front buzzer isn't working for some reason. Welcome to Sinful Pleasures. How can I help you?"

"We need some supplies." Bertrand said.

The man stared at the man in a flowing robe with an arm draped around the shoulder of the man dressed in pink and green. "Sure," the man said, quickly sizing up his customers. "I'm sure I can help you out there. What'll it be? Lotions? Creams? I just got a new shipment of toys in that you two might like." He pointed towards the leather section. "Or maybe some of our latest restraint devices might interest you. We're the sole central Texas distributor of the You Ain't Going Nowhere line. Trust me, they ain't kidding when they say that."

Bertrand scowled at the man and shrugged Dr. Randle's arm away. "We need a video. For a party."

"Then you've come to the right place," the man said. "Follow me." He led them through the beaded doorway, and they found themselves standing in a massive room filled floor to ceiling with porn.

"Wow," Dr. Randle said. "Talk about your growth industry."

"Yeah," the man said, admiring his inventory. "Billions a year and still growing. This country can't make a television or stereo worth a shit, but we sure know how to videotape people screwing, huh?"

"You should bring John here," Bertrand said. "Talk about your immersion therapy."

"No," Dr. Randle said, shaking his head. "I'm afraid that could result in a major setback."

"I think I've got just what you two are looking for. Follow me." The man led them to the other side of the room. He reached up and grabbed a DVD from a shelf and handed it to Bertrand.

"Top seller the last three months in your market," the man said.

"My market?" Bertrand said. He flipped the DVD over and read aloud from the back cover. "The Lonely Woodman. A forest ranger battles fire in the woods while refusing to succumb to heat in the bedroom. What is this?"

The man took a step back and pointed to another shelf. "And here, of course, is the always popular Nut Busters series. But I imagine you two have probably seen all of these."

Dr. Randle wandered off to another section of the room. Bertrand stared at the man in disbelief. "These are all men."

"Of course, they're all men," the man said. "What did you think I was going to show you?"

"Well, for starters, how about women?"

"Women? You? You two?"

"What are you talking about? Us two?"

"I'm sorry," the man said. "What with the way you're dressed and the arm around the shoulder. I thought you were a couple."

Bertrand took a step forward and glared at him. "A couple of what?"

The man laughed nervously. "You know. A couple."

"Well, we're not." Bertrand took another step forward.

"Okay, I got it. I'm sorry," the man said. "Follow me. The hetero section is over here.

Bertrand followed the man across the room until they were standing next to Dr. Randle, who was examining a DVD. He turned around and held it up. "I can't believe you have this one."

The man glanced down at the DVD in Dr. Randle's hand and smiled. "Oh, sure. That's a classic."

Dr. Randle handed it to Bertrand who read the title and tagline on the back. "The Adventures of Madame Palm. She does a lot more than just read them."

A confused Bertrand looked at Dr. Randle.

"I served as story consultant on that one," Dr. Randle said.

"Really?" the man said. "I'm impressed. I thought it was a very authentic take on the fortune telling industry."

"Thanks," Dr. Randle said. "They wanted me to play a minor role, but something told me it wasn't a smart career move."

"What did you use for that one? Erectomancy?" Bertrand said.

Dr. Randle's booming laughter reverberated through the room. "No, I'm afraid that's one of the most unreliable methods when it comes to the male species, Bertrand."

"Let me show you something I think you might like," the man said.

They followed him to another shelf and watched as he collected several dvds from a display case. He handed one to Bertrand, who after glancing at the trio of silicone-breasted beach blondes on the front cover, again read aloud from the back.

"Heavy Weather. An unending storm of big tropical fronts moves through creating havoc and mass hysteria."

"It's very popular." the man said. "But pretty derivative."

Bertrand handed the DVD back to the man. "Can we get on with this? How much do these go for?"

"Forty bucks."

"Forty bucks? Are you shitting me? I can get laid for forty bucks," Bertrand said.

"Yeah, in Altoona, maybe."

"How much for a rental?"

"I don't do rentals anymore. Too much of a hassle," the man said, shaking his head.

"Forty bucks?"

"It's for a good cause, Bertrand," Dr. Randle said. "I think I'll wander around while you decide."

Bertrand watched Dr. Randle depart then turned back to the man. "Don't you have anything cheaper?"

The man thought for a moment and then snapped his fingers. "You know, you might be in luck. I've got some old videos I'm trying to get rid of that might do the trick. You still have a VCR?"

"Yeah, I think we've got one around somewhere."

172

"Then follow me."

He led Bertrand out of the room, down a corridor and into a room filled with old magazines, deflated dolls, and boxes filled with videotapes. "I've been meaning to get this room cleaned up," he said, working his way through the clutter. He brushed a half-inch of dust off a box and pulled it open. He began scrounging through the contents and tossing video cassettes down on the floor near Bertrand's feet.

"You should find something here to your liking," he said. "I won't testify to the production values in most of them, but they should do the trick."

Bertrand began rummaging through the videos. "What's this one about?" Bertrand said, holding up a dusty video.

"Let's see what you've got there." He brushed away the dust and read the title. "Oh, yeah. I remember this one. Devil's Anytime Playtime Plaything. Good one. The devil has created this sex robot that goes on a rampage."

"Any good?"

"Well, if I remember, it wasn't bad. I thought the female star's acting was abysmal, but she totally put out. You know, now that I think about it, I can't remember ever seeing her in anything else. Yeah, it's not bad. I'd give it three dicks up."

"How much?"

The man shrugged. "Five bucks?"

"Deal," Bertrand said.

"Cool." The man wiped the dust off his hands. He led Bertrand out of the room, and they headed back towards the DVD room. "Do you need anything else?"

"No, this will do," Bertrand said. He then had an idea. "Hey, I don't know if you can help or not, but I also need to find a stripper for the party."

"You have come to the right place," the man said. "I don't advertise it, but I do run a bit of a sideline operation."

"Strippers?"

The man laughed. "All that and more, my friend. What are you looking for? Girl on girl? Mini-orgy? Or just a straight bump and grind?"

"That depends," Bertrand said. "How much?"

"Gee, that depends, too. At the top end, your basic mini-orgy will cost you three grand, not counting tips."

"Three grand? Yeah, right. Next."

"Your basic girl-girl option goes for six hundred an hour."

"That include tip?"

The man grunted, laughed and shook his head.

"What do you have for a man on a limited budget?"

"Gee, I don't know what else I can do for you," the man said. "These women get paid good money these days, plus I've got my overhead to consider. You know, transportation, security."

"What's the best you can do?" Bertrand said, anxious to close the deal.

"Well, there's Sally."

"Sally? She sounds nice."

"Nah, I don't think so. I better not."

"What's wrong with Sally?"

"Well, it's not like there's anything wrong with her. Sally's just a little…different."

"Dangerous?"

"Only to herself. Nah, you don't want Sally."

"How much?"

"You really don't want Sally."

"How much?"

"She's seventy-five an hour. Tip included."

"Deal," Bertrand said.

"You sure about that?"

"Done deal," Bertrand said, nodding firmly.

The man shrugged. "Okay. Just tell me the time and place and we're good to go."

"That's great," Bertrand said. "Hey, Doc. Let's go. We're out of here."

Dr. Randle waved, returned the DVD he was reviewing to its display case and headed in Bertrand's direction.

"Just one more thing," the man said. "Don't freak out when you see her dog."

"Dog? This isn't some weird animal act, is it?"

"No, nothing like that. Just don't act surprised when you see it. That's all."

"Dog, huh?"

"Yeah."

"I like dogs," Bertrand said.

"Good," the man said, shrugging. "Maybe it'll help."

Dr. Randle approached. "Find something good?"

"We're all set. And I've lined up the stripper as well."

"Well done, Bertrand," Dr. Randle said. "Let's get some lunch."

"Lunch?"

Dr. Randle smiled. "Don't worry, Bertrand. It's on me."

40

"Forget to pay the light bill, John?" David inched his way forward as John led him down the darkened hallway.

"Maybe I did. I guess I should go check that fuse box, huh?"

"I would say so. I can't see two feet in front of me."

"Tell you what. You wait here while I go check it out."

John gently pulled David's sleeve until he was standing in the doorway of the entertainment room, then reached out and flicked on the light switch. The room, now brightly lit, was covered with decorations and filled with food and drink.

"Surprise!"

David, overcome with delight, looked at the assembled group then back at John. "You guys. You shouldn't have."

"Hey, it's not every day you get married. Especially to someone like Margaret."

John pulled David into the room and sat him down in the chair of honor strategically placed in the center of the room.

"Get this man something to drink," John said.

Randolph, still in his robe and sprouting shaggy facial hair, reached into a small refrigerator next to him and tossed a can of beer in David's direction. David, not paying attention, caught it with the side of his head. Randolph frowned, waited until he had David's full attention and tossed him another. Bertrand approached with a bottle of tequila and handed it to David. Drinking straight from the bottle, David took a long pull and handed it back to Bertrand.

"Easy, big fella," Bertrand said. "You've got a long night in front of you."

"Speaking of which," John said. "What time does the entertainment get here?"

Bertrand glanced at his watch and said, "She should be here any minute now."

"Stripper," David said. "All right. Now you're talking."

"Yes," John said. "And after the main event, I thought we'd settle down to some serious drinking and a little poker."

"Cool," David said.

"And some porn," Randolph said.

"Yeah," John said. He frowned, glanced at Dr. Randle and said, "For those of you so inclined."

"You too, John," Dr. Randle said. "Consider it part of your therapy."

"Woo, woo," David said, grabbing the tequila bottle from Bertrand. "Can't have a bachelor party without porn."

John pulled Bertrand off to one side. "You're sure about this stripper? I mean, did you check her out? Talk to any references?"

"References? Jesus, John, it's not like we're hiring her to do your taxes. Relax. Sally's great. Trust me."

John raised an eyebrow at Bertrand but said nothing.

Dharna stole a quick glance in Monty's direction then inched forward to grab a spinach tart from the tray in front of him. He pulled his hand back when he felt the slap on his wrist. He sat back in his chair and looked sheepishly at Monty, who was waving a finger at him.

"You're working here," Monty said.

"Just one, please."

"And bring dishonor to a noble profession? No way. But keep up the good work on Randolph. Stay close to him tonight. I think he's close to cracking."

"Stay close? Have you caught a whiff of him lately?"

"Well, yeah. I know what you mean. But at least keep an eye out for chances to give him The Scream. That one drives him nuts."

Dharna nodded and stared longingly at the blue cheese oozing from the spinach tarts.

The doorbell rang, and the front door opened. "Hello? Anybody home? Who's ready to party?"

"Sally? Is that you?"

"C'est moi, mon cheri."

"French?" John said.

177

"For the right price," Randolph said. "I'm sure she'll do just about anything."

"We're in here," Bertrand said.

Everyone sat up and looked expectantly towards the doorway. A small attractive woman wearing black sunglasses and a short black leather skirt with matching bustier thrust one arm forward, rested it against the doorframe, and tapped the cane she was carrying on the floor. Her other arm remained out of sight. "Hello, gentlemen," she said in a husky voice.

"Hey," Randolph said. "Look at you. Say, what's up with the cane? You do the Can-Can?"

"But of course," she said. "If you can, my good man. I can too."

"I'm over here," Randolph said.

"What on earth is that smell?" she said, slipping out of character.

John continued to study Sally's movements and whispered to Bertrand. "What's the matter with her? She's staggering. Think she's drunk?"

John's question was put on hold when the group's anticipation was derailed by the introduction of Sally's other arm. Actually, it was what was attached to her other arm that got their attention. Sally stepped through the door and introduced everyone to the massive beast attached to her left arm. "This is Bluto."

The dog stepped through the doorway, slowly scanned the room, and emitted a low, menacing growl. Everyone slunk back in their seats without taking their eyes off the dog.

"What is that thing?" Randolph said.

"Rottweiler-dingo mix," John said, mesmerized by the dog's stare. "Big motherfucker, too."

"I would have guessed part leopard," Bertrand said. "How much does that thing weigh?"

"Only a hundred and fifty," Sally said. "But don't worry. He's fine."

"Is he friendly?" John said.

"Define friendly," Sally said.

"Can you pet him?"

"Well, I can," Sally said. "But if I were you, I'd stick with the verbal."

"No worries there, Sally," John said. "Come on in and make yourself comfortable."

John and the others stared in disbelief as Sally slowly made her way through the doorway tapping her cane in front of her. The dog stayed at her side and glanced back and forth growling.

John shook his head and looked at Bertrand. "She's blind. I can't believe you. You hired a blind stripper?"

Bertrand watched Sally's movements with one eye while keeping the other focused on Bluto. "What's the big deal? We're supposed to be watching her, not the other way around."

"I can hear you," Sally said. "My other senses are pretty sharp. What is that smell?"

Randolph, embarrassed, was unable to make eye contact with the others who were staring in his direction.

Sally made her way to the center of the room and commanded the dog to sit. It sat, but it didn't look very happy about it. Swivel-like, his head continued to scan the room as if deciding which one of them to eat first.

"Okay, here's the deal," she said. "I dance for an hour and make sure I give the groom-to-be a special treat. Other items, within reason, are available based on my set rates. And I need to mention that whenever I'm off in another room with one of you guys, someone will need to dogsit Bluto. Also, he's pretty protective so, while I'm dancing, it's important that you don't make any sudden movements."

"This is gonna be great." Randolph laughed. "Ready for your lap dance, David?"

David looked at Randolph and stared at the dog. He lifted both feet and tucked his legs up on his chair. "No hurry."

"Well, I need to get ready," Sally said. "Is there someplace I can change?"

"There's a bathroom right at the top of the stairs," John said.

"Thanks." She reached down and vigorously grabbed the dog's neck and scratched his ears. "Now you be a good boy, Bluto and stay here while mommy gets changed. Okay, schnookums?"

The dog thumped its tail on the floor and barked.

"Do you need any help finding it?" John said.

"No, I'll be fine." Sally gave the dog one final vigorous rub then turned and left the room.

The dog began to follow. "Stay, Bluto," she said. The dog whimpered softly and sat down in the doorway facing them. The dog resumed scanning the room, accompanied by a constant low growl.

"Well, you've done it again," John said to Bertrand.

"What are you talking about? This is fine. As long as all of us remember to avoid any sudden movements, I'm sure we'll have a great time. Isn't that right, David?"

"Huh?" David said. "Sorry, Bertrand. I wasn't paying attention. That's the biggest dog I've ever seen in my life."

"He's just a little protective, that's all," Bertrand said. "He's just a big puppy."

"Then you pet him," Monty said.

"Right. Like I'm going anywhere near that thing," Bertrand said.

"Lapdance," Randolph laughed. "Get ready, David. But I'd try not to get wood if I were you."

"Bertrand, I thought you had learned your lesson."

"Relax, John. Have another beer."

"Yeah, why not? If I'm going to get my throat ripped out, I sure don't want to do it sober. Randolph, grab me a beer will you?"

Randolph leaned forward and stretched an arm towards the refrigerator. He stopped when the growling intensified. Spying the dog only a few feet away, Randolph slowly drew his arm back and tucked himself back in his chair. "Sorry, John. You're on your own."

"Well, I hope she gets back soon," Monty said. "I gotta take a leak."

"Go ahead," Randolph said. "Just walk right past him. He probably won't bother you."

"I can hold it," Monty said.

"Here I come," Sally called from the top of the stairs. "Start the music."

Randolph reached for the remote sitting on the table next to him without taking his eyes off the dog. He clicked the remote and a loud dance number rumbled from the speakers. Sally eventually made her way back into the room.

"Bluto. Stay. I need someone to hold him. Two of you would probably be better."

All the heads swiveled back and forth in a unanimous no.

"I don't think we've got any takers, Sally," Bertrand said.

"No handler for Bluto, no dances I'm afraid."

"Bertrand will do it," John said.

"Like hell, he will," Bertrand said.

"You got us into this." John gently shoved Bertrand in the direction of Sally and the dog. Bertrand glared back at John but slowly approached Sally and waited for instructions.

"Slip around behind me and grab the handle of the lead. As long as you stay behind him, you'll be okay. But never, under any circumstances, get your hands near his mouth."

"No worries there," Bertrand said. He tentatively grabbed the handle with trembling hands.

"Got a good grip?" Sally said.

"I think so," Bertrand said.

"Okay. Let's have some fun. Bluto…stay."

Sally stepped away from the dog and began moving seductively to the music. She dropped the cape she was wearing around her shoulders and revealed a sexy teddy complete with stockings and garters. Everyone in the room watched the show using the same strategy.

Focus on Bluto; sneak a peek at Sally.

Focus on Bluto; sneak a peek at Sally.

Bluto apparently either didn't like the show or being constrained by Bertrand. The dog tried to inch his way closer to

Sally and his claws dug into the wood floor as the depth and volume of his growl swelled.

Bertrand struggled against the force and silently begged for help.

Monty shook his head no.

Dharna did The Scream; undoubtedly out of real fear.

John gave Bertrand an evil smile.

Randolph took the momentary lull as an opportunity to get a fresh beer.

David, despite his fear, admired Sally's dancing and opened his arms to her.

Sally eventually located David's chair with one arm, pirouetted and plopped down on David's lap. She ground herself into him. Hard.

David groaned.

Big mistake.

Bluto tore away from Bertrand like a band aid from flesh and headed directly for David.

Randolph, returning to his chair, screamed and tossed the unopened beer into the air which Bluto snatched out of mid-air. Bluto leaped at David at the same moment he bit through the metal can. The beer exploded, later recounted as the critical component in David's subsequent and relatively unscathed escape. Bluto, stunned and confused by the noise and blast of cold liquid, paused. And David, to his credit, scrambled onto and then on top of a large cabinet along one wall where he sat staring down at the beast.

Sally, drenched in beer, glared down at the dog who was now sitting quietly at her feet. "Damn you, Bluto. Bad dog. Bad dog."

Bluto's bottom lip quivered, and he stretched out and whimpered.

"Sorry about that, guys."

"No problem," Bertrand said. He looked down at the leash handle he was still gripping with both hands.

Sally examined the damage to her costume. "I'll need to go change."

"No, that's okay," John said.

"No, I insist," Sally said. "Don't worry. I'll take him upstairs with me this time. I won't be a minute."

John handed her the cane, and she was soon tapping and inching her way back across the room, Bluto in tow.

"John-," Bertrand said.

"Don't say a fucking word, Bertrand."

Bertrand shrugged and headed for the tequila bottle. John coaxed David down off the cabinet and settled him back in his chair. David accepted the tequila bottle from Bertrand and took a huge gulp. Gradually, his breathing returned to normal.

41

Emily, wearing a loose-fitting cotton dress with spaghetti straps, rang the doorbell and waited for the door to open. She smoothed imaginary wrinkles from the dress and bounced nervously on her toes. Margaret opened the door and smiled.

"Hi. Come on in. I love that print. Is that cotton?"

Emily smiled weakly and stepped inside. She looked around and nodded, impressed by her surroundings. "This is very nice."

"Thanks, I'll give you the tour later," Margaret said. "I have to give John most of the credit. He's the one with the magic touch." She laughed. "At least when it comes to houses." Margaret led them to two chairs on either side of the fireplace. "It's probably not cold enough for it, but I love a fire."

Emily settled into her chair. Margaret poured two large glasses of red wine. Emily took a sip. "This is good."

"Thanks. John's influence again. He taught me everything I know about wine. So what are the boys up to? And I don't use that term lightly."

Emily chuckled through a sip of wine. "Oh, they're being so secretive about it. Like a bachelor party is some big mystery."

"Strippers and porn and beer," Margaret said. "What imagination."

Emily laughed. "I was surprised when you agreed to this."

"Well, I've been thinking about doing it for a while and tonight seemed as good a night as any. Sort of a get to know you kind of thing." Margaret stared into the fire. "I feel like I owe you an apology for...well, for fucking your husband. Even though I had no idea at the time."

"Forget it. I should be thanking you. Although I don't see why you'd want him. Apart from the obvious reason, of course."

"You're probably a bit biased." Margaret held up a joint. "Smoke?"

"I can't even remember the last time I got high. What the hell. Girls night out, right?"

"Right," Margaret said.

She lit it, took a hit and handed it to Emily. Emily puffed, tentatively at first, then inhaled and held her breath. Eventually, she exhaled and handed the joint back to Margaret. "Wow, that's strong."

"Yeah, it's good," Margaret said. "I try not to do it too often. I get a little goofy."

"It always makes me horny," Emily said.

"Quaaludes do that to me. They're hard to find, but when I do, it's off to bed, see you Wednesday."

Emily laughed and accepted the joint from Margaret.

"You want to take the tour?" Margaret said.

"Sure."

Margaret stood up, refilled their glasses and led Emily into the dining room, through the kitchen, and past another room that contained a television.

"Very nice," Emily said. "It's modern, but it's still got some great antique pieces. I can notice John's touch."

"You're about to see my contribution to the décor," Margaret said, leading her upstairs.

On the second floor, Margaret's master bedroom dominated. A massive bed, surrounded by mirrors, including a large one on the ceiling, rested on top of thick carpet. Emily looked around the room, then up at the mirror.

"I like to watch," Margaret said.

"And David is into it?" Emily said.

"Sure."

"That's odd. I could never get him to do anything out of the ordinary," Emily said.

"At first, neither could I," Margaret said. "But he didn't have a choice once I pointed out a few things to him."

Emily sat down on the edge of the bed and looked up at herself. "Like what?"

"Basically that he was going to do what he was told. At least in this room," Margaret said.

"David? Submissive?"

"Oh, totally," Margaret said. "You never figured that out?"

"David? No way."

"I guess he just needed someone a bit more… forceful."

Margaret's eyes sparkled. Emily shook her head as she accepted the joint from Margaret.

"I can't believe it. He was always prolific but very traditional."

"Predictable," Margaret said.

"Yes, absolutely," Emily said. "It used to drive me nuts. I used to beg and plead with him to spice it up."

"Wrong approach. You should have demanded it."

"No," Emily said. "I could never do that. I think I'd be classified submissive as well."

"Two subs in the same relationship? Not a good combination. That's worse than two Gemini." Margaret gestured for Emily to follow her. "C'mon, I'll show you what I mean."

42

"That dog is not human," David said.

John considered the statement, then nodded. "David, when you're right, you're right."

Sally called from the top of the stairs. "Okay, guys. Let's try this again."

"What about the dog?" A question asked in unison.

"I'll slip back in and close the door. He should be fine in the hall." She paused. "Is there anything valuable there?"

John looked at the deep scratches Bluto's claws had left in the wood floor. "Not anymore."

"Okay, guys. Get ready for a real treat. Here I come," Sally said. "Easy, Bluto. Look out...you're standing on my foot. Get your nose out of there. Bluto...Bluto. Will you please get the hell out of the way? Aaaaahhhh!"

Sally's scream was punctuated by the sounds of a scantily-clad, blind stripper falling down a long flight of stairs. Then, silence ensued. Everyone jumped out of their seats and raced to the hallway. They traffic-jammed together in a heap at the doorway when confronted by the confused and angry Bluto. The dog slowly circled the unconscious Sally lying face down at the bottom of the stairs.

"Holy shit," John said.

"Man, she's out cold," Monty said.

"Think she's dead?" David said.

"I wish I could say, but I'm getting nothing," Dr. Randle said.

"What a waste of money," Bertrand said.

Randolph, hammered, stared down at her provocative landing position. "Nice butt."

"Jesus Christ, Randolph. What the hell is the matter with you?" John said.

"Well, it is nice." Randolph noticed Dharna standing behind him and elbowed his way to the other side of the doorway.

"Somebody should go check to make sure she's okay," Dr. Randle said.

John looked around the crowded doorway. "Any volunteers?"

Another round of silence ensued.

"Maybe we should draw straws," David said.

"The straws are in the kitchen," John said.

"I'll go get them." David started through the doorway. Bluto growled at David's first step. "Never mind."

"John, you should go," Monty said.

"Why me?"

"It's your hotel."

"Prove it," John said, working his way back inside the entertainment room.

"Look," Monty said. "If she's hurt, who do you think her lawyers are gonna come after?"

John fell silent and looked around the room. He spied a tray of appetizers on a coffee table. "Hand me that tray, Dharna."

Dharna stared at the food and reluctantly handed it to John.

"Think he likes spinach tarts?" John said.

"There's only one way to find out," Monty said.

John whistled, and Bluto looked at him and growled. He flipped a spinach tart through the air, and Bluto devoured it in mid-air. The beast gave John the slightest wag of his tail.

"I think he likes them."

John tossed another tart, this one a bit further and over Bluto's head. The dog jogged off, finished the tart with one bite, and returned to Sally's side. Slobber dribbled out the corner of his mouth onto the floor.

"Okay, here's the plan," John said. "Monty, you take the tray and keep firing tarts past him into the reception area. How many are left?"

"Eight," Monty said, then saw a hand snatch one off the tray. He glared at Randolph.

"Hey," Randolph said. "I haven't had dinner."

"Okay, we've got seven left," John said. "That should give me about a minute or two to check her out. Think that's enough time?"

"I guess we'll find out," Monty said. "Ready?"

John nodded and Monty fired the first spinach tart across the room. Bluto raced after it. John dashed out of the doorway and slid on his knees and came to rest next to Sally. He felt her wrist and watched for the dog.

"It's working," Monty said. "Two down, five to go. Hurry up. He doesn't chew his food.

John gently slapped the side of Sally's face, and her eyes opened. John, relieved, let out a loud sigh.

"Hurry up," Monty said. "I've only got three left."

"Are you okay?" John said.

Sally blinked and groaned.

"How many fingers am I holding up?" John waited for a response then realized what he'd said. "Sorry, forget I asked."

"What is that smell?" Sally said.

John turned towards the doorway.

"She's going to be fine."

"That's good because I'm out of tarts."

Bluto polished off the last tart, licked his chops and realized somebody had gotten into Sallyland. He kicked it into high gear, and John scrambled to his feet and made a beeline for the entertainment room. He slammed the door shut behind him. Seconds later, a loud thump was heard, followed by a soft whimper.

"Now what?" Monty said.

"Time to watch porn?" Randolph said.

"Go sit down, Randolph," John said.

Randolph sheepishly headed for his chair, grabbing a fresh bottle of tequila on the way.

"I better call an ambulance." John dialed 911 and waited. "Yes, I need an ambulance. No, I think she's going to be fine, but she will need to be checked out. Send it to Divorce Hotel at...what's that? Oh, you know the place. Your brother stayed here when he was going through his divorce. I see. Yes, I think I remember him. Short guy, no neck? Yeah? Glad to hear he's doing better. Please tell them to hurry...oh, one more thing. You better bring along someone from Animal Control."

43

Margaret led her down the hallway and opened a door. Emily peered into the darkened room and was stunned when Margaret flipped the lights on.

"Welcome to the playroom," Margaret said.

"What the…?"

"Nice, huh?"

Emily stared at the number and variety of machines, apparatuses, and various other items all apparently designed with some form of restraint in mind. But the item that got her attention, since it completely dominated the center of the room, was a gleaming silver metal ring that resembled a massive hula-hoop. Emily approached the ring, ran her hand across the cold metal and shivered. She glanced over her shoulder at Margaret, who had her hands on her hips and was staring proudly around the room.

"Is this what I think it is?"

"What do you think it is?" Margaret said.

"It looks like a big letter O," Emily said. "But I have a feeling it's a bit more than that. Sex toy?"

"Trust me; this is a very high-tech piece of machinery. It's definitely not a toy. It's my latest addition. I call it the Big O.

"But not because it looks like one, right?" Emily stared at the big metal circle.

An evil smile crept across Margaret's face. "No, not because it looks like one."

"Are you, what do they call it, a dominatrix?"

"Not quite," Margaret said. "I'm still finishing up my certification. But yeah, I know my way around a dungeon."

"How long have you been into this?"

"As long as I can remember," Margaret said. "I had the room built several years ago. John left shortly after that."

"So John was never into this stuff?"

Margaret laughed and shook her head.

191

"John? Mr. Let's Not and Say We Did? Not likely."

"But David is?"

"Yes, he's coming along nicely," Margaret said.

"Really? I'm shocked."

"So was he," Margaret said. "At first. Fortunately, we crossed paths when he was still somewhat trainable." Margaret lovingly ran her hand across the silver ring. "I had it custom built. It's a combination restraint and personal pleasure device. Completely programmable and runs on hydraulics. Want to try it out?"

Emily shook her head firmly. "No, that's okay. I'll take your word for it."

"C'mon, indulge yourself. You won't believe what this baby can do."

Emily continued to stare at the machine. She took a sip of wine and looked at Margaret. "Nah, I'd be too embarrassed."

"Who's gonna know?"

"You won't tell?"

"I never do," Margaret said. "Here, take a couple more hits first."

Emily took three long hits off the joint and held the smoke deep in her lungs. She exhaled and handed the joint back to Margaret, who inhaled several times in rapid succession. Margaret swayed for a moment and then crushed the roach out in an ashtray. "Wow," Margaret said. "That did the trick."

Emily rubbed her eyes and downed the rest of her wine. She held out her glass, and Margaret refilled it.

"I know I'm going to regret this."

"I seriously doubt that," Margaret said.

"What do I do?"

"Well, the first thing you need to do is remove that dress. Loose fitting clothing is a definite no-no around this thing."

Emily eyed Margaret suspiciously.

"Relax, sweetie. Estrogen does nothing for me." Margaret said. "I'm serious. If anything got caught in the hydraulics, you could get hurt."

Emily took a big gulp of wine, took a deep breath and slid the dress off her shoulders. It dropped to the floor, and she stood facing Margaret clad only in her panties.

"Nice," Margaret said. "Who works on you?"

"What do you mean?"

"Your doctor. Who does your body work?"

"Nobody," Emily said. "This is the real me."

Margaret slowly walked around Emily and nodded.

"I'm impressed."

"Okay if I leave these on?" Emily said, pointing to her panties.

"Sure." Margaret approached, and Emily flinched when Margaret put her hands on her.

"Relax," Margaret said. "You're worse than David."

Margaret reached up and pulled down a thick cable that was operated by a pulley system. Emily heard Velcro being pulled apart and watched Margaret fasten a leather restraint device around her wrist.

"I still don't see you and David together," Emily said.

Margaret paused from her work and said, "It's weird, but David is the first guy who ever truly got me. He's the only one I've ever met who's totally comfortable with me being myself."

"We're still talking about David, right?"

"It's taken him a while to get to this point."

Emily watched as Margaret secured her other wrist.

"And, of course, his size has to be a bonus," Emily said.

Margaret paused.

"Yeah, he's fine that way. Of course, he's no John. But then, who is?"

Emily cocked her head at Margaret and felt her arms being raised against the backdrop of a soft whirring sound.

"John? John who?"

"John. Our John. Or should I say your John?"

"He's not my John."

"Really? I thought you two would be going at it big time by now."

"No, not at all. John? Big?"

Margaret laughed and took a sip of wine.

"David is David. John is Goliath."

"No way. That's impossible," Emily said.

"Remember who you're talking to here, girlfriend. I should know," Margaret said. She knelt down and glanced up.

"Move your leg back a bit."

Emily complied and looked down as Margaret attached a large Velcro strap to one of her ankles.

"You're serious about John?"

"What? About his size?" Margaret shuffled across the floor to her other leg and grabbed the other ankle restraint. She held it in her hand and looked up at Emily "Sweetheart; you've got no idea." Margaret fastened the other restraint. "I can't believe we're talking about this."

"I can't believe we're doing this." Emily giggled.

"This? Just relax. Try to think of it as an amusement park ride."

"Disneyland for adults?"

"Exactly. Not too tight?"

"No, I'm fine."

Margaret sat down in front of a computer next to the machine and banged away at the keyboard. Emily's arms began extending further towards the edge of the metal ring, and her legs were pulled down and stretched apart. Emily, still upright, yet spread-eagled and immobilized, stared down at Margaret, who was studying the computer monitor.

"I'm still trying to figure out how to use all the features on this thing," Margaret said. "The manual that comes with it sucks." She approached the device and examined Emily's situation. She tested the taut metal cables that held Emily's arms and legs. She placed a hand on Emily's back and gently pushed against the tension. Satisfied, she grabbed the riding crop sitting on the desk. Margaret flicked her wrist, and the riding crop snapped in the air.

Emily gulped. "Now what?"

"How come you and John haven't hooked up?"

Emily glanced nervously at Margaret, who was tapping the riding crop against her palm. "Well, he's a mess when it comes to actual physical contact. Fear of intimacy doesn't float my boat if you know what I mean."

Margaret flicked the crop through the air several times. Emily cringed at the loud snapping sounds. Margaret continued to stare off into the distance.

"Don't tell me he's still using that 'Oh, poor me, I'm afraid of sex' crap."

"Yeah, he is. You don't buy it?"

"He's such a fucking baby," Margaret said. "He blames me. Says that I'm responsible for turning him into Frigid Man."

"But he is, isn't he…I guess you'd call it frigid? Almost phobic?"

"Well, he certainly was the last couple of years we were married. But come on, enough already."

"He's in therapy with Dr. Randle."

Margaret, wide-eyed, stood directly behind Emily and examined the riding crop. "He should be working with me. Give me a couple of sessions with him on this baby and he'll be beggin' for a cuddle." Margaret snapped the riding crop across Emily's ass.

"Jesus Christ," Emily said. "Margaret, that hurt."

"Sorry." Margaret's eyes sunk back into her head and Emily, flashing back to what she had observed behind the hedges, recognized the mood swing.

"I just get so pissed whenever I think about that son of a bitch blaming me for his problems with sex." Margaret again whipped the riding crop across Emily's ass.

"Ow! Cut it out!"

Margaret snapped out of her thoughts and glanced at Emily. "Oh, I'm sorry." Margaret tossed the riding crop onto the floor and sat down in front of the computer. She lit a fresh joint, puffed away while it hung from her lower lip, and resumed banging away at the keyboard. The apparatus refused to respond.

"I think I've had enough," Emily said.

"So soon? But you haven't even tried any of the attachments."

"I'll take your word for it. My legs feel like a wishbone."

"Hang on. I'll loosen up the tension."

Margaret entered another round of keystrokes. Again, the shiny apparatus remained motionless. "Damn computers," Margaret said. "Oh, now I remember." She tapped at the keyboard. This time, the apparatus responded. But instead of loosening the grip it had on Emily, the machine merely rotated ninety degrees. Emily, now stretched out across the horizontal axis, stared up at the ceiling.

"You're making me nervous, Margaret."

Margaret glanced at Emily and scratched her head. She removed the joint from her mouth and held it up in Emily's line of sight.

"Maybe later," Emily said.

"Let me get you out of there," Margaret said. She took one last hit off the joint, extinguished it, and resumed typing.

Emily felt herself begin to move. She exhaled and relaxed, but tensed again when she realized what was happening. The machine remained horizontal, but Emily found herself rotated 180 degrees and staring down at the floor.

"Shit," Margaret said. "I should finish reading the manual."

"Ya think?"

"Hang on." Margaret entered another burst of keystrokes. Emily now began to repeat her 180-degree turn.

Look up at the ceiling; down at the floor.

Up at the ceiling; down at the floor.

"Goddamn it," Margaret said.

She watched Emily rotate back and forth. "Are you okay?"

"I feel like a rotisserie chicken. Get me out of here."

Margaret nodded and tried to focus. She stared at the monitor, took a sip of wine, and rubbed her forehead.

"C'mon, Margaret," Emily said.

Margaret looked at her immobilized, yet still rotating, guest.

Up at the ceiling; down at the floor.

Up at the ceiling; down at the floor.

Margaret entered yet another round of keystrokes. The machine now began rotating around its axis. Margaret stared as Emily, in addition to the 180-degree turns, slowly revolved like an old turntable.

Rotate and turn.

Look up at the ceiling; then down at the floor.

"This thing's got a mind of its own," Margaret said.

Panic invaded Emily's anger. "Margaret, I'm losing it here."

"Hang on. Don't get your knickers in a knot."

"A knot? They're halfway up my butt. I think it's a little late to worry about a knot, Margaret. Will you get me out of this thing?"

Margaret turned back to the keyboard. She banged away and glanced back at Emily. The speed of the spinning and rotations increased. Margaret now panicked, stared at the rotating, flipping, freaking out Emily a few feet away.

"M-m-m-Margaret. I can't take much more."

Margaret rubbed her forehead. She then did what she had done many times in the past; she made a bad decision.

Margaret approached the machine, reached out, and grabbed the rapidly revolving outside metal ring. Immediately, she was pulled along by the force of the machine and soon found herself revolving wildly around the room, holding on, bull riding style, with one hand.

Halfway through one of her 180-degree turns, Emily caught a glimpse of Margaret as she whizzed by. She then heard the scream. Margaret, flying around the room rapidly with her legs stretched out behind her, reached up with her free hand and grabbed the metal ring. She pulled herself closer, hooked one leg over the top of the rapidly revolving ring and dragged her other leg up. Soon, she had both feet on the ring but was still holding on for dear life with both hands.

"Now what?" Emily said the next time she was able to make eye contact.

"There's a remote control for this thing somewhere." Margaret released her grip and slipped into a surfer pose and scanned the

197

room for signs of the remote. She spied it sitting on top of the computer monitor, steadied herself the best she could, and grabbed for the remote as she whizzed past. On the third revolution, she successfully grabbed the remote, readjusted her balance, and pressed the on button. ESPN appeared on the large screen.

"Goddamn it, David," Margaret said. "How many times do I have to tell you this room isn't for watching television?"

"He never listened to me either," Emily said.

"He's going to pay for this." She began pushing various buttons on the remote as she continued to spin around the room.

"Margaret, I'm gonna be sick."

"Hang on," Margaret said. She adjusted her balance and glanced at the remote control in her hand. "There it is. Here we go." Margaret pressed another button.

The metal ring continued to rotate but now began oscillating in a bizarre pattern similar to what a hula-hoop does before coming to rest on the ground. Margaret screamed and clutched the metal ring. Emily's view of the world changed as well.

Rotate, oscillate and turn.

Look up at the ceiling, then down at the floor.

Catch a glimpse of Margaret, watch SportsCenter.

And to make matters worse, Emily hadn't been joking about getting sick. Wine, pasta, and a trace of pot smoke spewed violently from her mouth.

Up at the ceiling, then down at the floor.

Margaret, both arms wrapped around the oscillating metal ring, frantically punched the remote with both thumbs. Finally, one of the sequences worked, and the machine stopped oscillating, then revolving. Emily stopped flipping back and forth and slowly, silently the machine came to a stop. Margaret dropped to the floor and glanced up at Emily, who was glaring at her.

"Get me down," Emily said.

Margaret scrambled to her feet and released the leg restraints. She helped Emily get her feet under her and released the wrist bindings. Emily staggered, grabbed the metal ring for support, and belched.

"You okay?" Margaret said.

"I've been better." Emily belched again and surveyed herself. "Why can't you just fuck like a normal person?"

Margaret, although embarrassed, still managed to chuckle. Then she began to laugh. At first, Emily didn't see the humor. But as she stood there in her panties and felt the sticky mess in her hair, she too began to laugh. Soon, the sound of both women's hysterical laughter filled the room. Gradually, it subsided, and Margaret pointed at Emily's shoulder. Emily glanced down to discover a perfect piece of penne resting in a red sauce on her shoulder. She flicked it away, looked at Margaret and both women lost it again.

"You need to get cleaned up." Margaret pointed. "The shower's right through there. I'll clean this mess up."

"You sure you don't want some help?"

"No, you've been through enough."

Both women laughed again.

"You gonna tell anybody about this?" Emily said.

"Not if you don't."

"Deal." Emily staggered towards the shower.

And it was this night the two women would remember forever. For this was the night that they officially bonded. These two strangers, unlikely affiliates, brought together by a strange set of circumstance and coincidence, that night formed a friendship that would last a lifetime. Despite their best intentions, over the years the story was retold many times by both women. They discovered, in the end, it proved itself to be one of those life events that simply needed to be retold, but not re-lived. And only told in select company.

To her credit, Margaret did eventually master the intricacies of the restraining, revolving, rotating, oscillating, you-name-it, it-does-it, metal ring sex-machine, now renamed, and hereafter known as, the Big Uh-Oh.

And Emily kept her solemn vow never to go near it again.

44

Thirty minutes, two paramedics, one confused veterinarian, and three shots of animal tranquilizer later, Sally and Bluto were finally ready for departure. Sally, immobilized and groggy, managed a brief wave as she was wheeled out the front door and down the steps to the waiting ambulance.

The veterinarian knelt down over Bluto and petted the snoring beast. "Good boy," she said.

"Yeah, he's a real sweetheart," John said.

"He's gorgeous," she said, glancing up before turning her attention back to the dog. "Yes, he's just a big baby."

"How are you going to get him out of here?" John said, staring down at the creature that spanned eight feet of carpet.

"One of the guys will be right back with another stretcher. I'll take him to my clinic until she's out of the hospital."

"Have fun with that," Bertrand said.

The tech burst through the door and soon Bluto was hoisted onto the stretcher and secured with three large straps. The veterinarian and tech waved goodbye as they whisked Bluto out the door and into the ambulance. John waved goodbye and closed the door. "Okay, guys, halftime's over," he said. "Bertrand, you ready with the movie?"

David, still visibly shaken, said, "Look, John, if you don't mind, I think I'll call it a night."

"No way," John said. "When I say I'm throwing a party, I'm throwing a party."

"Don't worry about it. My big bachelor party is in a couple of days, so let's just wait until the rest of my gang gets into town. We'll party then."

"David, throwing parties is one of my specialties. And it's something I take very seriously. The night is still young, and we've got more to come. Trust me. By the time this party's over, I think this night will be one you'll remember forever."

"It's been pretty memorable so far," David said.

"A minor setback," John said. His voice rose as he spoke towards one corner of the entertainment room where Bertrand was hooking up a video player. "And if I could just get a little cooperation around here."

"Relax, for chrissakes," Bertrand said. "How was I supposed to know she was blind?"

"What's that?" Randolph said, snapping out of his alcohol-fueled coma. "She's not blind; she's deaf."

"Okay, we're all set," Bertrand said. "Refresh your drinks and take your seats. It's show time."

Everyone settled back into their chairs and John stepped to the center of the room.

"A toast," he said, raising his glass. "To David. May you be a better man than I was."

"Here, here," Monty said.

Glasses clinked, and John dimmed the lights. He nodded at Bertrand who pushed the play button. A grainy black image appeared on all six big screens accompanied by the thunderous booms of a kettle drum. The film's title and credit sequence in bright red began to flash by as smoke appeared and wafted across the black background. A man wearing a devil costume and an evil grin appeared on the screen. The costume, nothing more than a pair of full-body red flannel pajamas, was already unbuttoned to the waist. A close-up of the man's face appeared, and he sneered and pointed with both hands to the plastic horns strapped to his head.

"Oh, now I get it," John said. "He's the devil. I'm glad he pointed that out. I might have missed it."

"Jesus, Bertrand," Monty said. "Where did you find this thing? It's ancient."

"Shut up, will you? It's a classic," Bertrand said.

The camera panned down a long head of blonde hair that stretched, Godiva-like, down a young woman's back. The hair bobbed up and down near the Devil's waist, and another close up of his face let everyone know that it was, indeed, good to be the Devil.

201

"All right," Bertrand said. "Here we go." He leaned forward in his seat.

"Okay," John said, getting up from his chair. "I think I'll go get started on those dirty dishes."

"No," Dr. Randle said. "Sit down. This is a logical extension of your therapy. And it's a natural expression of human emotion and desire."

"Do I have to?" John said.

"Yes, you do. Now sit up straight and pay attention. Be grateful I'm not making you take notes."

John, pouting, slumped back into his chair.

The Devil, apparently unable to stand anymore, stretched out on the bed and adjusted his horns. Godiva expertly adjusted her position until she was kneeling, legs-spread, in front of him. The blonde hair filled the screen, but an extreme close-up left no doubt what she was doing.

"Oh, damn. Now why did they have to go and show that?"

John winced and glanced at Dr. Randle, who glared back and pointed at the screens.

"Wow, six screens," David said. "I don't know which one to watch. I don't want to miss anything."

The others stared at David, caught each other's look of disbelief, and turned back to the screen.

The Devil pulled himself up in bed until his back was resting against the bed frame. This position gave him a tremendous vantage point to see Godiva's back that was still obscured by waves of blond hair.

"Man, she's really going at it," David said.

"Yeah, but I wish he'd move her hair out of the way so we can see some real action," Bertrand said.

On cue, the Devil began to clutch Godiva's hair. The image shifted to a close up of her foot, partially hidden by strands of hair. The hair slowly moved out of the frame, and the bottom of her foot came into view.

"Come on," Bertrand said. "Who wants to see her frigging foot?"

202

The camera began to pan slowly up until her muscular calf appeared, then the lower part of her thigh. Blonde hair continued to disappear from view, and soon both of Godiva's lower thighs appeared. Silence descended over the room as everyone leaned forward in their seats. Except John, who sunk into his chair and peered at the screen through hands-covered eyes. The boom of the drums intensified as the camera slowly made its way up the woman's legs.

"Well done, Bertrand," Dr. Randle said. "This definitely has some potential."

"Thanks," Bertrand said, unable to take his eyes from the screen.

Dharna, despite the large tray of shrimp on a table directly in front of him, gulped at the screen and winked. Nobody noticed.

The image changed to a close-up of the Devil holding a huge handful of hair. It then cut to another close-up, this time of Godiva's taut, upper-thigh.

"Here comes her ass," Bertrand said.

"Shhhh," Randolph said. "I'm trying to watch the movie."

"Wow, great legs," David said.

The camera continued its slow, inexorable march north as the drumming intensified. Another extreme close-up of the woman's mouthful and then all six screens were filled with the image of Godiva's ass.

"Oh, my God," John said.

"Now there's a surprise," Randolph said.

"Son of a bitch," Bertrand said.

David looked from one screen to another. After working his way across all six, he stared up at the image of Godiva's magnificent ass emblazoned with the 666 tattoo on the right cheek.

"Margaret?"

"I don't believe it," John said. "Don't panic, David. Maybe it's not her."

"Oh, you can believe it," Randolph said. "It's her. I'd recognize that ass anywhere."

"Margaret?" David was stunned and blinked several times as he stared at the screen.

"Now, I ask you," Randolph said, cracking open a fresh beer and pointing at the screen. "If you were sitting in that guy's position, wouldn't that look like 999 to you?"

"Randolph, will you please shut up?" John said.

"I'm marrying a porn star?" David said.

"Hey, David. Just relax. It's nothing to get excited about," John said.

Too late. David was already well into full panic mode. Wild-eyed he jumped out of his chair and began pacing. "I'm marrying a porn star."

"Hey, keep it down will you?" Bertrand said. "I'm trying to watch this."

"Wow," Randolph said, sitting down in David's vacated chair. "Look at her go."

"Guys, come on," John said. "Give it a rest." John caught a quick glimpse of the action and grimaced.

David stopped pacing, looked up at the action, and said, "Yeah, that's my Margaret."

Dr. Randle, unable to take his eyes off the screen, said, "You're a lucky man, David."

Margaret earned whatever money she'd been paid for this particular role. The Devil didn't stand a chance as she bobbed and weaved her way through the scene. He ended up staring down at Margaret with a goofy smile and then uttered the initial line of dialogue in the movie.

"Your training is now complete, Goddess Succulent. Go forth onto Earth and convert loyal subjects. Use what you've been taught to put them under your spell and bring them to me."

"Yo," Randolph said, raising a hand. "Right here."

"So that's where she came from," John said. "I knew it."

The camera slowly panned in for the close up of Godiva's face. A younger, smiling Margaret stared into the camera, licked her lips seductively and stretched out on the bed holding her arms up.

"Oh, master," Margaret said. "It is my honor to follow, lead the challenge, pursuit. Damn it. It's my honor to lead that pursuit for you."

"She's pretty bad," Dharna said.

"She has trouble with dialogue," David said.

"Well, it must be hard trying to talk after that," Randolph said.

Margaret did her best to recover. She spread her legs and beckoned to the Devil. "Yes, master. I will lead the attack on the people of earth at your bequest... behest... goddamn it. Who wrote this shit. I will suck. And you will see. I will go, I will do. But before I go, you do me."

"This is terrible," David said.

"What'd you expect for five bucks?" Bertrand said.

"Not the movie," David said. "The engagement."

"You spent five bucks? Bertrand, you cheap bastard," John said.

"I'm marrying a porn star," David said.

"Quit bragging," Randolph said, staring up at the screen.

"I'm marrying a porn star?" David said.

"David, relax," John said, draping an arm around his shoulder. "It's no big deal. So she picked the wrong vehicle. Made a bad choice. Even the great ones have done some nude scenes they regret later."

"Showing your tits is one thing," David said. "Chewing Big Woody on camera is something else altogether." He shook his head as if trying to clear cobwebs. "I'm marrying a porn star."

"Well, if it's any consolation, she's not actually a star," John said.

"Jesus Christ," Randolph said. "I think she's gonna do all three of those priests."

David glanced up at the screen and wailed.

"Oh, my God. What's my family going to say? What about my acting career? This could kill me in the industry."

"Maybe not," John said. "I've heard lately about how the porn industry is moving into the mainstream."

"Yeah," David said. "And the only people you hear that from work in porn. Don't expect to see Spielberg walk up to a porn star and ask if she's ready for her close up." He exhaled loudly. "I'm marrying a porn star."

"David, you just need to relax," John said.

David stopped in the center of the room and shook his head. "I'm not marrying a porn star."

"What?" John said.

"I'm not marrying a porn star."

"What are you saying?"

"You heard me, John. Look, I appreciate everything you've done for me, but I'm not marrying a porn star. The wedding's off."

David took one more look at the screen, caught a glimpse of a repentant Margaret trying to get closer to the church, and walked out of the room.

Dr. Randle approached and draped an arm around John's shoulder. "How are you doing?"

"How do you think I'm doing?"

"Oh, don't worry about that. He'll get over it. I meant about your situation and what you've just seen up on the screen."

"What? That?" John said. "That's nothing."

"I think I'm beginning to understand some of the pressure you felt during that time."

"What time?"

"When you were married to her," Dr. Randle said.

John thought for a moment and smiled.

"Hey, you're right. She must have made it during the time we were married."

"That's what I mean," Dr. Randle said. "So what do you think? Are you going to be okay?"

John stared up at the screen and watched as Margaret lost the last of her nun's habit. He looked back at Dr. Randle.

"What?" Dr. Randle said.

"This is beautiful," John said. He walked over to Bertrand's chair and stood next to the squinting figure peering intensely at the screen. Bertrand caught a glimpse of John out of the corner of one eye and flinched.

"Thank you, Bertrand," John said, slapping him on the back. "I'm sorry I ever doubted you."

Bertrand, confused but anxious to get back to the movie, glanced up briefly. "Whatever you say, John."

John smiled, patted Bertrand on top of the head and left the room with the strange, perverse smile fixed on his face.

45

Randolph, eschewing a much-needed shower, pulled on a dirty pair of jeans and a hooded sweatshirt. Despite his best efforts, he caught a glimpse of himself in the mirror, sucked in his stomach, and wondered what the hell had happened to him. Deciding the answer to that question could wait at least one more day, he grabbed his car keys, peered outside his bedroom door and spied the Dharna sitting with his back against the wall. He was reading the latest copy of Gourmet magazine and appeared to be drooling. When he spied Randolph, he closed the magazine, spread his arms and stared at Randolph with big, brown puppy-dog eyes. Randolph quickly closed the door and walked down the hallway towards the stairs. Dharna watched him go and trailed behind out of sight. Randolph entered the registration area and discovered a chipper John standing behind the desk shuffling a stack of papers.

"Hey, what's up?" John said. "You going to venture outside today?"

"Yeah," Randolph said, glancing back up the stairs to see if he was being followed.

"Work?"

"Bar."

"Shower?"

"Only if it rains."

John shook his head and resumed shuffling his papers.

"What's up with David and Margaret?"

"He's holding steady. Says there's no way he's going to go through with it," John said.

"You seem to be handling it pretty well. I'd have thought you would be in a funk over that news."

John smiled. "I'm fine with it. Either way. Margaret's got a hell of a problem she's not aware of yet."

Randolph watched John's smile turn evil and waited for him to continue.

"I have my divorce lawyer to thank. Way back when we were trying to finalize the divorce settlement, my lawyer kept holding out for what I thought was pretty strange at the time. A morals clause."

"Okay," said Randolph.

"Yeah, it's pretty bizarre. Anyway, he got to know Margaret pretty well during that time, and he was of the opinion that I should get something in writing that would invalidate our agreement if she ever did anything that could, how did he word it, cause emotional damage or any discredit to me or my name."

"And you think her going through half the Vatican in a porn flick qualifies?"

John's smile deepened.

"It's close enough. At least that's what my lawyer says. Plus, I don't think she wants something like that going public."

"Actually, it might help her career, what there is of it," Randolph said.

"It probably couldn't hurt," John said. "But I know Margaret pretty well. She might be incredibly prolific, but she prefers to keep her personal business private."

"Good luck with that."

"Thanks. I'll know soon enough. I asked her to drop by for a chat later. It's probably not a bad idea for you to clear out for a while. It might get ugly."

Randolph smiled, sucked in his stomach, and turned towards the door.

"Hey," John said. "If you end up having one too many, give us a call, and we'll come get you."

Randolph felt himself tearing up and his face flushed with embarrassment. He used a dirty sleeve to wipe his eyes.

"You okay?" John said.

"I'm fine. And thanks for asking." Randolph approached the desk with his arms outstretched in search of a hug.

John stepped back from the counter and stopped Randolph's approach with two outstretched palms. Randolph got the message and stopped.

"See you later," Randolph said.

John watched Randolph depart and shook his head at his friend's bizarre behavior. "What a weenie."

Randolph climbed in his BMW and slammed the door. He started the car, sniffed, and cracked a window. He turned on talk radio, heard some hack political commentators prattling on about Gloria Fontaine and changed the channel. The Beemer purred as he increased speed and he felt himself relax. Humming out of tune along with a country song he hated, he noticed he was approaching a road crew up ahead and decided to change lanes. He glanced in the rearview mirror.

"Aaahh! What the hell are you doing?"

Dharna, from the comfort of the backseat, smiled back at him through the mirror.

"Nice car. A man who can afford this should certainly be able to make good on what he owes."

"What do you want from me?"

"Why money, of course."

"Money? You've got to be kidding."

"I'm entitled to it."

Randolph looked at Dharna through the mirror and laughed.

"Well, someone certainly has a high opinion of himself. How much did you have in mind?"

"Ten grand."

Randolph laughed louder.

"Ten grand? Let me tell you something, pal. Randolph Tut has never paid for it in his life…well, not counting Vegas. And he's certainly not going to start now. Especially with you."

"We'll see about that, Randolph. Ambulance."

"Ambulance? What the hell are you talking about?"

"In front of you," Dharna said, ducking down behind the front seat.

Randolph glanced at the road, swerved, slowed down and merged back into the right lane.

"Look, Dharna. I can understand the attraction. I'm a good looking, successful guy but, quite frankly, you just don't float my boat if you know what I mean."

"Attraction?"

"Yeah. You and me. You know what I'm talking about."

Dharna winked and sat back in his seat thoroughly confused. He remained silent the rest of the trip.

Randolph found a parking spot in front of the restaurant. "You can stay in the car."

"You going to be eating in there?"

"I'm going to be drinking." Randolph slammed the car door and trudged towards the entrance. Dharna watched him go and stretched out on the back seat for a much-needed nap.

46

"What are you smiling at?"

"I'm just glad to see you, Margaret."

"Yeah, sure you are. I'm here. What do you want?" Margaret closed the front door and removed her sunglasses. She arched her back, testing the cotton fabric of her tight T-shirt, and walked into the registration area and sat down in a chair. She crossed her legs and twirled her sunglasses.

John came out from behind the desk and sat down opposite her. "You're looking good."

"Tell me something I don't know," she said. "Where's David?"

"I think our poor lovelorn friend is probably avoiding you."

"I know he is. Do you know what his problem is? He hasn't said anything to me since you threw that stupid party. Except call and tell me that the wedding's off. What did you do to him?"

"Me? I didn't do anything." John beamed at her.

"I guess I should go find him and see what's rung his bell this time."

"I think we should chat first. That is if you have a second."

Margaret's eyes narrowed. "What do you want?"

"Oh, it's nothing," John said. "It's just that I had an interesting chat with my lawyer this morning."

"That idiot? I can't believe you're still even speaking to that cretin."

"He has his moments."

"Yeah, one can only imagine," she said. "That reminds me, the first of the month is coming up. Why don't you write the check while I'm here? Save yourself a stamp."

John's smile intensified. "That's what I wanted to talk to you about."

Margaret stiffened in her chair.

"What about it?"

"I just thought I should tell you in person that you won't be getting any more checks out of me."

Margaret roared with laughter.

"Just try it, John. In fact, I'd love for you to try it. And so would my lawyer. By the time he finished with you, you'd be paying me double."

"I don't think so, Margaret."

"And what makes you think that?"

"Just a little something I like to call my get out of jail free card. But you probably remember it by another name."

"I don't have a clue what you're talking about," Margaret said. "But I'm too busy to sit here and play games with you." She stood, but made no attempt to walk away.

"The Devil's Anytime Playtime Plaything," John said. "It's a little wordy, but it definitely captures the essence of the film."

Margaret flinched, just for a second, but John caught it. She eased herself back down into the chair.

"I don't have a clue what you're talking about."

John stared up at the ceiling.

"What is it?" Margaret said. "The name of some cult?"

"Well, there is some group activity involved, but I don't think it could be accurately called a cult."

Margaret chewed her bottom lip, hard. "So what is it?"

"C'mon, Margaret. Cut the crap. We both know what it is."

"That's impossible," she whispered. "I bought up all the copies."

"I think you missed one," John said.

"I mean…I've never done anything like…fuck."

"You certainly did. From what I hear, you were outstanding. I think the guys nominated you for Best All Around."

"Goddamn it," she said. "That was years ago. Shit. That was back when we…"

John leaned forward in his chair. "What was that, Margaret?"

"Nothing."

"Back when we were married? Is that what you were going to say?"

"Forget I said anything."

"No, I'm not going to forget this one," John said. "And neither will my lawyer."

Margaret rubbed her forehead, then sat back in her chair and sighed. "You're talking about that damn morals clause in our divorce agreement, right?"

"You bet your overworked ass I am."

"Jesus, what a mess."

"I think it's great."

Margaret shook her head and stared out the window. Eventually, she looked back at John. "What do you want me to do?"

"Well, for starters, I'd suggest you agree to dissolve our alimony agreement."

Margaret thought for a moment.

"And then what?"

"I suppose you could try and get David to take you back. Although I have no idea why."

"How about because I love him?"

John sat back in his chair as if hit by lighting.

"Love him?"

"Why is that so hard to believe? He gives me everything I've always wanted in a man."

"Total subservience?"

"That... among other things." Margaret drummed her fingers on her leg. "How would you suggest I go about it?"

"Oh, I don't know. Maybe try some humility and contriteness."

Margaret frowned.

"I know it's a stretch, but you're an actress. Try faking it."

She gave John the death stare. He smiled back.

"I want you to help me get David back."

"Now why on earth would I want to help you do anything?"

"Well, for one thing. I happen to know that Emily has threatened to quit if he isn't out of here pretty soon."

John caught off guard, fell silent.

"And I'm sure you don't want that little cutie pie walking away. Not that you'd know what to do with her."

"You should try and be nice to me, Margaret."

"Now that's a stretch," she said.

"I'll help you, Margaret," John said. "For a hundred grand."

"A hundred grand? Forget it," she said. "Give me an hour with him and he'll be begging to come back."

"That's not what I'm talking about. The hundred is for my pain and suffering for the past several years. That's about a year of alimony. And that's the amount that will keep me from suing you for everything I've given you since the divorce. It's also the same amount that will keep my mouth shut about your previous adventure into hell."

"You'd reopen the whole thing? After all these years?"

"Margaret, I've given you close to eight hundred grand. You bet your ass I'll reopen it."

Margaret, beaten, stared down at the floor.

"You can be a real son of a bitch, John."

"Well, I learned at the foot of the master, Margaret. What can I tell you?"

"All right," she said. "Deal."

"Beautiful. I'll have my lawyer draft something up."

"I don't think we need to involve the lawyers, John. What's the matter? Don't you trust me?"

John stared at her in disbelief.

"Forget it," she said. "Drop it off and I'll sign it." She stood, adjusted her T-shirt, and put on her sunglasses. "This is a new side of you I'm seeing. Where was that backbone when we were married?"

"I think you removed it during our honeymoon."

"Oh, yeah," she said, heading towards the door. "Now I remember."

John waited until he heard the sound of Margaret's heels fade, then leaped in the air, danced a jig, did a victory lap around the room and pulled a hamstring

47

Randolph stepped through the front door, removed his sunglasses and blinked until his eyes adjusted to the light. He headed to the bar and waved to the bartender who was chatting up a waitress. The bartender ignored him, finished his story then strolled in Randolph's direction. Halfway down the bar, he smiled in recognition. "I was beginning to think you'd fallen off the edge of the earth. Where you been, Randolph? Without your tips, I thought I was going have to refinance my condo."

"I've been busy. How you doing, Mike?"

The bartender extended his hand across the bar then paused and sniffed the air. "Say, Randolph, far be it for me to say anything bad about one of my best customers, but you stink."

"So everybody keeps telling me." Randolph eyed the long, multi-level rows of bottles. "Bring me a Glenfiddich."

"Single or double?"

"Bottle," Randolph said, looking around the empty bar and restaurant. "What's happened to your lunch crowd? This place is always packed."

"It's 9:30, Randolph."

Mike slid the bottle in Randolph's direction, put a glass on the bar and took two steps back. Randolph tossed back a large shot and poured another. "So you've been busy, huh?"

"Yeah." Randolph coughed. "Can't you tell? Say, have you seen Randy Van Swalo around here lately?"

"He's here," Mike said. "But then, when isn't he? I think he just went to the bathroom."

Randolph took a sip of scotch. The bartender walked away and resumed his conversation with the waitress. Van Swalo, a short, unkempt man in his early forties, returned to the bar, spotted Randolph and made a dash for the door.

"Hey," Randolph said. "Get your ass over here."

Van Swalo stopped in his tracks and glanced back. "Randolph Tut. Long time, no see. Whatcha been up too?"

"Licking my wounds. No thanks to you."

Van Swalo took a seat next to Randolph. He noticed the strange smell but said nothing. He reached for a glass on the other side of the bar and helped himself to some Glenfiddich. "Yeah, that was too bad about Toy's campaign. A bit of bad luck there, huh?"

"Oh, you mean the part about Fontaine's deaf mother," Randolph said, downing another shot. "That's the bit of bad luck you're referring too?"

Van Swalo chuckled nervously and played with his glass. "Eh, yeah, sorry about that one. My source was pretty good, but I guess the message got a little...garbled."

"Yeah, just a little."

"But what the hell, huh? Toy's a total asshole and deserved to lose. But I'm sorry you got caught up in it. What are you working on these days?"

"What am I working on? Shit, I can't get a phone call returned."

Van Swalo polished off the last of his scotch and poured another. "Yeah, it's been tough on me, too," he said. "I've been forced to resort to doing background checks for some hygiene consortium. Talk about your boring gigs."

"Who's got time for hygiene?" Randolph said. "You haven't heard of anybody looking for help, have you?"

"What, for someone like you? Nah, it's pretty quiet at the moment."

The sound of the front door opening caught Randolph's attention. He watched the small entourage enter. "Unbelievable. What's she doing here?"

"Breakfast meeting, I imagine," Van Swalo said. "She's adopted the place. Says it brings her good luck."

Randolph watched Gloria Fontaine, surrounded by several other people, remove her sunglasses and glance around the restaurant. She noticed Randolph and walked towards the bar.

"I think I'll have a cigarette," Van Swalo said. "She makes me nervous." He hopped off his chair, nodded at Gloria on his way out and disappeared through the front door.

"My, how the mighty have fallen," Gloria said, giving Randolph the once over.

"Did you stop by to gloat, Senator?" Randolph said, staring at her over the top of his glass. He took a large swallow and wiped his mouth with a sleeve.

"Isn't it a little early in the day for Glenfiddich?"

"Actually," he said, topping up his glass. "I'm a bit behind schedule."

"I see," Gloria said. "I just came over to ask about Margaret's wedding. I got an invitation; then it was called off. But when I talked with her the other day, she said to keep my weekends as flexible as possible. What's the deal?"

"I think it's off at the moment," Randolph said. "But I'm a bit out of the loop."

"I want to go, but it's getting pretty hectic. Some days I wonder why I ran in the first place," she said.

"How do you know Margaret?"

"College," Gloria said. "We were sorority sisters. You think she's a piece of work now; you should have seen us back then."

Randolph arched an eyebrow. Gloria noticed and laughed.

"Forget it, Randolph. I bought back the last of those photos a long time ago."

"I'm sure you did, Senator," Randolph said.

"Randolph," Gloria said. "I'm not an ogre. I just wish we had met under different circumstances."

"You mean other than online dirty talk?"

Gloria laughed, and Randolph found himself drawn to her. "No, not that," she said. "Although that was the most fun I had during the entire campaign. Talking with you relaxed me. I meant us meeting in the middle of the whole political thing. It's such an ugly process. By the time a campaign's finally over, forget about your enemies, you end up hating your friends." She laughed again and glanced at her waiting entourage. "I need to get in there.

Another fundraiser. I just spent millions getting elected, and the first thing I have to do is start raising money. Nice seeing you, Randolph."

"You too, Senator," Randolph said, extending his hand. "Good luck in D.C."

"Thanks, I'll need it," she said, accepting the handshake. She began walking away but stopped and turned.

"And one more thing, Randolph."

"Yeah?"

"You stink."

She walked away with what seemed to be an extra dash of sway. He admired the rearview profile, drained his glass and dropped a fifty on the bar. He walked to his car and discovered Dharna sleeping peacefully in the backseat. He tapped on the window. Dharna opened his eyes and sat up as Randolph climbed in the passenger seat. He tossed Dharna the keys and leaned back in his seat. "Make yourself useful and drive me home."

48

John fired a dart, heard the thump, and smiled at the result. He repeated the process with his last dart and sat down next to Emily.

Emily laughed. "I thought you two were getting along better. That you were going to help her out with David."

"It helps me think," John said. "I just wish I could come up with something. David's not making it any easier. Says that she betrayed their trust."

"All this coming from a guy who cheated on me for a year with her."

John looked at Emily and caught the white-heat of her anger. "I know. Just hang in there, we'll figure something out."

"You better hurry," Emily said. "I heard that he paid you in advance for next month. I can't last that long, John."

"Where'd you hear that?"

"Is anything a secret around this place?"

John sighed and leaned back in his lawn chair. He stretched his legs and looked out at the sun disappearing behind the trees. "Nice up here, isn't it?"

"Yes, it's very peaceful." She finished her beer, grabbed two more from a nearby cooler and handed one to John. He tossed his empty into the cooler and opened the fresh one. They sat sipping in silence.

"I just wish I could think of something about Margaret we could exploit in some way," John said.

"How so?"

"Well, if she had a real weakness that we could use to our advantage. Something that might cause David to come to the rescue."

"She's pretty fearless." Emily laughed.

"Oh yeah, it's been so crazy around here I forgot to ask you about the other night. How did that go?"

Emily sipped her beer and glanced up at the sky.

"Oh, it was uneventful."

John studied her face.

"Why do I get the feeling you're not telling me something?"

"It was just your basic girls' night," Emily said.

"Uh-huh."

"It was. We sat by the fire, had a few drinks and chatted. Then she gave me a tour of the house."

"Did she show you the entertainment room?"

"She certainly did."

"The last time I saw that place it looked like something right out of medieval times. Perfect for burning someone at the stake. Is she still using Middle Ages theme?"

Emily casually sipped her beer.

"I'd say she's going for more of a high-tech look these days."

"I don't even want to know," John said.

"Good."

John caught her small smile but said nothing. John jiggled a leg up and down.

"What to do? What to do?"

"Maybe if she threatened to do something drastic," Emily said. "You know, John, after you strip away all her bluster, she's pretty vulnerable in a lot of ways.

"Margaret? We are still talking about Margaret, right?"

"She is. And as strange as this is going to sound coming from me, I like her."

"What did she do to you over there? Threaten to remove a limb?"

Emily laughed.

"She's okay. She's just quirky."

"You say quirky; I say she's nuts. I just wish we could figure how to use it to our advantage."

"How about suicide?"

"Margaret's? I'm all for it." John laughed.

"No, I mean if she somehow threatened to end it all if David wouldn't take her back. That just might play into his machismo in

221

some way. I don't think he gets much of a chance to show that side off very often."

John considered the idea. "Interesting. How would we pull that off?"

"Well, we'd have to put her in jeopardy and have David ride in like the white knight."

"Margaret in jeopardy. I'm starting to like this idea."

Emily laughed again. "But we couldn't do anything that might cause her any harm."

"You're ruining the moment, Em."

"I'm serious," she said. "But what if we put her in a place where it looked like something tragic might happen. How do you think David would respond?"

"You tell me," John said. "You were married to him."

Emily remembered what Margaret had told her about David and their relationship.

"I used to think I did. Now, I'm not so sure," she said. "But suppose we put Margaret in a place where David was nearby. She could profess her undying love, but threaten to do something drastic, and he would be forced to respond."

John nodded along with the conversation and she continued.

"We could do it in front of a group of people, so he also had peer pressure to deal with. David's a real weenie when it comes to the possibility of being publicly embarrassed."

"I like it," John said. "But what's the situation? Pills?"

"No, too risky," she said. "Guns?"

"Too tempting."

"Car accident?"

"Too public."

"Hunger strike?"

"Nah, that's been done to death."

Emily laughed. "That poor little guy is wasting away. How long is Monty going to keep this up?"

"As long as it takes. He's having so much fun watching both of them think they're trying to get each other in the sack, he doesn't want it to end."

222

"Randolph," Emily said, shaking her head. "What a piece of work he's turned out to be."

"It's the booze. He's not very lucid lately."

John fell silent. The leg started jiggling again.

"What to do? What to do?"

He walked to the dartboard and retrieved a fresh supply of ammunition. He fired a dart past the board that headed off into the night. John held his breath and waited.

"Ow. Jesus, John. That's my foot."

"Sorry, David."

49

Bertrand sat down in the chair and cracked his neck. Thursday afternoon and already forty-five hours into his work week, he was tired and mentally exhausted. And cranky.

"Thanks for stopping by, Bertrand," Walter Harrison said.

Bertrand couldn't miss the huge smile on the man's face. "No problem," Bertrand said. "I hope this won't take too long. I'm trying to get out of here. We're having a barbecue tonight."

"Won't take long at all," Harrison said. "It could probably have waited until tomorrow, but it is such good news, I thought you'd want to hear it right away."

"I could use some good news."

Harrison leaned back in his chair. "As I'm sure you know, Bertrand, for some time now, we've been getting ready to launch No Offense into the market."

"Yes, it would be hard not to know that since that's all you've been talking about lately."

"Yes, well, it's an exciting time. What can I say? Anyway, one hour ago, we finalized the negotiations on the endorsement side. It will be announced tomorrow, but I am at liberty to tell you that we have signed a contract with a celebrity endorser for two million."

"Two million dollars?"

"Well, we're certainly not paying in rubles."

Bertrand didn't find the humor and scowled.

"You're going to pay some idiot two million dollars to stand in front of a camera and rub my product under their arms?"

"Well, there's more to it than that, but, yeah, that's the basic concept."

"Unbelievable. Who is it?"

"I can't tell you that."

"Why not?"

"Because it's a secret."

Bertrand scowled at his boss.

"Relax, Bertrand," he said. "That's just the first part of my news."

"Oh, good. There's more. I can't wait."

"This is good news. We've decided that since you were such an instrumental part of this, I mean, you invented the damn thing, so without your efforts, we wouldn't have much of a campaign, would we?"

"No, you wouldn't."

"So we've decided to give you a much-deserved bonus."

Bertrand sat up in his chair.

"Now you're speaking my language."

"Yes." Harrison laughed. "I'm sure I am."

He handed Bertrand a sealed envelope. "For all your hard work and amazing creativity, I thank you."

Bertrand grabbed the envelope and tore it open. He removed the check and stared at it. He then stared at Harrison.

"What's wrong?" Harrison said.

"I think there's been a typo," Bertrand said.

"I don't think so."

"Yeah, it's missing at least one zero."

Harrison chuckled but stopped when he saw the look in Bertrand's eye.

"Three thousand dollars? You've got to be kidding."

"Bertrand, I'm afraid that's the best we can do. But if the product launches successfully, you have my word that we'll be revisiting the size of your bonus."

"Revisiting? I come up with the hottest idea to hit the personal hygiene market in ten years, and you'll be revisiting it? I don't think so, Walter. I think you better revisit it right now."

Harrison returned Bertrand's glare. "I'm sorry, Bertrand. But I can't do that. We've already completely blown the budget for this product already."

"But you just happened to find a couple of million lying around for a spokesperson."

"Bertrand, you know how it works. Marketing's the key."

Bertrand clenched his fists until they turned white. He slowly released the fists, interlocked the fingers of both hands and cracked his knuckles. A loud snap punctuated the dead silence in the room. "That's it. I quit."

"You what?"

"You heard me. I'm done. Fuck this place. And fuck you too, Walter."

"You can't talk to me like that."

"Not as an employee, no. But as an ex-employee, I can say pretty much whatever I want."

"Fine. If that's the attitude you're going to cop, go."

Bertrand stood and glared menacingly across the desk. Small beads of sweat began trickling down Harrison's forehead.

"You're sweating, Walter. Isn't that ironic?"

Harrison flashed a crocodile smile.

"Well, thanks to you, Bertrand, it's a good thing I've got a new deodorant to take care of it, huh?"

Bertrand, at a total loss for words, wheeled and stormed out of the office.

50

John finished cutting the final vegetables for the salad, tossed them into a large bowl, and wiped his hands. He glanced over at Emily who was shaking a healthy dose of a spice mixture onto a tray of large steaks. Satisfied with the status of the preparations, John leaned back against the kitchen counter and took a sip of beer. Margaret appeared through the back door and John panicked.

"Margaret, what are you doing coming in the back? David didn't see you, did he?"

"No, he's oblivious. Relax. Hey, Em."

"Hey, Margaret. Nice shoes. Where did you get them?"

"I found them at Macy's of all places. Can you believe that?"

"Very cool."

"You should check it out. They're having a big sale."

"I just might do that. You free tomorrow afternoon?"

"Yeah. Let's hook up for lunch and then we'll go spend some of John's money. I'm afraid I don't have much of it left." Margaret forced a laugh.

John stared in disbelief at both women.

"Can we focus here, please?"

"I still can't believe I let you talk me into this," Margaret said.

John peered out the kitchen window and saw David sitting at the picnic table, pounding a beer. Dharna sat staring at the appetizer tray. John turned back to Margaret.

"You think you're ready for this?" he said.

"Yes, but it's the stupidest idea I've ever heard."

"Well," John said, turning coy. "If you don't think you have the acting ability to pull it off."

"Don't have the ability? Just watch me."

Dr. Randle entered the kitchen, smiled at everyone and checked out the tray of steaks. "Very nice, I definitely see one of those in my future," he said. "And how is everyone this evening?"

"I'm a little nervous, Doc," John said. "Big night ahead."

"Something I should know about?"

"No, but stick close. You never know when we might need you." He then turned to Margaret. "You ready?"

"Lead the way," Margaret said.

"Em, why don't you and Doc start taking that stuff outside? It's show time," he said.

Dr. Randle caught John's conspiratorial tone and studied him closely. John led Margaret out of the kitchen. Emily grabbed the tray of steaks and headed out the back door. Dr. Randle walked to the fridge and was rummaging for a beer when Monty walked in.

"Hey, Doc," Monty said. "What a day. Forget the beer. Come and join me in a glass of champagne."

51

John opened the door that led to the roof, waited for Margaret to step outside and closed the door behind them. Margaret shuffled her feet as she inched her way out onto the rooftop.

"Jesus, Margaret. Move it. It's going to be dark in an hour."

"I don't like this. When you told me about this, you never mentioned I'd have to get on the roof."

"Well, it wouldn't be much of a suicide attempt if you tried jumping off the picnic table."

"I don't like this."

John, surprised by her fear, smiled. "Margaret, don't tell me you're afraid of heights."

Margaret's knees shook as she slowly maneuvered her way towards the center of the roof. "I don't usually share that with anybody." She glanced towards the edge of the roof still twenty feet away.

"I had no idea," John said. "This is gonna be fun." John strode towards the edge of the roof and looked back at her.

Margaret glared at the mischievous grin on John's face and put both hands on her hips. "Don't fuck with me, John. I'm warning you."

"Relax. Come on," he said, motioning to her. "Over here, to the edge."

"Can't I just do it from over here," she said.

"Yeah, sure," John said, shaking his head. "We'll do the first voiceover suicide attempt in history. Get your ass over here."

Margaret dropped to her knees and crawled the last twenty feet. John watched her snail-like progress and laughed. When she finally arrived, she wrapped her arms around his legs and held on for dear life.

"On your feet, Diva," John said.

"No fucking way," Margaret said.

229

John dragged Margaret to her feet and she stood shaking and clutching one of his arms. "What happens if I fall?"

"Just make sure you land on your airbags."

"You're not making this any easier, John. And trust me, I won't forget it."

"Keep breathing," John said, prying loose from her death grip. "It's not so bad." He gently grabbed her by the shoulders and purred into her ear. "That's it, just relax. Now it's simply a matter of getting comfortable up here."

"Are you sure?" she said, still paralyzed.

"Absolutely. The secret to overcoming one's fear is to confront it," he whispered.

"Okay. What do I do?"

"Just try to relax and slowly lean forward." John, with a gentle touch, massaged her shoulders and guided her closer towards the edge. "That's it. Now you've got it. See, that's not so bad." John suddenly tightened his grip and cried, "Watch out!"

Margaret launched herself backwards, rolled and ended up glaring at John from her knees ten feet away. "You son of a bitch." She climbed to her feet and the intensity of her glare deepened in direct correlation with his laughter.

"I'm sorry, Margaret," John said. "I couldn't resist."

"You'll die for that."

"Come on, let's get this over with."

Margaret slowly worked her way back to John and steadied herself with one arm against his. "God, this is frightening." She peered out over the edge of the roof. "Now how does this work again?"

"Jesus, Margaret. You must be a director's worst nightmare. Look, I'm only going to go through this one more time. You stand by the edge, profess your undying love for David, threaten to jump and end it all, he talks you down, and we cut to the big happy ending. For chrissakes, use your imagination. Didn't you ever do Romeo and Juliet?"

"Hardly. Shakespeare's for hacks. Hey, wait a minute."

"Now what?"

"I never do my own stunts."

"I'll do it," said a voice from a far corner of the rooftop.

John and Margaret looked in the direction of the voice and discovered Randolph slumped against the wall holding a half-empty bottle of scotch.

"Ah, Jesus. What are you doing up here?" John said.

"Just enjoying my last few moments on earth," Randolph said. "Hey, Margaret."

"Hello, Randolph," Margaret said.

"Not now, Randolph, please. I'm a little busy here at the moment," John said.

Randolph took a long swig from the bottle and slumped further down the wall.

"I am not doing this without adequate safety precautions," Margaret said.

"Goddamn it, Margaret," John said, his teeth clenched.

"I'm serious. You get me some sort of safety rope or I am simply not going to do this."

"Safety rope? Jesus Christ, Margaret, I'm surprised you didn't ask for your own trailer."

52

Dr. Randle and Monty were at the kitchen table working their way through the first of three magnums of champagne Monty had brought home.

"You're kidding." Dr. Randle laughed. "He really said that?"

"Yeah," Monty said. "Dexter is a piece of work. I almost fell on the floor I was laughing so hard."

"Must be nice to be young and rich."

"It is, Doc. What can I say?"

Dr. Randle raised his glass in toast. "To you, Monty."

"Thanks, Doc. Well, should we open a fresh bottle and head outside?"

"Why not?"

Bertrand burst through the back door. Both men took a step backwards when they saw the look on his face.

"Bertrand," Dr. Randle said. "You look distressed."

"I just quit my job. Those bastards are through sucking me dry."

"Quit? Gee, I thought things were going well for you," Monty said. "Sit down, have a glass of champers, and tell us all about it."

Bertrand slumped into a chair and accepted the glass from Monty. He downed it and held up his glass for a refill. Monty poured three glasses and sat down next to Bertrand.

"So what's up?" Monty said.

"We finally closed the deal on this new product I developed and they gave me a bonus of three thousand bucks."

"Three thousand? That sucks. How long did you work on the thing?"

"Well over a year." Bertrand drained half of his second glass.

"Cheap bastards," Monty said. "Well, that kind of takes the edge off my day."

"What do you mean?"

"I had a big day."

232

"Of course you did. But then, you have them all the time." Bertrand polished off the second glass and refilled.

"Yeah, I closed a very nice endorsement deal for Dexter today."

"How nice," Bertrand said, half-heartedly. "I'm so happy for both of you."

"Yeah, it took forever. And I had to maintain strict confidentiality the whole time. Actually, it's right up your alley."

"Yeah?" Bertrand took a large gulp of champagne. "How so?"

"It's with a consortium for a new deodorant called No Offense."

Bertrand dropped his glass and it shattered. "What did you say?"

"No Offense. That's what they're calling it. And get this. These idiots are paying Dexter two million bucks to promote it. Well, a million eight after I take my ten percent."

Bertrand's shoulders began shaking uncontrollably. He gripped the table with both hands and screamed. Dr. Randle and Monty stared at the raging monster now before them. "That's my product you're talking about," Bertrand whispered.

"What did you say? I didn't hear you," Monty said, leaning closer.

"That's…my…product."

This time, Monty heard him loud and clear. "Uh-oh." Monty hopped out of his chair. "Bertrand, I had no idea."

"Two hundred grand? That's how much you're making off this deal? Two hundred grand?"

"Minus expenses, yeah."

"What expenses?" Bertrand said.

"Well, this champagne sure ain't cheap."

"You son of a bitch. That overpaid imbecile is going to be endorsing my product?" Bertrand hopped to his feet and began stalking Monty.

"Bertrand, take it easy." Monty eased his way around the table towards the door that led to the hallway. Bertrand lunged, missed securing a hold on Monty's shirt, and fell onto the floor with a loud thud. Monty, dredging up his football instincts, ran a deep crossing route across the kitchen and down the hallway. Bertrand scrambled to his feet in full pursuit.

Dr. Randle watched them disappear, poured himself another glass of champagne and headed outside to join the others.

53

John dragged a long, yellow device from the storage shed and draped it across his shoulders. Struggling under its weight, he closed the door with his foot and made his way back to Margaret. Margaret, confused, watched him approach and felt her legs shake. She ventured a quick glance over the roof's edge then refocused her attention on John. She eyed the yellow contraption suspiciously. "What the hell is that?"

"Your safety rope." John caught her scowl and shrugged. "It's the best I can do on short notice."

"Is that what I think it is?"

"Yeah. It's a bungee cord."

Margaret stared at him and waited.

"From last year's Halloween party," he said.

Margaret raised an eyebrow.

"Don't ask," John said. "Okay, let's get you hooked up."

"Hooked up? I thought you were trying to get me back with David."

"What? Jesus, Margaret, does your vagina even have a pause button? I was talking about the damned bungee cord."

He dropped to his knees and fastened one end of the cord around Margaret's ankle.

"How's that?" he said, climbing to his feet.

"Fine, I guess," Margaret said.

"I can always loosen it if it's too tight," John said.

"Very funny, John. Just keep it up."

John chuckled as he fastened the other end to a long metal pole attached to the rooftop. He placed his hands on his hips and nodded. He walked over to Margaret and slapped her on the back. She staggered briefly, replanted both feet and glared at him. "Knock it off, dickhead."

"Okay, I think we're ready," John said.

"When I jump, believe me, it won't be with a safety rope," Randolph said, still slumped against the back wall.

"Well, let me know when you're going so I can sell tickets, Randolph." She flipped her hair back from her face, took a deep breath and inched forward. She peered over the edge. She shuddered and looked at John. "I'm not happy about this. How far up are we anyway?"

"Fifty feet."

"And how long is this cord when it's fully extended?"

"About sixty."

Margaret's face turned a shade of purple.

"I'm just kidding, Margaret. What happened to the carefree woman who was always telling me to lighten up?"

Margaret ignored the question, opting for another glance over the edge. She shuddered and cursed under her breath.

"You'll be fine, Margaret. Don't worry. David will be up here before you know it dragging you off the roof."

"For your sake, he better be."

"Okay, I'm out of here," John said. "Break a leg."

John dashed for the door that led back down into the house, laughing the entire way. Margaret watched him go and snuck another peek over the edge.

John raced down the stairs and was headed towards the backdoor when Bertrand's voice, coming from the registration area, caused him to stop short. He walked in and discovered Bertrand in a rage and on the prowl.

"I know you're in here somewhere," Bertrand said. "Come on out, you fucking coward."

"What are you doing?" John said.

"Looking for that bastard, Monty. Have you seen him?"

John watched Bertrand continue to search the room. "I don't have a clue where he is."

"Well, help me find him," Bertrand said. "I need to have a little chat with him."

"Sorry, Bertrand," John said. "I'm a little busy right now. Maybe later."

Bertrand waved him away as he continued his search. John dashed towards the backdoor.

Once outside, John quickly sized up the situation. David was sitting at the picnic table that had been moved to a spot close to the edge of the house. He had four empty beer bottles in front of him and seemed determined to increase the size of his collection. John sat down on the other side of the table which provided him with an unobstructed view of the roof and Margaret's head as it intermittingly appeared, then disappeared, from sight.

"How you doing, David?"

"I'm fine," he said. "I'll be fine."

"Nice night," John said.

"Yeah, I guess." David finished his beer and reached into the cooler for another. John glanced up at the roof, caught Margaret's eye and motioned for her to move closer to the edge. John tracked her movements while keeping one eye on David. Eventually, Margaret, from the waist up, came into view. John gave her a thumbs-up. Margaret closed her eyes, took several deep breaths, and looked down at the picnic table. Emily wandered over, noticed Margaret on the roof and sat down next to John.

"Jesus Christ," John said. "She's playing herself and she still can't get into character."

"What's that?" David said.

"Nothing."

And then a voice from above caught everyone's attention.

"Oh life, what good is it without the love of my beloved?"

David paused mid-sip and cocked his head. "Did you hear something?"

"Be still my beating heart, for you will not have to beat much longer," Margaret said.

David turned around and looked up. He stared in disbelief. "What the hell are you doing up there?"

"If the end can be seen as the beginning, I now know where to start the finale of this final tragedy that began at inception."

David, bewildered, continued to stare up at the roof.

"Where the hell did she come up with that?" John whispered to Emily.

"As far as acting goes, she should have stayed in porn," Emily said.

Monty burst through the door with Bertrand in hot pursuit. "Bertrand, calm down." Monty glanced over his shoulder as he raced across the lawn.

"That's my money, you bastard."

Monty did a lap around the picnic table then raced back inside. Bertrand was gaining on him. John glanced up at the roof and noticed Margaret studying a handful of notecards. She slipped them back into her pocket and stared out towards the horizon.

"Soulful sorrows sip succulent...damn, what the fuck is it?"

Margaret rechecked her cards. Then it was back to the horizon.

"Soulful sorrows slip silently surrounding streams softened by tears." Margaret clutched her chest and wailed.

"Man," Emily said. "If she keeps this up much longer, I'm gonna jump."

"Wow," Dharna said. "She sucks."

"No one's listening, Margaret," David said, not looking up. "No one cares."

"Hark," Margaret said. "Who listens without hearing? Who speaks without talking? Who feels without touching? Who smells without...?" Margaret grimaced. "What the hell is that smell?"

John looked at Emily and said, "Randolph's up there."

"This day, so dear, that has turned into this good night, will be the last day I ever say...goodnight, dear."

John reached across the table and grabbed David's arm. "My god, she's going to jump."

David gave Margaret a quick glance then returned to his beer. "Nah, she's bluffing. That's straight out of the third act of that turkey we did in summer stock last year." David took a long swig of beer and burped. "I got great reviews."

54

Bertrand almost got hold of Monty's pants leg as they raced up the stairs. Monty continued to take two stairs at a time but was tiring. He reached the top of the stairs and ran past his room, deciding to continue up another flight to the third floor. He glanced over his shoulder at Bertrand. "Tenacious little bastard, aren't you?"

"Just wait until I get my hands on you."

Monty continued up the stairs, noticed the open door leading to the roof and ducked through. Seconds later, Bertrand followed. Monty spotted Margaret and the bungee cord attached to her leg, but Bertrand's latest lunge recaptured his undivided attention. Monty inched backwards as Bertrand began circling, preparing to move in for the kill.

Margaret glanced at both men and looked down at the ground and saw John gesturing at her to pick up the pace. She studied her notecards and tried to concentrate.

"Oh, my beloved, David. Without you, my life is as empty as...as..." The last of her concentration was broken by Monty and Bertrand.

"What the hell is the matter with you?" Monty said.

"I'm going to kill you, you sonofabitch."

"Hey!" Margaret said, wheeling to face them. "Can you guys keep it down? I'm trying to kill myself here."

Monty and Bertrand glanced at her and fell silent, but Bertrand continued to stalk Monty. Monty, still walking backwards, noticed Bertrand closing the gap.

"You're a dead man," Bertrand whispered.

"What the hell did I do to you?" Monty whispered back.

The stalking continued.

"Without your love, what is left?" Margaret said.

Pleased with her latest effort, Margaret smiled and continued.

"Without your love, what is right?"

She paused for effect.

"Right or left? Which way do I turn?"

Bertrand was slowly maneuvering Monty towards the edge of the roof. Monty kept one eye on Bertrand while repeatedly glancing back, carefully monitoring his steps.

"I bust my ass and you make two hundred grand," Bertrand said.

"Bertrand, will you please calm down?" Monty said. "Look, some people spend their lives in pursuit of money and success. Other people get a PhD."

"How dare you." Bertrand lunged at Monty. And missed.

"For life without you is not worth-"

Margaret's latest effort was cut short when Bertrand, off balance, attempted to catch himself by using the closest object he could find. Unfortunately for Margaret, the object happened to be her. Bertrand bounced off Margaret and fell with a thud onto the rooftop. He looked up at Margaret, now teetering precariously on the edge of the roof.

"Uh-oh," Bertrand said.

Margaret frantically wind milled her arms to regain her balance. Tippy-toed on both feet, she arched her back, and flailed. She almost made it safely back onto the roof.

Almost.

She teetered back and forth, clutched the air and her eyes rolled back in her head as she tumbled off the roof. Her screams filled the air and reverberated throughout the neighborhood.

Randolph, who had staggered over to watch the proceedings, stared down then looked at Monty. "Wow," he said. "She jumped."

Watching from down below, John shook his head in disbelief. "Goddamn it, Margaret. "If it's not one thing, it's another. Can't you follow a simple set of instructions?"

David watched Margaret's free fall and raced from the picnic table. He dove across the lawn, righted himself on one knee, positioned himself under the most probable flight path and stretched both arms out in an attempt to catch the rapidly descending woman of his dreams. He glanced up at the approaching Margaret, saw the terror in her eyes, closed his, and braced himself for impact.

"Catch me, David."

Eyes still closed, David said, "I got you, sweetie."

The bungee cord exhausted its last bit of stretch and tightened. Margaret, only inches away from David's outstretched arms, now felt herself being propelled skyward. Another piercing scream echoed through the neighborhood.

David, fully prepared for Margaret's weight, opened his eyes and discovered his arms were still empty. Baffled, he turned left, then right. "Margaret?"

"I'm up here, you moron."

Apparently, David was out of earshot because he maintained his catching position and continued to scan the ground for signs of Margaret.

"Man, that thing's like a rubber band," Emily said, studying Margaret's trajectory.

"Yeah, the guy I bought it from warned me about that." John looked up towards the roof. "Hey, Randolph. Make yourself useful. Catch her on the way up."

"How about that? Just like last year's Halloween party," Randolph said, as he worked his way to the edge of the roof. He knelt down and extended his arms. Margaret's speed seemed to be increasing but Randolph managed to grab her as she sped past the top of the roof. However, instead of stopping her ascent, Randolph, his arms now wrapped tightly around Margaret's back, was dragged skyward. His face was buried in Margaret's breasts. Despite his fear, he couldn't resist nuzzling them. "Just like old times, huh, Margaret?"

Margaret, not in the mood for a cuddle, cringed from the sight and smell of her new traveling companion. She screamed and kicked at Randolph. "Unhook me from this thing."

Being untethered from her sole connection with anything resembling solid ground was probably not a wise choice on her part, but Randolph complied. He fumbled with the Velcro strap around her ankle, eventually worked it free and wrapped it around his arm; in hindsight, probably another poor decision.

Margaret stared up at the approaching treetops, had a sudden change of heart. "Hook me up! Hook me up!"

Asking Randolph to unhook something in his current state of booze-fueled depression was one thing, asking him to refasten it was something else altogether. He fumbled with the strap but soon felt Margaret begin to slide slowly down his body. He felt her desperate tug on one leg of his pants and then heard her scream as she began a free-fall. Randolph, still ascending, approached the trees.

Monty and Bertrand, their personal differences suddenly taking a back seat, knelt on the edge of the roof and watched as Margaret plunged past.

"Think he'll catch her?" Monty said, staring down at the ground.

"A hundred bucks say no," Bertrand said.

"You're on."

David, still kneeling on the ground with outstretched arms, shook his head and glanced around the lawn. "That's odd," he said.

Margaret, caught a glimpse of the rapidly approaching lawn, looked skyward, and offered a prayer. "I'll be good. I promise I'll be good."

Seconds later, she dropped into David's arms. Technically, it wasn't a catch. But David did do two things: He broke her fall; and broke both his arms.

Randolph clenched his teeth as he neared the top of his ascent. The bungee cord snapped tight and hurtled him back towards the ground. Oak leaves brushed his face and fluttered in the breeze Randolph created as he began his descent. Suddenly sober, he sized up his chances of survival. Deciding they were no better than fifty-fifty, he did what most people would do when faced with a similar challenge. He screamed.

John glanced at David who was writhing on the ground. He looked up at Randolph and trotted towards the probable landing area. Emily and Dharna followed closely behind and soon all three were staring up at the incoming bundle of joy.

"How do we do this?" Emily said.

John nodded at David rolling on the ground in pain with the quivering Margaret draped around his neck. "Well, whatever we do, we're not gonna copy him."

Dharna, transfixed by the recent events, stared up and caught Randolph's eye. Randolph glared down at him and Dharna, overcome with fear, winked. Randolph added extremely pissed-off to the mixture of fear and panic he was experiencing.

"You. You son of a bitch."

Randolph approached the ground and reached for Dharna with his free arm. Randolph grabbed him just as the bungee cord tightened again and they felt themselves violently jerked skyward.

"Man, you're light as a feather," Randolph said.

"Thanks," Dharna said. "I try to watch what I eat."

Then Randolph and Dharna realized they were locked together in a tight embrace. This time, the scream punctuating the early evening air was a duet.

"Get off me, you pervert," Randolph said, struggling to break free.

"This is probably not the best time to bring this up," Dharna said. "But about that money. Whoa."

The bungee cord again tightened near the treetops and both men closed their eyes as they felt themselves launched downward.

"Come on," Monty said, glancing up at the latest descent.

"What?" Bertrand said, eyeing Monty suspiciously.

"Let's catch a ride."

"You're joking, right?"

Monty wasn't, and he dragged Bertrand by the arm closer to the edge to prove it. "Get ready."

"For what?" Bertrand said, wide-eyed.

"To jump on. We need to add some weight to slow it down," Monty said.

"No way am I-"

Monty didn't give Bertrand a chance to finish as he dragged Bertrand by the arm and jumped off the roof. Bertrand and Monty landed on top of Randolph and Dharna and managed to hold on as the speed of the drop accelerated. Dharna wasn't quite as successful. About twenty feet from the ground, he lost his grip, went into free fall and bounced off John who tried unsuccessfully to catch him. He landed on top of the picnic table, face-down in a bowl of potato salad. Dharna didn't seem to mind in the least.

The stretched bungee cord was unable to overcome the combined weight of the three men. It gently bounced and hovered near the ground, Monty removed the safety strap from Randolph's arm and they collapsed in a heap onto the ground. The bungee cord bobbed until it came to a stop dangling harmlessly from the roof.

"Hey. You with the hand," Randolph said, from the bottom of the pile. "Move it or lose it."

Margaret gave David a passionate kiss. He grimaced and groaned. "Darling, you were magnificent," she said. "Hold me, sweetheart."

"Maybe later," David said, both arms drooping from the elbows. "After I get back from the emergency room."

Margaret helped David to his feet. David, his face white with pain, said, "I'll see you guys later."

"Give us a call if you need anything," John said.

"Thanks, John," David said, following Margaret towards her car.

"Yeah, thanks, John," Margaret said. "It was pretty weird, but it looks like everything worked out. But the next time you decide to throw a party, don't worry about inviting us."

John waved and watched them walk away. "It's been a while since we've had any broken bones."

"Yeah, not since Randolph broke his ankle when he fell off the roof," Monty said. He looked at Randolph. "You ready to pay off your debt?"

Randolph, beaten, nodded. "Yeah, I'll write you a check as soon as we go inside."

Monty turned to Bertrand. "And you owe me a hundred bucks."

"What are you talking about? That wasn't a catch," Bertrand said. "Don't stand there and try to tell me that was a catch. He trapped her."

"Bertrand, do I have to sick Dharna on you?"

Bertrand fumed but dug a hundred dollar bill from his wallet and handed it over. Monty smiled and looked around. He spotted Dharna, a hot dog in each hand and potato salad smeared all over his face. "Hey, Dharna. You're off the hook."

Through a mouthful of hotdog, Dharna said, "Way ahead of you, Monty."

55

It was a day of color matching.

A cloudless blue sky matched a quiet sea that rolled onto the nearby sand. Lavender tablecloths matched the crisply folded napkins perched on top. Crimson roses matched the bridesmaid's dresses. A hundred, black-clad guests matched each other. The bride's shimmering white gown matched the two casts that stretched from David's shoulders to his wrists bent forward at a ninety-degree angle from the elbows.

The only thing that wasn't matched, wasn't capable of being matched, was John's mood. He smiled as he half-listened to Dr. Randle, dressed in a black cape with his goatee dyed jet black, work his way through the wedding vows. Never had the ocean air smelled this pure. Never had the gentle breeze that drifted across his face brought such contentment. Never had anything tasted as sweet as the simple glass of water he had savored earlier. Never had his entire range of senses, emotions, and thoughts been so closely matched in perfect harmony.

"What a perfect setting," Emily said.

"Margaret had to do it out here on the coast. Her agent told her it was the only way the industry press would even consider covering it."

"I only see one camera crew," Emily said, glancing around.

"And I'm sure Margaret hired them."

Emily laughed and gently punched his shoulder. "Did you know Dr. Randle was an ordained minister?"

"No," John said. "He's full of surprises. What was he telling you before the ceremony started? I noticed he was whispering in your ear."

"Oh, he was just demonstrating something to me," she said.

John shrugged and looked back at the ceremony. Emily took another quick glance at the surroundings "This is beautiful."

"It's perfect."

"This is exactly the sort of-"

John gently cut her off with a wave of his hand. "Shhh. I need to hear this." He leaned forward and listened to Dr. Randle.

"Now," Dr. Randle said, "if anyone here has any reason why these two people should not be forever joined in holy matrimony, let them speak now or forever hold their peace."

John leaned back in his chair and slowly slid a hand inside his jacket. Emily glanced down and was startled by what she saw. The sun glistened off the silver Beretta. John's hand rested on the pistol.

"What on earth are you doing with that thing?" she said.

John, scanning the crowd for naysayers, waited until he was satisfied with the silence, then relaxed back into his seat.

"Just making sure there aren't any last minute problems."

Emily giggled, grew embarrassed by the annoyed looks she was receiving from nearby guests, and bit back her laughter. She placed a hand on John's thigh and he flinched. Emily prepared to pull her hand away, but eventually he relaxed and smiled at her. She left her hand where it had fallen.

"Hearing no objections," Dr. Randle said, "I hereby pronounce that you, Margaret and David, are now...husband and wife."

John leapt from his chair and thrust a fist into the air. "Yes!"

A round of applause broke out along with laughter provoked by John's outburst. Grinning from ear to ear, he loudly clapped along with everyone else. Margaret and David eventually broke their kiss and waved to the crowd as they made their down the aisle.

Tears of joy streamed down John's face.

56

Dharna, gorging himself at the buffet table, watched Margaret and David perform the obligatory first dance. Senator Gloria Fontaine walked up next to him and picked at a tray of vegetables.

"You the one they call Dharna?" she said.

Dharna nodded at her through a mouthful of food.

"I've been hearing a lot about you. I think we should have a little chat."

Randolph, standing nearby admiring the Senator's profile, decided to move on. He smoothed the lapels of his tux, checked his freshly-shaven face and new haircut in the mirror and smiled at himself. "Welcome back, big guy." He spied Monty off to one side of the room talking on his phone. He wandered over and stood nearby waiting for the call to end.

"Gee, three and a half million," Monty said. "That's a lot of money for not that much house." Monty listened and then laughed. "Yeah, I guess you're right. What else are we gonna do with it?"

Monty spied Randolph and waved him closer. Randolph approached and Monty draped an arm around his shoulders and squeezed. Randolph smiled and returned the hug.

"When? Well, this thing is probably going to go all night if I know this group." Monty listened and laughed again. "Oh yeah. He's standing right here. Want to say hi? No problem. I'll tell him."

"Who's that?" Randolph said.

"It's Dexter," Monty said.

Randolph continued to wait patiently as Monty finished the call.

"I'll catch a flight back sometime tomorrow afternoon. With a killer hangover too, most likely. Yeah, you know the drill. Okay, I gotta run. Go ahead and make the offer, but tell that realtor not a penny over three and a half. You bet. Love you, too."

248

Randolph flinched, not quite sure he heard Monty correctly. Monty closed the phone and put it in his pocket.

"You tell all your clients you love them?" Randolph said.

"Nope," Monty said. "Only Dexter."

Randolph attempted to slide out from underneath Monty's arm but gave up as Monty increased the pressure.

"Is there something you want to ask me, Randolph?"

"Not really." Randolph squirmed and shuffled his feet.

"Relax, Randolph," Monty said. "If I had found you the least bit attractive, you would have known about it a long time ago."

"No way," Randolph said, shaking his head firmly. Then a thought crossed his mind. "Hey, what's wrong with me?"

Monty laughed and released his bear grip. "Oh, Randolph. I'm going to miss you."

"Where are you going?"

"Dexter and I are buying a house up in the Bay area. We want to try living together. Coming out could be a career killer, the way the football deals with the issue, but he's adamant about the house. Hopefully the press will think we're just two more wild and crazy bachelors."

Randolph looked like he'd been hit in the face with a brick. "How long have you…?"

"A very long time," Monty said.

"No way. But you were such an animal on the field."

"I still am." Monty laughed. "A big puppy."

"Who else knows?"

"A couple of people. John, for one. And I'd appreciate your discretion."

Randolph smiled and extended his hand. Monty accepted it and Randolph's hand disappeared. "You're leaving the hotel?"

"I guess we all have to grow up sometime, huh?"

Randolph smiled at his friend. "Just don't ask me to dance later, okay?"

Monty laughed. "Don't flatter yourself." He wandered towards the bar but turned back. "And thanks for the check. I put it to good use. I used it for a down payment on Dexter's new Mercedes."

Monty jabbed a 'gotcha' finger in Randolph's direction, chortled, and sat down at the bar.

Randolph stood watching the dance floor and frowned at the lack of activity. He noticed Gloria Fontaine walking in his direction and realized he couldn't take his eyes off her. As she approached, he caught a whiff of perfume and stared at her as she brushed her hair back. She took a sip of wine. "Nice ceremony don't you think?"

"It's been pretty weird up to this point, but it seems to have worked out all right."

"I guess they make a good couple," Gloria said, not at all sure.

"I think I'm going to stop making those sorts of judgments," Randolph said, glancing over at Monty who was now doing shots with Bertrand and Dr. Randle. "I don't seem to have a clue these days."

"Well, it looks like you've cleaned yourself up. You look good.

"Thanks. I decided it was time. My life flashed before my eyes the other day and I can't say I liked what I saw."

"I see," she said. "Well, I do need to talk to you, Randolph. I want to ask you for your help."

"Me? What could I possibly do for the woman, excuse me, for the Senator who has everything?"

"I could use your talents. You're still on the market, aren't you?"

Randolph eyed her suspiciously. "You are talking about work, I assume."

"Yes." She laughed and took another sip of wine. "For now anyway."

"Me, work for you? Now that's a switch."

"When you think about it, it's not a strange idea at all. It's probably safer for me to have you working my side of the street."

"What would you want me to do?"

"There's a ton of work that needs to get done. Plus, if the franchise goes through, that's a whole other area that will need to be worked on. I know you love sports."

"I think I'll stick with the political side. Play to one's strengths and all that."

"Okay. How would you feel about living in Washington?"

Randolph considered the prospect. "I could probably be convinced."

"Good," she said. "We'll figure out the particulars later. Let's just enjoy the rest of the day." She began strolling back towards the crowd with Randolph walking next to her. "One thing you will need to jump on as soon as you start is the national debt issue. It's was a central theme in my campaign so I better try and do something about it."

"Yeah," Randolph said, nodding. "I could spin that one."

"Actually, I've just hired someone to help out with the debt issue. I think you'll like him."

"I can't wait to meet him."

"Well, let me introduce you." She gestured at someone standing behind them.

Randolph turned and found himself face to face with Dharna who was about to stuff a chicken leg in his mouth. He stopped short when he saw Randolph.

"You?"

Dharna shrugged and began working on the chicken. Gloria laughed. "I know you'll find his approach fascinating, Randolph."

57

John and Emily were standing next to Margaret and David along with Bertrand and Dr. Randle chatting amiably. Margaret glanced over her shoulder at the empty dance floor and frowned.

"What is wrong with these people," she said.

"They'll be fine once they get a few more drinks in them," David said.

"So," Emily said. "What about your honeymoon plans?"

"Well, we've decided to wait until David's casts come off," Margaret said. "Then we're thinking about an island somewhere."

"Yeah," John said. "It's probably a good idea to eliminate as many of his escape routes as possible."

"You just can't help yourself, can you?" Margaret said.

"Sorry," John said. "Force of habit." He grabbed a puff pastry from the silver appetizer tray that had been placed on top of David's casts and chewed in Margaret's direction. She glared at him and then focused on David. "But in the meantime," she said, "it doesn't mean he's excused from his duties."

"But, Margaret," David said. "I can barely move with these things."

"It won't matter, sweetie," she said. "I've already scheduled a repairman to make the necessary equipment modifications."

Emily spit a mouthful of wine out and coughed. David, flushed with embarrassment, pawed the floor with one of his shoes. John, thoroughly confused, looked at all three and squinted. "Did I miss something here?"

"Nothing you'd appreciate, John," Margaret said. She smiled at Emily and said, "Good luck with that, Em." Margaret removed the tray sitting on top of David's casts, set it down on a table, and dragged David by the coat towards the dance floor. "Come on," she said. "Let's see if we can help jumpstart this thing."

"What did she mean by that good luck comment?" John said.

"Just a little girl talk we had earlier," she said. "A little tactical adjustment in strategy."

John didn't have a clue what she was talking about but Emily tapped him on the shoulder and beckoned him closer. He leaned in and she began whispering in his ear. He jerked his head away, but Emily pulled him back and resumed the soft whisper. John nodded, slowly at first, then more vigorously as the whispering continued.

"I need to sit down," John said.

Emily led him to a table, sat down next to him, and resumed her whisper. John listened for a few moments, paused to drain the last half of his wine and leaned in for another round of soft talk.

Dr. Randle watched the gentle seduction begin to play itself out and smiled at Bertrand who was staring out at the dance floor.

"My work is done here," Dr. Randle said. "I'm so good, sometimes I scare myself."

Bertrand, not paying attention, shook his head in disgust. "This party sucks," he said. "She should have let John organize it."

Dr. Randle followed Bertrand's eyes out to the floor. "It is dead. Somebody should do something."

Bertrand glanced at Dr. Randle and watched the evil grin appear. The light went on for Bertrand, and soon he matched his new friend's grin.

"You didn't happen to bring them with you by any chance, did you?" Bertrand said.

Dr. Randle reached inside his cape and withdrew a small wooden box. "Of course, I did. I never go to a party without my boys."

"You think we should?"

Dr. Randle grinned mischievously at Bertrand and waited.

"Absolutely. Let's do it," Bertrand said.

Dr. Randle knelt down, opened the box and watched four furry tarantulas scurry away. Dr. Randle returned the box to his pocket and put his hands on his hips. He smiled as the last of the tarantulas disappeared underneath tables filled with wedding guests.

John's head continued to rest on Emily's shoulder as she whispered softly into his ear. "Feel like dancing?"

John shifted uncomfortably in his seat and shook his head.

"I think I'm going to need a few minutes."

Emily smiled, glanced at the dance floor, and resumed her conversation with John's ear.

The band ended the ballad it was playing and launched into an up-tempo number that got everyone out of their chairs and onto the floor. Soon the entire room was filled with gyrating individuals of all shapes and sizes.

From a distant corner of the room, four furry beasts huddled observing the proceedings. Deciding their work was done, they scurried off in tandem towards the kitchen.

The party was rolling.

And had it not been for David's feverish, misguided attempt at breakdancing where he managed to shatter a kneecap, the entire day would have gone down as an unqualified success.

"You know, Bertrand, I've been thinking about hitting the road."

"Already? We just got here."

"No, I mean later. After the party. But soon. An extended road trip. What you do think, care to join me?"

"Me?"

"Sure. Why not? It's a big world out there and most of it could certainly stand to smell a whole lot better."

"Gee, leave the hotel? I guess I've never thought about it," Bertrand said.

They began strolling away from the dance floor, side by side, at a casual pace.

"I've been thinking about the possibilities surrounding Aromatherapy," Dr. Randle said.

"Interesting," Bertrand said, nodding.

"Yes. And why should it be limited to only relaxation and stress-reduction?"

"Yeah, good point."

"How does the term, Aromamancy, grab you?"

"I like it."

"Yes, so do I," Dr. Randle said. "Fortune telling using smell. Let's face it. With your scientific abilities and my marketing skills, I think we could make a fortune."

"Who knows what the future might hold for us?"

"My sentiments exactly. I was thinking about heading to Europe. Or maybe South America."

Bertrand considered the possibilities as they continued towards the exit. "You know," Bertrand said. "Maybe I could use a change of scenery. The hotel has lost some of its excitement lately."

"I know. It's a special place, but I think everyone needs to take a chance now and then to shake things up."

"Makes perfect sense to me."

They came to a stop directly in front of a large mirror. Both men stared at each other reflections.

"Of course," Dr. Randle said to Bertrand's reflected image. "You will need some therapy. We need to start working on managing your anger. It's just not healthy."

"I guess I could go along with that," Bertrand said.

"I thought we might start with some Enoptromancy," Dr. Randle said.

"That's the one with the mirror, right?" Bertrand said, staring at himself.

"That's the one," Dr. Randle said, nodding. "If you can make it past the mirror, Bertrand, you can do anything."

Bertrand stared intently at himself in the mirror. He glanced at Dr. Randle's reflected image then looked at the real thing.

"You know, Doc, I think I see a bright future for both of us."

Dr. Randle smiled and gently rested an arm on Bertrand's shoulder.

"See, you're making progress already."

Be sure to check out B.R. Snow's Damaged Po$$e series.

American Midnight – The Damaged Po$$e #1

http://amzn.to/SUTrYm

Doc White wakes up in a Las Vegas hotel suite a very confused man with a massive tequila hangover. As he reflects on the previous day's events that included his wife walking out on him and with their joint savings, the return of the voice in his head, his subsequent loss of another $150,000 at the blackjack tables, and then waking up next to a total stranger, Doc's already damaged life has taken another serious dip downward.

In order to pay off his new debt, Doc is forced to do something he vowed years ago never to do again; take a corporate job. Doc's new boss, an octogenarian Chinese casino owner with a taste for curling and political intrigue, along with the return of an old love help to reenergize Doc as he tries to rebuild his life in Sin City. At a major crossroads, Doc draws on the expertise of Merlin, his coke-addled, phobic colleague from a prior life and Summerman, a part-time ghost who is certain he can help Doc deal with the voice in his head. By the time this initial installment in B.R. Snow's Damaged Posse series is wrapped up, Doc, Merlin, and Summerman have joined forces and are armed and ready to wreak havoc on the bad guys as well as themselves.

Larrikin Gene – The Damaged Po$$e #2

http://amzn.to/10tqmMa

Gene has a bit of a problem. Several actually. He's wrapping up a year-long, high-end matchmaking scam that has proven to be most profitable but, in the process, he's lost the love of his life to a billionaire. Now to help mend his broken heart, he's back in Las Vegas finishing up another lucrative scam. But the FBI is on his trail and Gene discovers that the agent in charge is none other than the hapless Roger Gentry, a high school acquaintance with whom he shares a tenuous past. To make matters worse, Gene is soon sleeping with the other agent on the case who turns out to be Gentry's fiancé.

To cool things off, Gene decides it's time for a well-deserved vacation Down Under. He brings his father along, an ex-convict whose biggest wish in life is to work one scam with his son before he dies. And before Gene can even get a chance to catch his breath and enjoy his time off, he finds himself running the ultimate con; one that threatens to irrevocably change his life. Fortunately for Gene, the Po$$e needs his help and Doc, Summerman and Merlin follow him to Australia to do a little recruiting and provide Gene with a possible way out of his current predicament.

258

Sneaker World – The Damaged Po$$e #3

http://amzn.to/VUnhnP

Sir Bentley Carruthers, sneaker magnate and exploiter of the poor on four continents, has decided to expand his empire into the lucrative field of biopiracy. He's purchased a small group of islands from the Indian government ostensibly to assist with recovery efforts after a devastating tsunami. So he's built a sneaker factory on one of the islands along with a high-end resort that caters exclusively to the uber-rich. Unfortunately for Sir Bentley, Doc and the rest of the Damaged Posse are well aware of what his real motives are. And the fact that Sir Bentley has been selling off weapons technology to the highest bidders also hasn't gone unnoticed. After the Posse arrives on the island, they embark on their strangest and funniest adventure yet that is filled with dense jungles, a lost tribe, cantankerous girlfriends, shoulder-fired missiles, and a safari suit wearing antagonist you'll love to hate.

Summerman – The Damaged Po$$e #4

http://amzn.to/SqukAk

In the eagerly anticipated fourth book in B.R. Snow's popular Damaged Po$$e series, Summerman finds himself staying close to home and, of course, he isn't shy about enlisting the help of his three cohorts in crime. Set in the magnificent surroundings of the Thousand Islands, Summerman needs to juggle several problems simultaneously and each one brings along its own challenges and predictably hysterical outcomes. Summerman is faced with stopping his uncle's Senate campaign along with the plan he and his defrocked priest partner in crime have come up with. Summerman also has to deal with the return of his ex-girlfriend, Grace, and her two daughters as well as his nephew's plan to put Summerman's band back together. On top of all that, Summerman's grandmother, Mamo, has a few surprises in store as well. Doc, Merlin, and Gene are all back as is Murray and, unfortunately for Uncle Dick, he is in particularly fine form.